A Great State: The Rescue Book Three

by

Shelby Gallagher

Prepper Press

Post-Apocalyptic Fiction & Survival Nonfiction
www.PrepperPress.com

A Great State: The Rescue

The third book in the *A Great State* trilogy.

ISBN 978-1-939473-92-9
Written by Shelby Gallagher
Copyright © 2019 by Shelby Gallagher
All rights reserved.
Printed in the United States of America.
Prepper Press is a division of Kennebec Publishing, LLC

Glen,
Thank you for sparking off this trilogy with a hammer.
I love you, Shelby.

Chapter 59
Pink Slips

Steve opened his eyes to the dome light inside his car. He was reclined in the driver's seat and Addison was asleep on his chest. Her head rested just below his chin, and he inhaled her sweet, baby scent. The early morning sun poured into the car and he was surrounded by silence.

He had struggled to make it through his first night in the SUV, after spending many restless hours trying to get comfortable and relaxed enough to sleep. He'd had minimal success in the sleep department, particularly due to the dead silence of the junkyard, which was a quiet Steve was unaccustomed to. After two months of living with the constant hum of city noise and traffic, the silence was deafening.

Yet in the silence, Steve was certain he heard something. He struggled against the urge to sit upright, which would alert anyone outside of the vehicle to his presence. Steve slipped his right hand under his thigh and felt the hard handle of the knife. He gripped the knife, pulling it from beneath him, and laid it between his legs, still in its sheath.

Slowly, he rolled to his right and gently laid Addison in the front passenger seat. She cuddled into the curve of the seat as if it were a human body. Steve took the knife and continued to roll to his right until he was on his stomach. He slowly lifted his head up until he could peer out the windows and see what was out there making noise.

At the rear of the SUV stood the same man from several nights ago, with the same distinctive beard and jean jacket. He wore a khaki ball cap and aviator glasses.

"Dude, I know you have the knife. I gave it to you, remember? Don't even think of it. Open the back," the man demanded as he tapped on the window.

"Who the fuck are you?" Steve hissed.

"Your chauffeur. Pop the back. Now," the man demanded again.

He's early. I didn't expect him now, Steve thought, his mind racing. He hadn't been expecting his escort north for a few more days. Yet this was the same guy who had delivered the knife he asked for.

"Dude. Your dad is Bentley. Your baby is Addison. We're going to Pierce Point soon. Open the fucking door, or I'm out of here."

Steve felt his shoulders relax. No one except Amanda and Jody knew that information.

"Why are you here before the agreed time?" Steve asked as he cracked the side window.

"Need to prep you and the vehicle. Need to store gear," the man answered back. "Last time. Open the door."

Thump. The SUV's hatch slowly rose, and the man watched it lift.

"Dude, you're a sitting duck sleeping in plain view like this. You're lucky no one saw you last night," the man said as the door reached its peak.

Steve had no answer. He had figured he was hidden just by being in the junkyard.

"Call me Shawn. This car needs work. *A lot* of work," Shawn said as he began pulling the few items in the back of the SUV out onto the ground.

Steve watched intently. He didn't know what to do except watch.

Shawn cleared out almost everything until the entire back hatch was empty. Then he threw in a large duffel bag and tossed a tarp over everything. He walked away for a few moments and returned with full garbage bags. They were dusty and dirty.

"Come here," Shawn ordered, pointing his gloved index finger at Steve and motioning it toward him over his shoulder.

Like an obedient dog, Steve quickly exited the driver's door. As he approached the rear of the vehicle, Shawn pointed to the tarp.

"Crawl under," Shawn commanded.

Steve didn't move.

"Wise to be suspicious, though I'm your ride. Try this. Your entire inheritance is funding this little effort to get you and that baby to Pierce Point. My job is to get you there, though I get paid regardless of whether that happens," Shawn said in a monotone, staccato tone. "I am not going to kill you. But… you make me repeat myself one more time, and I might punch you before I head to my next job." Shawn's expression was stoic as he pointed to the space next to the duffel bag and under the tarp.

Steve grabbed the edge of the entrance and slowly slid into the SUV, tucking himself under the tarp. He watched Shawn work quickly to place paper garbage all around him.

"Where is your stuff?" Shawn asked.

Steve pointed to the front passenger seat, and Shawn went to the front of the car. Steve felt himself grow apprehensive, knowing that Addison was in the passenger seat. Shawn hesitated as he looked in the passenger window and noticed Addison. He quietly opened the door. Shawn's head disappeared into the foot space to pull out Steve's bag and Addison's supplies. Shawn closed the passenger door, not making a sound.

How does he do that? Steve wondered, impressed by Shawn's stealthy movements.

Shawn walked around the car and opened the door behind the driver's side. He levered the driver's seat upright and tucked the bags behind the seat under the tarp and trash. By the time Shawn was done, the car's interior was full of trash.

"You crawl into that void at night when you sleep. Take the baby with you. Look around—this now looks like a car that belongs in a junkyard, not a car *parked* in a junkyard." Shawn pointed as he spoke.

He bent over into a large, black duffle bag, and pulled out sheets of metal and a vest. From Shawn's exertion, Steve quickly surmised that the equipment was heavy.

"Grab that car seat and come here," Shawn said, motioning to the back of the car.

Steve immediately complied.

Shawn moved confidently and quickly. "Spread out your arms," Shawn commanded, and slid a heavy vest onto Steve.

Steve immediately felt the pull of the twenty pounds of level IV body plates. Steve stood still as Shawn strapped the Velcro enclosures for the armor.

Shawn looked up at Steve, and half punched him in the chest. "Feel good?"

Steve coughed. "Uh… yes. Protected."

Shawn didn't wait for Steve to answer. He grabbed the car seat and started peeling off the cloth cover. Carefully, he fitted various-sized plates he had over the back and sides of the bucket of the carrier, until he found sizes that fit. Next, he took straps and tightened the plates down to the seat using holes already in the seat's frame. Before putting the cloth cover back on the seat, Shawn laid down a piece of cloth that had "velocity backer" written on a label.

"What is that for?" Steve asked.

"If that plate gets hit," Shawn said, pointing to the metal plate, "it might splinter and cause spalling… spalling is like shrapnel. That is a layer to protect from spalling."

Steve's felt his eyes grow large. "Well, I would imagine that the vests already have that inside," Steve stated, trying to sound knowledgeable.

"No," Shawn said, unflinching.

Steve's eyes grew bigger. "Oh."

"Grow a pair, dude," Shawn said. "Of course it does. Everyone on this detail has the same armor."

"Everyone?" Steve asked.

"Yes, everyone," Shawn said. He pulled the cloth cover over the car seat.

"Got a baby carrier? You know, the thing you strap her into to hold her to your body? Not a car seat," Shawn described.

"Oh! Like this?" Steve took a few steps to the car, reached under the back seat and pulled out a soft baby carrier. It looked like an octopus with all the straps dangling from it as he held it up.

"Put that on, with your armor," Shawn commanded.

Steve extended all the straps, slid the carrier on and held out his arms.

Shawn pulled a knife out of nowhere and walked toward Steve. Steve froze. Being around Shawn was like being around a tame lion. At any moment, all the training in the world could go out the window, and in one swipe, he could strike to kill.

Shawn's gaze fixated on the back of the baby carrier. He slid his knife along the top of the back, opening the layers of fabric. Bending over, he picked up one of the many pieces of metal and slowly slid it into the baby carrier. It was snug—too snug. Bending back down, he found another piece, along with a piece that said "velocity backer" on it. He slid both pieces into the carrier.

Shawn shook his head once. "Gonna have to do," he muttered. "This carrier is to be used as little as possible. Your best protection is the vehicle. This is shit for protection right here, but it's better than nothing. If you flee the vehicle, it's because everything has gone south and the vehicle no longer offers protection. This is a last resort. You might hand it off to the baby's mother when you get there. That detail might use it."

Steve was taken aback to hear Julie referred to as Addison's mother.

"We leave tomorrow. Be ready at zero-six-hundred. Sleep with the armor on. Have the baby sleep in that seat," Shawn directed.

He raised his hand, giving a slight wave, then walked away, quickly disappearing between vehicles.

***

At six o'clock the following morning, Steve sat in the driver's seat, wide awake. Addison was asleep in the car seat. She had been fussy most of the night. Steve held two backpacks for the trip. One contained the few personal items he had left in the world, including the parental release forms he'd promised his dad he would present at Pierce Point. The second pack carried Addison's supplies: diapers, formula, and a few changes of clothes. Steve had strapped the baby carrier around Addison's bag, attempting to streamline the number of items that needed to be carried.

The morning was chilly and damp, even with the sun well above the horizon.

Shawn, as usual, appeared out of nowhere near the passenger side of the vehicle. "Grab your bags," he commanded as he opened the door behind the front passenger seat and gingerly slid Addison out of the vehicle, still in her car seat.

"Follow me," Shawn ordered as he started walking away.

"Wait! The car? Where are you going?" Steve called out.

"Armored vehicle. Yours is staying here," Shawn said over his shoulder.

"That wasn't the agreement," Steve called, trying not to yell, and realizing he sounded like a complaining child.

"We are taking an armored vehicle. Any other questions?" Shawn stopped and looked directly at Steve.

Steve had several questions, but felt stupid asking any of them. What would happen to his car? That was part of the agreement, wasn't it? The car was valuable, so if no one wanted it, could he come back and get it? Mitch? What would Mitch think if the car was here after he said he wouldn't be?

As Steve's mind raced, he followed Shawn about fifty feet to an older, beat up, Toyota 4runner.

"But my SU—" Steve started to say.

"Shut up," Shawn interrupted, glaring. "Your hipster SUV isn't armored. I'm starting to repeat myself again. Get in."

Shawn opened the backdoor and slid Addison onto the seat. He pointed to the space on the opposite side of her, saying nothing, but glaring at Steve.

***

At zero seven hundred, Shawn and Steve were parked near the Airport Way overpass, pointed north. It was the last exit before crossing the I-205 bridge. In regular times, it was simply an overpass, but that was no longer the case. The I-205 had double chain-link fencing crossing it, with temporary buildings serving as booths for checkpoint agents. A military tank sat next to one of the buildings. Steve could not believe his eyes. He had no idea this checkpoint even existed, let alone in such an armed state.

Shawn looked in the rearview mirror and noticed Steve's wide eyes as he clutched Addison tightly.

"Shut up when I speak to anyone. If anyone speaks to you, be quiet. I'll answer for you. Clear?" Shawn commanded, which was met with a nod. Shawn settled into his seat and pulled a small radio and antenna out of a pocket in his chest. He turned up the volume.

"Eight-zero-eight to three-four, in position. Visual on you," Shawn said.

"Three-four. Copy," the man on the radio replied.

Shawn watched the guards intensely as they mingled around. They spoke to each other casually, pointed to the lined-up cars, and held large rifles to their chests.

Shawn was not alarmed by the rifles, but Steve's gawking told another story. Shawn watched every move the guards made—how they handled their firearms, how they communicated, who they pointed to, and their general routine.

Cars were motioned to approach the booth one at a time. Sometimes they were searched. Other times, they were completely emptied. Many car occupants didn't hide their annoyance or anger. Some were unperturbed and simply waited as their belongings were strewn on the pavement. One man got angry and started yelling and strutting around, waving his arms in the air. It didn't take long before he was tackled, handcuffed, and pinned to the ground as his car was searched. Thoroughly.

"We here to watch, or go through the checkpoint?" Steve asked from the backseat. "Seems like this is taking longer than necessary."

Shawn didn't answer.

Bang! Bang! Bang!

The baby immediately started to cry at the sudden sound, and even Shawn jumped slightly. He pressed the button to roll down the driver side window.

"Dude, thanks for scaring the kid." Shawn stared hard at the twenty-something-year old male standing at the door. Addison was now screaming, and Steve murmured quietly as he tried to calm the infant.

The guard scanned Steve and Addison, then looked at Shawn. Shawn glared. The guard took a slight step back.

"Uh… you're up," the young man said sheepishly as he pointed for the car to head to the booth.

Shawn's glare continued as he rolled the window up and slowly drove to the booth.

"You going north?" the guard asked.

"Yes, sir," Shawn replied.

He handed Shawn the telltale piece of pink paper. Shawn quickly took it and stashed it in his pocket. Shawn reached under his seat, pulled out two cartons of cigarettes, and handed them to the guard before slowly pulling away.

"Who are the guards? They don't seem like Portland police," Steve whispered.

"This is a state police checkpoint to control the traffic on I-205, and eventually I-5 farther north. The only authorized traffic is for essential supplies, infrastructure or 'humanitarian purposes,'" Shawn explained. "People like us have to convince those deputized millennials in charge that *we* are humanitarians."

"This took so long. How come there isn't a line backed up to Salem?" Steve asked, referring to Oregon's capitol, fifty miles south of them.

"People quit traveling north once the president's domestic immigration policies went into effect and settled in. The Feds govern this bridge and the I-5 bridge between Washington and Oregon, but the responsibility to police it is on the local law enforcement. Portland took up that baton and contracted it to the state patrol. Portland police have their hands full with whatever events happen downtown. You know more than anyone how corrupt that whole outfit is." Shawn looked directly at Steve in the rearview mirror as he emphasized his last statement. Shawn communicated without speaking that he was aware of what Steve did downtown.

"Yes, I do," Steve muttered, and nodded slowly.

"When the state decided to make it a toll bridge, it just opened up the door for them to have complete control over citizen travel by escalating prices. In January, it cost ten dollars one way to cross it. The governor said it was to pay for 'infrastructure' that the Feds refused to fund," Shawn described. "Mandates of who could pass came down slowly over the spring. And now, here we are. Just another layer of corruption. Our passage across this bridge is much more than ten dollars. Someone, somewhere, will get a wire transfer from your trust fund after we cross," Shawn said.

"Let me get this straight. In six months, this toll bridge — that started out with a ten-dollar toll — is now what... a hundred dollars? Five hundred dollars?"

"Add another zero," Shawn said. "Yes. Imagine if you had left Portland in December, when most families did. Business is booming for me," Shawn grinned.

"Jeez," Steve said with an audible sigh.

"Some call it a 'decline.' The media calls it a 'recession.' The governor blames the president. I call it what it is — a collapse. I like telling myself the truth, don't you?" Shawn looked at Steve and felt a stab of pity for the pathetic man, cowering in the back seat with a baby in his arms.

Chapter 60
Memory Lane

Julie stared at the computer monitor as she waited for all six hundred and eighty-four of her emails to load. She took a deep breath and watched the spinning clock pointer slowly tick, indicating that emails were loading. *This is going to take a while*, she thought as she leaned back in the chair of the Smoky Flats library.

Stretching her arms above her head, she looked at the ceiling. She leaned back down on her elbows and her gaze rested on Ned. He stood at the glass doors by the entrance, talking to Victor. His hands were in his jacket pockets and his demeanor was relaxed. From Julie's vantage point, the conversation appeared casual, but important. There wasn't urgency in their body language or volume level, but their faces were serious. Victor nodded intently as Ned seemed to describe something, occasionally taking his hands out of his pockets to gesture. Watching the two men talk reminded her of watching them deep in discussions before city council meetings, months before when she had first arrived at Smoky Flats.

She wondered what Ned was like as a father. She had seen him interact with Johnny, but Johnny was practically an adult now. *What was Ned like when his kids were little?* Julie wondered. *Did he wake up in the middle of the night? Did he gag at disgusting diapers? Did he make every time he changed a diaper seem like a major sacrifice of his time?*

Julie knew that Ned had imparted wilderness skills to his kids; she had seen that firsthand in Johnny. Julie hoped she could impart a fraction of what she had learned from Ned to Addison.

Julie was startled by this line of thought she hadn't considered before. Ned, just by being Ned, had shown Joel so many new skills in the short time they had been in Smoky Flats. Joel had learned things without even realizing he was learning them. He simply enjoyed being around Ned, and Ned enjoyed Joel.

What would it be like when Addison was around? Would Ned come by as often? Would he show the same friendly interest in their family as he did now? Summer would be a great time for evening walks around the lake. Julie was enjoying those walks as an almost daily routine. They were a pleasant and welcome punctuation mark to the end of a day. Julie was keenly aware that Ned liked her — a lot. He had made it clear in a reasonable and undramatic way. Julie was beginning to feel the same, but she was still fighting it.

I have got to get to Pierce Point and get Addison home. It's that simple.

The rest will take care of itself, Julie told herself. As she collected her thoughts, she caught Ned's eyes. He looked at her, smiled warmly, and waved. Julie's heart fluttered. She smiled, winked and waved back. The computer beeped. Her emails had loaded. Looking at the screen, she began to scan the list of senders.

"Ah!" Julie muttered to herself. There was one from her insurance company.

> *Ms. Atwood:*
> *Thank you for your continued patience as we process your claim. A claims adjustor surveyed your property recently. After the report is reviewed, your claim will be considered. We will notify you in the next sixty days as to the results of our investigation and the resolution to your claim.*

"Well that wasn't useful." She looked up and saw that Ned hadn't stopped looking at her. Julie's cheeks felt suddenly warm. She waved at him and gave him the "one more minute" sign. He nodded.

Julie scanned her emails for anything else that seemed urgent. Many caught her eye.

"I'll have to come back later and read those," she said with a sigh as she signed out and closed the browser.

Heading toward Ned at the library door, Julie couldn't help but smile. Ned's smile warmed her as he opened the door for her to exit. He extended his elbow to her, and she took it. They started the evening walk home.

"Victor was telling me the bank that owns the trading post sent him an email," Ned said, as he and Julie turned down the road leading to Western Lakes.

"Oh!" Julie was surprised. "What did they say?"

"Since people have been traveling through Smoky Flats, apparently word has gotten to them that the building is occupied, and not by squatters," Ned explained. "They want those who are occupying it to either pay rent or purchase the property."

"Well, that might be the end of the trading post then," Julie said, suddenly feeling worried.

"Victor said the same thing. He indicated several people in Smoky Flats benefitted from the trading post, and it made all the difference in how lean their winter was," Ned said.

"Think of Barbara," Julie pointed out. "She's an example of someone who should have used it more."

Ned nodded, and then quickly changed the subject. "Don't worry

9

about the property. Victor is going to contact the bank and point out to them that the property is in better condition now than it has been in years. The town's use of it improves the property value for them in the long run. He'll use his political skills of diplomacy and maybe smooth things. He's hoping he can keep the bank at bay until he can find a way for it to be purchased here locally. It's the same problem the property has had since it was abandoned," Ned said and squeezed her hand.

"On any other day, I'd worry. Right now, I honestly can't. I need to get to Pierce Point. When I get back with Addison, I'll worry," Julie declared.

"I'll worry with you when we return," Ned said, and flashed Julie a reassuring smile.

***

"This is becoming a ritual, Ned," Julie said, as they stood over their spread of gear. Just like three times before, she and Ned were surveying their gear for the trek to Kenney Reservoir the next day.

"It's a good ritual," Ned said with a nod as he strapped his sleeping bag to his pack.

"Yes," Julie almost whispered, nodding.

Ned looked at her. He could sense that Julie was growing more introverted and serious as the final trip approached. *She's got a lot to think about*, Ned reminded himself.

"I think a walk around the lake tonight would complete the ritual," Ned replied.

"That would be nice." Julie smiled softly.

"We'll go soon," Ned said. "Let me get this packed up."

Julie layered freeze dried food in her pack tightly, and nodded.

With only the sound of the evening breeze in the towering evergreens, Ned and Julie organized their packs. They had packed and repacked their things, not only to prepare for trips, but so that during trips, there was little need for words. They knew what each other was carrying, how it was packed, and where it was in each pouch and slot. For anyone watching, it was a synchronized dance to witness them prepare.

In unison, they stood up and stacked their packs against Ned's work bench. Ned grabbed a water bottle from the bench, turned to Julie and extended it to her. Julie took it as they headed down the drive for a walk around the lake.

As the gravel crunched under their feet, Ned scanned his brain, looking for a way to break the silence with words.

"Julie, tell me what you're thinking," Ned said, when he couldn't think of anything new or noteworthy to bring up.

"Oh, jeez, Ned, that's complicated," Julie said. "We might need to take laps around the lake tonight for that." Julie giggled.

"I'm all ears, and we have a long walk ahead of us. Try me," Ned said.

"I'm a mess of 'what ifs' right now. What if we miss the plane? What if one of us is injured? What if we are ambushed? What if we encounter a predator? What if…? What if…?" Julie spun her index finger in the air, as though the words she said were a constant swirl in her mind.

Julie continued before Ned could allay her anxiety. "That is one train of thought. Another train of thought I have is *you*," Julie said softly, looking forward, avoiding Ned's gaze. "I've said it a thousand times. Thank you. You're taking a huge risk to do this with me. To this day, I do not understand why — why would you leave the safety and comfort of your home to travel cross-country to this crazy place, to pick up a baby you have no connection to, only to turn around and do it all again in reverse. And that's not the half of it. You will also be trekking across Colorado's high country with this strange woman and even stranger baby for the final leg of this trip. Why? And yet, I'm so grateful. I wonder if I'm crazy for questioning your generosity, for fear you'll regain your sanity."

Julie's shoulders visibly shrunk as she blurted out the words. A burden had been released.

"And yet another train of thought is Joel. I've talked to him a lot about having a baby around. He seems excited. My dad seems excited. Babies are exciting. But babies are also a drain. I'm no fool. I know we are living in tenuous times with no guarantees of the future. I worry that she will feel like she was the redheaded stepchild we took in out of charity. I realize that's a bit emotional and irrational, but I want her to know she is loved and cherished. I need to make sure Joel and Dad conduct themselves that way." Julie whispered her final thoughts, "No one would have gone to this kind of risk if she wasn't worth it."

Julie sighed and squinted her eyes. Ned could see the worry all over her face. "On the other hand, I'm excited. It's the same excitement I had when I was in the final stages of pregnancy. I am ready. Everything is prepared. The baby just needs to come. Isn't that silly? I feel like a huge, pregnant woman about to give birth, who just needs to go into labor," Julie described with a tender smile on her face. She looked up at Ned. "I'm all over the place. At any given moment, I'm somewhere between worried, grateful, and excited."

"Julie," Ned said with a sigh, "I can't see into the future and tell you this trip will be a walk in the park. I worry about the same things. I have prepared us as much as I can, and I'm hoping we have covered everything, but I know we haven't. It's not possible. I do know this, though—the chances of success increase a hundred times by having two of us go prepared, versus you by yourself. Not sure that helps."

"What you say is true," Julie agreed.

Ned continued. "As to my motivations for doing this…" He paused, waiting for Julie to say something. After a moment had passed and the silence started to feel awkward, he pressed on. "You don't know?"

Julie shot him a confused look. "No, I don't," she answered.

"Julie, it's you. I know you don't feel the same, and that is fine. But if you want something, I want it for you. I know it's juvenile for me to insert myself in all the things you want to do. However, by traveling to Pierce Point, I knew I could help. If that is something you want to do, I want it for you. I want to help you. Does this make sense?"

"It does. Still very risky, though," Julie replied.

After a long stretch of silence as they watched the sun kiss the mountaintops, Julie asked quietly, "Ned, you know those conversations from last November and a couple of months ago?"

"I do." Ned's curiosity was piqued.

"You just reminded me of what you said," Julie mused. "You're saying your feelings for me haven't changed at all since then. This isn't a passing thing."

"Oh, wow, Julie. No. If anything, they have grown richer as I've gotten to know you. I stand by what I said that first dry run trip. I know you're fiercely independent. I understand my role is to get Addison home. I have not only made that promise to you, but to your dad. No one knows what will happen after we return. I don't expect anything from you once we get home. At the very least, I hope you'll join me for summer evening walks and an occasional cup of tea. I enjoy evenings with you and your family, and I would miss them," Ned said.

"I would miss them, too, Ned. I enjoy them very much. I think Dad and Joel do, as well. I don't want our evenings to ever stop," Julie said as she squeezed Ned's arm.

Ned smiled.

"Ned, I was thinking about babies today. Imagine that? Tell me what you were like when your children were babies."

"That's a good question. You might want to know that, since we'll be sharing a tent with a baby soon, huh?" Ned joked. "Wow, let me think. That was a lifetime ago."

Ned looked up to the sky as though he were pulling memories out of the universe, and that *was* what it felt like. His memory hadn't waded into those waters in many years.

"Well, Barbara had a homebirth for both Rachel and Johnny. Takes too long to get to a birthing center. The thought of trying to get to one was more stress than it was worth. Easier to do it at home."

"Wow, that's pretty impressive!" Julie exclaimed.

"What a moment — to watch them enter the world and take their first breath," Ned said. "Those are moments that cameras don't capture. It's a memory in my heart. Watching them with their mother in those first moments. Cutting the cord. Feeding them. Oh, man..." Ned smiled deeply as he recalled the moment his children were born.

"You had a midwife?"

"Yes. There was a lady over in Lucky Ranch who was a licensed midwife. She birthed a whole lot of kids in Smoky Flats over the years. She retired about five years ago. What was her name?" Ned wondered out loud. "Regardless, she retired and moved to Denver, I think. Something about health issues."

"Tell me about when Rachel walked for the first time," Julie prodded.

"Rachel was an early walker. She walked at nine months old. It was strange to see such a small baby walking," Ned said. "I'd plant her on her feet in the dining room and she would toddle to her mom in the living room. She was so determined, and yet so gangly." Ned laughed. He looked at Julie, who was smiling. "Then Barbara would turn Rachel around and send her back to me. I'd catch her as she came toward me and give her a toss in the air. One time she spit up in mid-flight. I got a mouthful of Rachel-spit-up. That was horrible, but we were laughing so hard, the horribleness was short lived."

"Tell me a story about Johnny," Julie pressed.

"Let me think." Ned looked up at the sky to pull another memory out of the universe. "Rachel was hell on wheels as a baby and toddler. She was always in motion, and didn't have time for a hug or a kiss. Johnny was the opposite. He loved to cuddle and hug. Going to bed was an hour's worth of cuddling. He wasn't fussy, but he was cuddly, and needed that time to settle down to sleep. I did the bedtime routine so Barbara could have an evening break from children after a full day. I enjoyed it. I got an hour to relax and cuddle my son. I know that isn't as exciting as spit up in my mouth, but that is what I remember about Johnny as a baby. I loved quiet evenings with him. In a way, we still have our quiet evenings now."

Ned took a deep breath as he felt raw emotion bubble up in his chest. "Babies are a blessing."

"I love it when you say that. It keeps the purpose of this trip in sharp focus for me," Julie said.

"Addison is a blessing, Julie," Ned said determinedly. "Babies are worth fighting for. That may be my best answer for why I am helping you. Babies in a collapse, in a big city, are in danger. If helping you gets your daughter here, then it's worth it. She's worth it."

"Yes," Julie agreed, smiling. "It's nice to hear you say 'daughter.'"

"I can't wait to meet her and bring her home," Ned said decidedly.

"Me neither," Julie said.

Chapter 61
Kandi's Place

Jon sat at the bar inside Kandi's, a long-forgotten nightclub in downtown Portland. It was an unusually quiet evening. Since the collapse, business had slowed considerably, but tonight was exceptional. Kandi's was once a thriving, bustling club, nationally recognized for its drag queen shows. At one point, decades ago, the club's cabaret style shows were glitzy, glamorous, tasteful, and amazing. Kandi's made headlines. This was back in the days when cross dressing was taboo, so while the general public was outraged by its success, Kandi's helped make dressing in drag mainstream — and profitable.

In recent years, Kandi's had become a magnet for patrons from all walks of life. Marvin, or "Kandi" as "she" was known when "he" was in full drag regalia, was an icon of not only the downtown bar scene, but the pinnacle of success for Portland's gay and lesbian community. Kandi's success, popularity, and publicity legitimized the gay and lesbian community in an era of secrecy.

As the collapse and decline of downtown Portland began, and only worsened, success waned at Kandi's. Every business in downtown felt the decline. Those in the restaurant and bar scenes were hit hardest. No one had money to spend on necessities, let alone a high-priced meal with an even more expensive beverage.

Normally, Kandi's attracted all things edgy and strange. Thursday through Saturday featured male strippers. A patron would enjoy drinks — creatively named with subtle innuendos to the atmosphere — and a full pub menu. Kandi's was an avenue for all members of the LGBTQ community to meet others in the community, while avoiding the strictly swinging gay scene. Going to Kandi's was entertainment first, hooking up second. Once gay marriage was legalized in Oregon, the bachelor and bachelorette party business took off at Kandi's. A new population of marriage seekers wanting to start their lives with a swinging, hedonistic party gave Kandi's a shot in the arm of new business. On any given weekend night, Kandi's banquet rooms were booked with parties that would make Roman orgies pale in comparison. Food, drink, and debauchery.

Kandi's downtown location also offered convenience. Professionals who spent days in the high-towered, professional offices — grinding out metrics and numbers — could easily go to Kandi's, enjoy a drink, meet a new friend, and head home. Kandi's was not seedy. To be seen there as a professional meant that you were simply enjoying the progressive offering Portland embraced. If anyone questioned a professional's presence at Kandi's, they were frowned on for their "judgment" and "intolerance."

Banquet rooms could be reserved for drunken bachelor or bachelorette parties. Strippers of any gender could be booked for any event. Strippers were arranged, alcohol flowed freely, pictures were snapped, Kandi made an appearance, swishing a feather boa, and more pictures were snapped. Such parties offered an aura of legitimacy and discretion. Photos were splashed all over social media, and Kandi reveled in the publicity. Partygoers were elevated for being open-minded and progressive. To be employed by Kandi's as a stripper was a highlight in the performer's career.

While Kandi was always the featured drag queen, her performance slots were given to the younger talent as she aged. Kandi's website profiled a dozen different drag performers and their talent.

Local politicians and elected officials made sure to shake hands and snap pictures with Kandi during any given election. A picture with Kandi was as good as an official endorsement. It guaranteed the vote from many in Portland's gay and lesbian community. It guaranteed the majority vote of over thirty-two thousand people. Kandi knew it, too, and used her influence to make sure her club was taken care of by local government officials. Kandi's venue was never checked for liquor control violations, health code violations, or scrutinized by the police for sex crimes. Ever.

This was convenient, because the unspoken secret known to everyone—including elected officials and lawmakers—was that Portland's strip club community was a gateway to the sex trafficking world. Stripping was lucrative and profitable if the performer was smart and stayed out of trouble. Working at Kandi's offered safety and legitimacy that no other strip club could offer—and money. What happened just outside Kandi's doors was never discussed.

Tonight, Jon wanted to relax and have a drink. He had been struggling with chronic bronchitis. Getting to a doctor had grown increasingly difficult—and expensive. Since he had lost his job at a local credit union, seeing a doctor without insurance was impossible. Paying for antibiotics out of pocket was out of the question. If he could find them on the street, he might be able to afford the street prices. Tonight was a lucky night. He had managed to find a full bottle of antibiotics on the street. He could take a full course, not just a few. He stood a chance of ridding himself of the bronchitis.

Jon took the bottle out of his jacket pocket, rattled out his first dose, and swallowed it with a sip of his potent drink. He knew there was a rule somewhere about antibiotics and drinking, but he didn't care. The drink would feel good until the medication kicked in.

"Hey, handsome."

Jon felt a tap on his shoulder. Pivoting on his chair, Jon recognized Patrick, a younger man Jon knew from his building. Jon had always assumed he worked in another office, because he saw him regularly in the lobby and/or in the elevator.

"Hey," Jon replied, extending his hand to shake Patrick's.

Patrick ignored Jon's gesture, and extended his arms for a hug.

Jon was unnerved by the personal gesture, but responded in kind. *We're in Kandi's after all*, Jon thought, *and I need to relax*.

"You look like you need another drink," Patrick said as he sat next to Jon. "Can I join you?"

Patrick was magnetic—his smile and his spirit. Jon welcomed the man's warmth and company—anything to get his mind off his endless worries.

The men flowed into an easy conversation, and Jon didn't notice as the sparse crowd thinned out even more. He didn't even notice when he and Patrick were the only patrons left at the bar. Time had escaped him while he was engrossed in conversation. Patrick was fun and easy to talk to. He was cheery, bright, and smart—just what Jon needed on a night like this. Patrick was young and professional. His whole life was still ahead of him. Jon had been worried about his job and health, so talking to a sympathetic person was like drinking from a well in a dry desert.

The bartender indicated it was last call, and an overhead light went up near the kitchen.

"My pumpkin has arrived," Patrick said, and his eyes sparkled.

"Where is your pumpkin taking you?" Jon responded flirtatiously.

"It's not a fancy pumpkin. The city bus will take me to the Lents neighborhood tonight," Patrick said dejectedly.

"Let me give you a lift. I have a few gasps of fuel left in my car. I'm parked in the garage two blocks away. Let's go." Jon stood up. He tried not to seem too eager but felt a ping of excitement at the prospect of moving to a more private location with Patrick.

The men slowly walked the street to the parking structure. Some of the street lights weren't working. Jon thought it gave the streets an old-movie look. He was sure Humphrey Bogart and Lauren Bacall would stroll by at any moment. The night was warm with a slight breeze.

Is the antibiotic working? Is it the drinks? Or is this really a wonderful evening? Jon wanted to pinch himself. He hadn't felt this good in a long time.

He and Patrick found the stairway entrance to the parking structure. The elevator hadn't worked in months. Jon didn't mind. His heart raced for many reasons as he rounded the switchback going up the stairs. On level four, the door to the stairs opened.

Four cars were parked on the level. Jon noticed a couple in a hybrid as they pulled out of their spot. He turned to look at Patrick, and was met with an overpowering embrace, as Patrick grabbed him before he could say a word.

***

Five days later, a homeless person made a police report about a partially clothed man, dead, in the parking garage stairway. He appeared to have fallen down the stairs and died from massive head trauma, but it was difficult to ascertain, since the body was in advanced stages of decomposition.

The deceased man's pockets were turned inside out, and identification was difficult. Police officers indicated that the man appeared to have fallen down the stairs drunk, and suffered head trauma. The lack of identification and personal items were attributed to the lag-time of police response in critical times. Homeless people — and regular people down on their luck — had no problem scavenging whatever was necessary these days.

An artist's drawing was formulated to locate anyone who might be able to identify the deceased man. His case was filed away. His picture was profiled on an obscure page of the Portland Police website, alongside numerous other John and Jane Does.

***

Two nights later, Bruce and Matt sat at a pub table at Kandi's. As fellow realtors, their day was marked by trying to keep squatters out of empty listings, calling mortgage companies in Great States to quell fears, and finding buyers in an ever-shrinking market.

Both men were concerned for the future of the housing market, and their careers. This night was for celebrating, however. They had secured a property management gig, which would compensate them for managing a small apartment complex that was owned by someone out of the state. The tenant turnover had become unmanageable for the owner. Squatters had ruined two of the apartments, and the repairs had been costly. Bruce and Matt welcomed the contract and income — even if it was managing difficult tenants and overseeing repairs. Money was money. Employment was something to cherish these days.

Bruce and Matt were more than just business partners — they were married. Kandi's was a favorite spot for them to unwind after work. During their dating days, they had spent many wild nights partying at Kandi's. Their bachelor party was in one of Kandi's infamous banquet rooms. Recently, Kandi's had become a place to reminisce and enjoy life's small celebrations.

As Bruce and Matt raised their glasses, Matt felt a tap on his shoulder.

"Hello, gentlemen. This must be the table reserved for only those who are exceptionally handsome."

"Patrick! Good to see you. Join us!" Bruce exclaimed. "Matt, this is Patrick. He works in the KOIN building. I see him when I go there to make deposits." Bruce gestured to Matt. "We're celebrating good news tonight!"

Chapter 62
Know the Enemy, Know Yourself

"If you know the enemy and know yourself, you need not fear the result of a hundred battles. If you know yourself but not the enemy, for every victory gained you will also suffer a defeat. If you know neither the enemy nor yourself, you will succumb in every battle." ~ Sun Tzu

Patrick left the office building. His week was over, and the long journey home was ahead. He braced himself for the two-hour city bus ride. Patrick always braced himself for that experience.

"Shit holes are less disgusting than a Portland city bus," he mumbled to himself. "Oh well."

Patrick preferred to ride a bicycle to work, but it had been stolen months ago. Without a car of his own, the city bus was his only option for getting into downtown. While trendy, cycling in Portland's wet winter months made the trek less enjoyable.

"At least I don't pay outrageous parking fees," he would brag to his acquaintances in an attempt to sound upbeat as his feet sloshed in the inevitable standing water.

In reality, Portland's city busses had become a petri dish of human waste, disguised as a mode of transportation for everyone who wasn't part of the elite class who could afford to put gas in their vehicles.

Patrick had dumped the hybrid car he scored last week. It ran out of gas, and he couldn't hustle enough money to fuel it up. He was frustrated by the loss. Hybrids were great for their gas mileage and he'd had his eye on that one.

Jon had been an acquaintance, which created a loose alibi for Patrick if questioned. Patrick could simply say, "Jon leant it to me. I have the smart key," and hold up the key. He could position himself in the same workplace as Jon. With the level of chaos in the city, investigators didn't bother to chase down the minute details that would reveal his dangerous scam.

Patrick was mad at himself. He was hoping he could sell Jon's antibiotics on the black market and get enough money for gas. Since he planned to travel so little, the car should have kept him moving for weeks. No such luck.

In the struggle with Jon, the pill bottle was broken, sending pills scattering throughout the stairwell. Since Jon had little left in the gas tank, the car didn't do much for Patrick. Patrick knew if he kept the car for too long in one place, it would draw attention, so he simply pushed it off a boat slip on the Columbia River near Jantzen Beach late one night.

He was back to square one: hating the bus ride he was sentenced to. He needed a new gig. As he rounded the corner, he noticed a young man standing at the bus stop near Kandi's. The young man nodded and smiled at Patrick. Patrick took a deep breath. *Could this be tonight's project?* he wondered as he smiled back and turned toward the young man.

"Hi, handsome," Patrick said, flashing his signature smile.

"Hello, there," the young man answered, not matching Patrick's enthusiasm, but smiling nonetheless.

"You going home?" Patrick asked pointing to the bus stop sign.

"Naw. Enjoying a cigarette," the man said, waving his left hand to show a cigarette.

Who can afford cigarettes these days? Patrick wondered, intrigued.

"My name is Patrick. I don't think I've met you around here, have I?" Patrick asked flirtatiously.

"I've been around. I've seen you," the young man said with a smile.

Patrick felt his cheeks grow warm. "If you've seen me around, and you know my name, then what is your name?"

"My name is Qaatel. And, you're right. I come here often," he answered.

Patrick instantly felt at ease. *Good, he's part of this community*. Patrick had wondered if Qaatel was a straight man just waiting at the bus stop.

"Well, since you seem to know me so well, let me buy you a drink, Qaatel," Patrick answered.

"Sure thing," Qaatel answered. He dropped his half-used cigarette and crushed it with his heel. Qaatel warmly patted Patrick's shoulder as they headed into Kandi's.

The late afternoon sun soon turned to dark, but Patrick didn't notice. He was too engrossed in the conversation, and something about Qaatel intrigued him, drew him in. The evening had started out flirty and superficial. Patrick gave his typical resume of what he did for a living. It wasn't so much of a living as a location.

"I work in the KOIN Tower. Not sure how much longer it will last, but I'll hang in there as long as I can," Patrick described. "What do you do?"

"I'm a head hunter," Qaatel answered with intense eyes.

Patrick felt his stomach jump a little as their eyes locked for an extended moment.

"Oh, wow, so you seek out employees for employers?"

"I seek out a lot of people, yes," Qaatel answered with a smile.

"What business are you in?"

"I'm in the people business! That's why I'm here with you," Qaatel answered flamboyantly, and with a tap on Patrick's knee.

The tit-for-tat conversation carried on. Qaatel seemed particularly skilled at answering questions with questions of his own. Patrick felt sucked in by this man's mysterious aura. Qaatel shared cigarettes freely with Patrick, who was impressed by the luxury item. Patrick was also impressed when Qaatel gave a sign to the bartender that he would pay for the pair's tab for the night. The drinks flowed freely.

The men sat at a pub table near a window, and ordered not only drinks, but a hearty dinner. Patrick hadn't had a decent meal for weeks, and enjoyed not only the full feeling in his stomach, but the surge of energy from the nutrition beginning to course through his body. He was beginning to feel "normal" again. After two strong drinks and his dinner, Patrick felt satisfied and content.

"Tell me more about this mysterious 'headhunting' you do, Qaatel," Patrick said as the wait person took his plate.

Qaatel moved in closer to Patrick. "I'm looking for the sorts of people you look for, Patrick." He stared intently at Patrick.

Surprised, and suddenly suspicious of this charming man, Patrick sat back in his seat. *What does he know about me – what I've done?*

"Oh? And what sorts of people do I look for, Qaatel?" Patrick countered, trying to be coy.

"Oh, my dear man," Qaatel said and waved his hand. "You look worried. No need to be. I have watched your game, and I am impressed." Qaatel was flirty in his words and gestures.

Patrick was put at ease a bit, but remained unsure about what he said. He knew he needed to keep his guard up.

"I don't know what you're talking about," Patrick replied dismissively.

"Oh, stop—you do too. And again, I'm impressed. I'm looking for someone with your skills. I was smoking a cigarette outside earlier, but in all honesty, I was waiting for you."

"Skills, huh? Tell me what skills you see in me." Patrick was trying to sound casual, but his alcohol buzz made it impossible to keep a poker face. He knew that Qaatel could tell that he was nervous. He felt like he was losing at a game he didn't even know he'd been playing.

"You come here often. Everyone here knows you, as do most people in your work building. You make a point to shake everyone's hand. Not just shake, but give everyone the illusion they know you, and you belong in their world. You keep track of who comes to Kandi's and you make sure you know them, and they know you, or at least they feel like they know you. Right? But in reality, you don't work in the building. You *troll* the building, but you don't extract a paycheck."

It took all of Patrick's energy to keep a straight face and remain nonresponsive. His game was up if he gave away anything. Qaatel could have him arrested. Portland police rarely arrested anyone due to their lack of resources, but if Qaatel took what he knew to the police, he'd be arrested easily. While Qaatel seemed to know plenty about Patrick, he was unsure if Qaatel knew *everything* there was to know.

"Patrick, you don't need to worry. I like you. I like you a lot." Qaatel moved in for the kill. "Like I said, I need someone with your skills. If we can put together a gentlemen's agreement, I think we'll both get what we want."

"Gentlemen's agreement?"

"Yes," Qaatel said and leaned back, motioning to the wait person. "We need another round. We're about to celebrate."

Qaatel leaned in, locked eyes with Patrick, and whispered his offer in a seductive tone. "Patrick, I can make this easy for you. You bring me the people you ensnare, alive. They must be alive. You get their spoils. That simple. Come to think of it, this will make your job easier. Less messy? Maybe?"

"What will happen to them?" Patrick asked.

"Really? I've seen what you do to them. Why do you care?"

Patrick felt the color drain from his face. He had figured up to this point that Qaatel had observed his hustling in the KOIN Tower and Kandi's. That meant Qaatel knew the ultimate end of Patrick's hustle.

"What do you say, Patrick?" Qaatel pressed.

"I don't know," Patrick answered in a loud, frustrated whisper.

"Let me make it easier for you, then. You have a second choice. I can call the police and inform them that I know John Doe's identity. He is Jon, without an H. And that I remember seeing him the night I sold him antibiotics a few blocks from here when he told me he was headed to Kandi's. I might also tell him about the two men who manage an apartment complex near me that aren't returning my call," Qaatel warned. "You and I know they will simply write down this information and file it away. However, I can also point out that I saw you back a car into the Columbia River at the Jantzen Beach boat slip. Once they have that car, you're in police custody. I hear that court cases are backed up by years. I hope you don't choose the second option, Patrick. I like you and I want us to be friends. That option would immediately make us enemies. Can we be friends?"

Qaatel's eyes were intense and he never blinked as he laid out Patrick's options.

Patrick studied him as he spoke. Qaatel couldn't be older than thirty. He was nicely dressed, but blended in with everyone. Not fancy, but well kept. He was clean. Patrick realized he probably took regular showers. The cigarettes and open tab. Qaatel had money and connections, Patrick realized. Qaatel's offers had resources to back them up. His skin was dark, and his hair was black and curly. His features communicated Middle Eastern descent, and his accent was American.

"Deal," Patrick said and swallowed hard.

"Wonderful!" Qaatel answered with glee.

"Wonderful," Patrick responded in a low tone.

***

"Hello, handsome!" Patrick greeted.

Two men turned, surprised expressions on their faces.

"Hello!" one replied. "Do we know you?"

"I've seen you two here often. I have to say that it's great celebrating special couples like you. I think I remember seeing guests going into your bachelor party here… when was it… last fall, maybe?" Patrick looked up as though he was trying to remember.

"Close. Late last summer! Oh, wow, you should have said something then, you could have joined us. That was a par-tay!"

"Well, I didn't know you then, but I see you here so often that I feel like I know you. Not to sound like a stalker," Patrick said with a grin. "I'm Patrick."

"Patrick, this is my husband, Trevor. And I'm Adam." Patrick leaned in and hugged both men.

"So nice to have the chance to talk to you two! Tell me! I've seen you, now tell me all about how you met and got married." Patrick looked up with a flirty smile. "I need some hope that a perfect person is out there for me."

Patrick motioned to the wait person for a new round of drinks.

"Gentlemen, since we're celebrating, dinner is on me," Patrick offered.

"How lovely, thank you," Trevor answered, reaching out and rubbing Patrick's forearm.

Food and drink flowed and Patrick listened intently as Trevor and

24

Adam told their story. Trevor would finish Adam's sentences and carry the story. Trevor would tell a side story, like, "But then my sister, she lives in LA, came to the wedding. Let me tell you about her for a moment. She is my rock!"

Patrick listened with enraptured attention, but not for the reasons Adam and Trevor would have expected. Patrick learned from the story that Adam worked at Oregon's Department of Human Services as a field-based social worker. Trevor was a freelance artist. He had been working hard to grow his international footprint since the collapse. He was getting some commissions, but business was tough. He was considering looking for other work.

Patrick learned that the couple had downsized to one car since the economy tanked. So far, they were living comfortably, compared to others, relying on Adam's state income. They were wary of the constant threat of layoffs that Adam had managed to avoid so far.

"DHS will be one of the last departments to close down, I'm sure of it. I feel good I'll be employed for the foreseeable future. I'm looking around, but no one is hiring," Adam said.

"We love it here in Portland! It's so diverse and LGBTQ friendly, we don't want to move. We'll cross that bridge if it comes," Trevor added.

Adam and Trevor indicated they were also dipping into some trust fund money that Adam's father had left for him when he passed a few years ago. "We wanted to get the car paid off," Adam explained.

"I have only heard of trust funds. I'm not so lucky. How exactly do they work?" Patrick asked doing his best to sound sincere, resting his chin on his hand looking genuinely interested. He knew exactly how trust funds worked. He wanted the details of Adam's trust fund. The conversation and drinks continued.

"It's late, my dear," Trevor said pointing to his wrist as though he had a wristwatch on. "Patrick, it's been a wonderful evening. Thank you so much for dinner and drinks. We need to head home. Can we give you a lift?"

"That would be wonderful. Yes, please," Patrick said with a smile.

The three men went outside on the warm, summer night. The sky was a dark, azure blue.

"We're in this parking garage," Adam said as he pointed to the stairwell.

"This one? Really! I have something special to show you. This is perfect!" Patrick exclaimed. "There is an upper deck to this garage that is perfect for watching sunsets like tonight's. We should go up to the top deck to see the lovely skyline in this light."

"Okay," Trevor said, shrugging.

The men went up the multiple stair switchbacks to get to the top deck. As they opened the door, everyone stopped for a moment to catch their breath, not only from the stairs but also from the view of Portland's skyline—the buildings, the Willamette River and the last of the sunlight brushing against the west hills.

All three men approached the handrail. Patrick and Trevor put their arms around each other. It was quiet and serene as they took in the panoramic view.

"Don't move!" said an unfamiliar voice from behind the three men. In a flash, Trevor and Adam had knife blades held to their throats. They froze.

"Take off your clothes! Don't look at me. Keep looking at the railing. If you look at me, your face will be sliced in half," barked the person holding the knife to their throats. "I'm right behind you. If you don't do as I say, the knife goes through you."

Adam and Trevor looked at each other desperately. Adam's chin quivered. Trevor's eyes were red.

"No problem, but please just take our things and let us go," Adam begged.

"Take off your clothes, now!" the man snarled.

Both men methodically took off their clothes, down to their boxers, and hesitated.

"Patrick! *Where are you?* Are you okay?" Adam called out as he scrambled out of his clothes trying to make side glances to locate Patrick.

"Shut up! All of your clothes!"

Both men complied, and then stood up straight with their hands out to their sides, looking at the Portland skyline. Adam scanned the area, desperately looking for Patrick.

"Step forward," the man commanded. Adam and Trevor stepped over their clothes, pressing their bodies to the railing.

"Stand up on the ledge."

Both men hesitated, stretching their peripheral vision to see the other. A tear dropped from Trevor's nose.

"Now!"

They scrambled up and stood on the ledge, still looking at Portland's beautiful skyline.

Patrick rushed up behind them, and shoved Trevor until he fell over the ledge. Before Adam could respond, Patrick's hands were on him, too, as he sent the man flying, following his lover to the ground.

Patrick found the key fob for the car in Adam's pocket. When he activated it, he heard the car beep on the second floor of the parking structure. After rushing down the stairs, he quickly popped the trunk and shoved the men's clothes inside.

He slid into the driver's seat and pressed the "start" button. A sly smile grew on his face as he saw the gas gauge go up to the three-quarters-full line. It wasn't a true hybrid vehicle, but it was a fuel-efficient model. Plus, Patrick knew he could access bank accounts to keep the tank full for weeks or months.

"Sweet!" Patrick said under his breath.

He could hear the commotion and screams on the street. *Time to bounce*, he thought, putting the car in reverse and quickly leaving the structure.

As the nose of the car pulled out onto the street, the stairwell door opened. Qaatel stepped out. Patrick caught his eye and held Qaatel's intense gaze for a moment. Patrick looked both ways, then pulled out into the street and disappeared into the dark night, as blaring ambulances stopped at the building.

After leaving downtown, Patrick pulled off to a parking lot near the decrepit Lloyd Center Mall. It had been closed for months, and the lot was a haven for the homeless. Patrick couldn't wait.

He climbed into the backseat and pulled the tab that brought the seat down, giving him access to the trunk.

Riffling through the pockets, he exclaimed, "Ha! Got it!"

He pulled out a large billfold. It wasn't a billfold so much as a pocket-sized briefcase. Unzipping the enclosure, he found neatly organized identifying documents to the trust fund, identification, and social security numbers. The trust fund was in Kansas, not Oregon. *Even better*, thought Patrick.

Continuing the search, he found a paystub with an address on it.

"I know where I'll be sleeping tonight," Patrick said to himself.

Quickly looking up, he decided he had seen enough. He pushed the seat back up and climbed to the front seat. Without hesitating, he clicked open the GPS screen and punched the "home" button, checked it against the address on the paystub, and followed the directions.

Chapter 63
Hand Slapping

"Dad, how are you doing?"

Floyd hadn't been sure what to think when the phone rang. The only time the phone rang these days was when Steve made one of his scheduled calls. Julie and Ned had left two days before for Kenney Reservoir, so he wondered what Steve could possibly want. But, as soon as he heard the voice on the other end, he knew it wasn't Steve.

"Seth," Floyd said as his heart jumped. "I am well. How are you? It is great to hear your voice."

"I'm not good, Dad." Seth spoke with a frantic tone. "Chicago is crazy and I don't know how much more I can take."

Floyd knew exactly where this was going. "Seth, are you high?"

"What? What the fuck, Dad! I tell you how I am and you ask me if I'm high? How about this, how about this... are *you* high? I mean, my God, Dad!" Seth exclaimed.

"I can hear it in your voice, Seth. You're high," Floyd answered calmly, trying to keep from joining his son's heightened emotions.

"Of course, I'm high! I'm in fucking Chicago. It's what keeps me sane in this shit hole!" Seth yelled.

"What do you want?"

"I want out of Chicago. Now! Please help me. I don't have anything." Seth lowered his voice. "They are after me. This place is fucking crazy." He slurred the last words of his screed.

"Seth, nothing I can do will get you the help you need," Floyd answered.

Floyd bit his lip. It killed him every time he had conversations like this with his son. In previous discussions, Floyd would concede and arrange to get money to Seth. The money would be used to buy drugs instead of paying for whatever emergency Seth said he needed it for. Floyd had helped Seth so many times, to the tune of thousands of dollars, only to end up with the sobering conclusion that he had simply helped his son get his next fix.

"What? What do you mean? This is easy. No, really, I mean it," Seth said, turning on his best salesman voice. "Just get me to Colorado. Where you are? Easy. Then I'm out of here and away from this place. No drugs in the Rocky Mountains, right? I can get clean. Easy. Seriously, just get me to Colorado and everything will be okay."

Floyd took a long pause before responding. "Seth, nothing I can do will get you the help you need." Floyd had rehearsed this response repeatedly, anticipating Seth's drug-addled call. He had been down this road before where heartfelt, emotion-tugging promises were made, assuring him that his money would be used for a designated purpose — a purpose Floyd desperately wanted for Seth. Never once had the money been used for its right purpose, though. It was always, always drugs.

"Oh my God, Dad! Seriously! Wire me some money, and I can get the fuck out of here. You have no idea how bad it is!"

"No. I don't have access to money right now. In case you haven't noticed, there's a collapse happening right now," Floyd replied.

"Sure you do! Just go to the bank and wire it to me," Seth begged.

"No. The closest operating bank is hours away by car. No one uses their car to go to the bank to wire money. People use their cars for emergencies — like a someone-is-bleeding kind of emergency," Floyd explained calmly, though he could hear his voice crack. It killed him. Every fiber in his body wanted to extend help to Seth, but he knew any help would be wasted and snorted.

"The bank is hours away? What are you talking about? It's in town. Are you lying to me, Dad?"

"The bank is not operating in Smoky Flats. The closest bank is Denver."

"Oh my God, Dad! You have to help me!"

"Seth, if you can get to Smoky Flats, I'll see if I can find some place for you to stay here. There are lots of outbuildings or abandoned homes. You just can't stay here at the cabin — we do not have the space or resources. Actually, to be clear, you are not welcome here, ever. Even for dinner. Do you understand?" Floyd's voice cracked as he finished his firm command. Tough love was not something that ever came easily to him. *I'm giving him the same requirements I gave for Steve. I must be fair,* Floyd rationalized to himself.

"Dad, I'm your son!" Seth yelled.

"Yes, you are my grown son," Floyd agreed. He couldn't say much more without his voice cracking again.

"Oh my God," Seth said, resignation in his voice. "So, that's it? That is all?"

"If that is all you want to talk about, I suppose so. It's good to hear from you." He had a feeling it would be a long time before he heard from Seth again, and that horrified him, though not enough to give in to Seth's demands. He braced himself for what would come next. It happened every time.

"Fuck you, Dad," Seth said. The line went dead.

29

Floyd set the phone's handpiece onto the cradle, and choked back his emotions.

***

"What happened?" Ramona demanded as Seth closed the door to the rundown RV.

"Nothing. Nothing happened. He won't help," Seth said, directing his irritation at Ramona. "Shut up."

"What you are going to do? Oscar is going to be pissed," Ramona demanded, her voice scratchy and hoarse.

"Shut up!" Seth reached over and slapped Ramona, hard.

"God! You're a prick!" Ramona yelled.

"God, you're smart," Seth said sarcastically.

"Oscar is going to fuck you up. You know it," Ramona taunted.

Seth towered over Ramona, his right arm across his chest as though he were going to backhand her. "I told you to shut the fuck up," he yelled, right in her face.

Ramona flinched and cowered, visibly bracing herself for the blow that usually came next, but Seth couldn't find it in himself to hit her as hard as he wanted to.

"You have work to do tonight, or else Oscar is going to be up your ass," Seth yelled as he backed away from Ramona.

Seth sat down hard at the tiny table. The grimy windows let in little light. The RV was cluttered and dingy. His mind was racing.

Seth and Ramona lived in a neglected, sometimes operational, RV in a city-designated parking lot for people who live in RVs. It was one of many lots referred to as "low income housing" for the "displaced." It was a place for the nearly homeless to park decrepit RVs and live in squalor. It was a haven for drugs, crime, and prostitution. Seth and Ramona were some of many purveyors and partakers of the goods and services offered in the lot.

They had known each other for years. In the early years, they were a couple. They had tried the sobriety and twelve-step path together, hoping to build a "normal" life. Ramona had wanted to get married and live happily ever after. Seth tried, too, but ended up arrested for domestic assault in one of his drunken benders. His stint in jail introduced him to drugs, which were plentiful behind bars.

Once out of jail, Seth and Ramona never seemed to be sober at the same time. They grew apart, but were always together. Neither would say they were *with* each other. In fact, the suggestion could create an angry

30

outburst. But they orbited each other, and depended on each other, never fully able to break free from one another. They were bound by loneliness, circumstance, and substance abuse.

Oscar was a pimp who offered Ramona a life of steady income. He'd supplied the RV and provided for Ramona's basic needs... barely. Eventually, Seth became a low-level drug peddler for Oscar, but he wasn't very good at it. He always seemed to use the drugs, not sell them. Oscar put up with the bullshit, for the most part, because Ramona couldn't seem to function without Seth nearby. It was a dreadful, stereotypically toxic relationship, full of drugs and homelessness, with little hope of escape.

Seth owed Oscar — drugs. Again. It was that simple. He had taken a "loan," agreeing to pay it back without any idea of how he would. He just needed the hit, and desperation would lead him to say whatever would give him his fix. Normally, when he would take a drug loan not knowing how to pay it back, he did one of two things: he split town, or robbed houses or cars. It was simple, and everyone did it. Seth had done it his whole life.

Historically, Oscar was patient and gave Seth a set time to pay it back. Now, though, Oscar's patience had run out. Seth knew Oscar was sick of him — knew Oscar saw him as a drain on his business — and it was worse since the collapse. Seth could tell he was skating on thin ice with the man, but didn't see a way out. The crisis made his usual options difficult. There was no one to rob anymore. The rich people had either left Chicago, or had armed security.

Seth had been shocked by the level of security he'd discovered while trying to rob an upscale neighborhood: armed security guards as people left their homes; armored vehicles; caravans of armed security; armed guards on multi-point-watches surrounding homes and property; communications, radios, ARs and AKs, and more. Obscured by manicured shrubbery, Seth had watched the methodical movements of armed security guards at a house he had planned to hit. *This is out of my league*, he'd thought to himself, his eyes wide.

Most typical security measures — a barking dog, motion detector lights — were simple for him to slip past to score a computer, tablet, and whatever else he could snag in a few moments. An armed security detail was too much for a regular street thief.

Grocery or convenience stores weren't an option, either. If any were open, they had no merchandise to sell, and very little cash on hand. He would need to rob hundreds of stores to get enough money to pay his debt.

Other criminals had the same idea, and store owners had taken measures. Chicago was infamous for being "gun free," but in the crisis, the line between "legal" and "illegal" gun ownership had blurred. The police were overwhelmed by the lawlessness. In the void of police presence and enforcement, the few grocers that were open had armed themselves—heavily. Criminals knew it.

It only took a few incidents of criminals being leveled at a cash register by an armed store owner before store robberies dwindled to the levels that had been normal before the collapse. The startling crime statistic was not spoken of in the local media.

Seth had heard the chatter on the streets about armed grocers. The typical options to pay his drug debt were dwindling. Fast. Floyd sending help had been his last option. Now, his only choice was to hide from Oscar. The last time he tried to hide from a debt, he was hospitalized from the beating he received from Oscar's cronies. Seth forgot many things in the fog of his drug usage, but he never forgot that beating.

Ramona was the liability in that plan. Oscar was Ramona's pimp, but part of Seth's agreement with Oscar was to keep eyes on Ramona so she wouldn't get any ideas of leaving or hiding. Seth knew Ramona's services were a cash generator for Oscar. Seth got free rent in the RV for keeping an eye on Ramona.

Seth could feel his world squeezing in on him. The paranoia from whatever drug concoction he had coursing through his veins didn't help, either. Seth allowed himself to be distracted from his fear of a beating by retreating to a dark corner of the RV as he watched Ramona transform herself. Normally, her features were pale and her hair and eyes were crazy. Her baseline demeanor was chaotic. Chaos oozed from her. Years of drug use had done irreparable damage to what was once a beautiful, youthful woman.

Preparing for her nightly work was a sight to behold. In normal times, she would take hits of meth. Seth couldn't remember the last time he had seen meth. These days, however, Ramona drank a half a bottle of whatever she could get her hands on. She preferred hard liquor.

With a sleepy, wide smile, she would say, "It burns going down. Once inside, it keeps me warm."

She didn't like drinking the liquor because it could be detected on her breath. Johns and cops didn't like smelling booze on prostitutes. Ramona would drink her bottle at the beginning of her ritual, and then swish it away with mouthwash.

The first thing she would do was clip her hair away from her face and take out her "paint box," as she called it. It looked like a tool box. *It was probably a toolbox at one time*, Seth thought.

She would start with her eyes. In a flourish of pencils and brushes, they were transformed from sunken and lifeless, to bright and engaging. She blinked at herself in the mirror, checking for perfection.

Next, she would take out four different brushes and paint her checks, forehead, and chin. To Seth, it was like painting a house: a base coat, followed by two or three top coats, for full coverage.

There had been many times when Seth had hit Ramona hard enough to leave a bruise. He didn't worry about her doing her job well after watching the layers of paint she would apply. She was highly adept at hiding many of the marks on her skin. Between the smacks Seth gave her, and the fast-paced aging process—courtesy of the drugs and prostitution—there were many blemishes Ramona's paint covered up.

After painting her face, Ramona was no longer the hollow-eyed, old, drug addict. The booze had settled into her bloodstream. The eye makeup had perked up her tired lids. Externally, the persona was complete. Internally, Ramona was broken beyond repair.

Next, she combed her hair out. Sometimes she used a hot iron to straighten it. Other times she used a curling iron to make perfect ringlets, transforming her rough hair into bouncy, flowing ribbons. Seth counted four different styling products she would use in the hair transformation.

The final step was her clothing. Ramona stood up and pulled off her dingy sweatshirt, exposing her sunken breasts. Bending down, she pulled off her shorts and panties in a quick motion. She reached up to a shelf above the small stove and pulled out a black slip adorned with sparkles. She slipped it over her head. Looking at the slip, Seth noticed that several of the sequins were missing, and there was a faint milky stain near the hem.

Except for a few details, Ramona was a fabulous looking prostitute. Her costume hid a multitude of flaws.

"Do you wash that?" Seth asked, pointing to her skimpy slip, his lips curled in semi-disgust.

"With what? Show me the laundry room," Ramona retorted, giving Seth a middle finger with a nail that was freshly painted pink.

Ramona slipped on a pair of stiletto heels. She took one last look in the mirror, pressed her lips together and smiled. Looking at Seth, she quipped, "You watch yourself. See you later."

Seth watched her out the window as she walked with ease in her stilettos toward the road, into the night.

***

Ramona crossed the parking lot and stepped onto the sidewalk. This step up was her cue to add a little sway to her hips and put on her persona. She could be anything and everything to anyone who would hand her money. Cash. Her smile was programmed to express sultry interest and mystery. Her voice changed to a lower register and slower pace. Her sentences were short, and only indicated interest in the person who was about to become a paying customer. If she didn't receive an offer from someone within a few exchanges of pleasantries, Ramona knew it was time to say goodbye and move on. Her goodbyes were as charming as her hellos. As she walked away, a toss of her ribbon-like hair and an extra sway in her hips was Ramona's clear message: "You'll regret that you didn't make this purchase."

As Ramona approached her familiar corner, she delivered an imperceptible wink and nod to a person in the shadow of a stairwell.

"Come here," she heard from the shadow.

Ramona knew immediately that it was Oscar. She slowed her walk and approached him, staying several feet away. He remained in the shadow and enticed her to come closer by offering a cigarette. Like an obedient puppy, Ramona stepped closer and took her treat.

"He there?" Oscar demanded.

"Hmmm…" Ramona said, and nodded as she took a long drag from the cigarette, closing her eyes tight as the smoke warmed her lungs.

"Get to work, bitch. You have your own debt to pay," Oscar snarled.

"I always pay, Oscar. Fuck you," Ramona said, unflinching.

She had heard Oscar's threats for years, and knew which ones to take seriously. She knew she owed him—she always did. However, tonight Oscar was after Seth more than her. Seth also didn't generate income for Oscar. Ramona did. While Ramona might get a beating on occasion, she knew Oscar would never jeopardize cutting off the money stream she provided him.

Ramona also knew that as the city continued to decline, the trailer and Oscar's protection was invaluable. She was no fool. *Oscar is only a slightly bigger fish than Seth. Not much difference between a thief and a street-level drug dealer*, Ramona thought as Oscar yammered something about Seth. Her housing and small supply of food teetered on managing the chaos of the chaos.

34

Seth sat in the dim light, not moving. His world squeezed a little tighter as Ramona's shadow disappeared in the darkness. His mind raced. Where could he go if he left town? What would he do once he got to said imaginary location? Who could help him? Seth had no answers to any of his questions. Not even a *maybe*. He had run out of options... He pondered the hopelessness of his situation as he felt his eyes grow heavy, offering him temporary salvation from his endless thoughts.

Seth jumped up with a start. His eyes focused on his location. He wondered how long he'd been asleep. He quickly realized that the loud noise was someone trying to pull open the cheap door. The RV was dark. Someone had cut the electricity, or it had gone out—both were common occurrences.

Seth tried to think. He had opted to stay in the RV after Ramona left, hoping no one knew he was there. Seth had left the lights on just as Ramona had when she left. He purposely hadn't moved from the chair while he'd had spent the last few hours there, thinking and sleeping. He didn't want to inadvertently create shadowy silhouettes, giving anyone watching from outside a clue that someone was in the RV.

Right now, his immediate thought was that it would only take a few more hefty yanks at the doorknob before the door would be breached. Seth had no options for avoiding his debt now. His only choice was to face it as it came through the door in the form of Oscar, who was clearly displeased.

"You little fuck!" Oscar roared as the door lock broke. Oscar rushed up to Seth who was cowering on the dingy sheets. "You have my money?"

Seth swallowed hard. "Oscar, you don't need to worry. I mean it, I made a call today...."

"Oh, you made a call? Tell me about this call," Oscar yelled. Seth could detect sarcasm and disbelief.

He froze. Normally, telling Oscar that he had made a phone call and giving him a string of lies would be enough to calm him down. This time, he feared that Oscar wouldn't listen to the story. This was the angriest Seth had ever seen them man.

"Well, uh... I have some sticks in the fire. Made some contacts. I will have it tomorrow, no problem," Seth said with shaky, feigned confidence. He had no idea what he would do tomorrow. Seth's immediate goal was to get Oscar calmed down and out of the RV.

Oscar sat down hard at the tiny table and smacked his hand on its surface.

"Sit down," Oscar yelled at Seth as he pounded the table with his hand again. The Formica tabletop shook under the blows.

Seth quickly scrambled to the table and slid into the chair — terrified. He was so scared that his legs were numb and he could feel prickles running up his neck.

"We gonna talk, Seth." Oscar looked at Seth across the table with fire-hot intensity radiating from his eyes. The bloodshot lines almost looked like evil flames.

Oscar's demeanor suddenly turned friendly. "You seem stressed, Seth. Let's play a game. Remember that game you played as a kid? You held your hands out, and the other person would try to slap them, but if you were quick enough, you'd pull them away before getting slapped. You play that game, Seth?"

Seth nodded. "I did."

"Well, then let's play! Put your hands on the table. Come on." Oscar pointed to the table. "Let's see if I can get you."

Seth was nervous. He didn't like the idea of receiving a slap from Oscar. *If he hits my hand hard, that is much better than getting the shit beat out of me,* he reasoned to himself. He blinked his eyes hard trying to clear his head to play the game.

Oscar's arm flinched as his muscles flexed. Seth watched closely. After a few flinches where Oscar was bluffing, Seth felt better. Since Oscar's hands were under the table, Seth would have plenty of time to pull his hands back. Seth knew he would need to let Oscar get a few licks in. He braced himself.

The next several minutes, Seth and Oscar played the silly game. Sometimes Oscar would get a lick in and laugh diabolically. Seth exaggerated how hurt he was by the hit. He wondered for a split second why they didn't switch so Seth would get a turn to smack Oscar, though he couldn't imagine slapping Oscar's hands even in a friendly game setting. Seth was happy to allow Oscar to play this game if it kept Oscar happy and bought Seth time.

Seth's thoughts distracted him, and Oscar knew it. Oscar made his move, and it was swift.

Oscar had just missed Seth's left hand. Seth's eyes were focused to his left as he snatched his hand back. That split second allowed Oscar to slap at Seth's unprotected right hand.

But — it wasn't a slap. Oscar drove a rusty kitchen knife through Seth's right hand, pinning it to the table. Oscar's hand remained on the knife's handle. In the motion of stabbing, Oscar's eyes had grown red-hot with anger.

Seth could only grab his right wrist with his left hand and scream. Oscar reached over with his right hand and boxed Seth hard.

"Shut the fuck up, you little shit!" Oscar roared. "You are such a shit!" Oscar boxed Seth again.

Seth was helpless. He was dazed by the blows and his ears were ringing. He couldn't move from the table. He frantically grabbed at the knife to release his hand. Seth was certain he was at the mercy of Satan in front of him... with no options.

***

Ramona knew that something was different—and she wasn't surprised—as she approached the RV. Her conversation with Oscar the previous night had left her on edge.

The door to the RV was ajar. Her pace slowed as she approached. While she knew Oscar wasn't after her, she was no fool. Unless you were one of the rich people with hired security, a person was unsafe from any number of criminals trying to make a buck to feed themselves. Ramona knew that Oscar's problem with Seth was solved—she just didn't know *how* it had come to resolution. In the meantime, she needed to see who was in the RV.

She pulled the door back slowly. No one was in her line of sight. Dead silence. She knew she had to step up three stairs, and by doing so, she would be spotted before she could see anyone in the room. Instead of popping her head over the railing, she leaned low to the floor and peeked around the railing. Her eyes were quickly drawn to a pool of crimson blood on the floor. Ramona gasped and froze.

"Anyone here? It's just me," Ramona called out. No answer.

After a moment, she let her eyes follow the path of gore, ending at the blood's origin. She saw Seth's feet under the table.

Even under the table a few feet away, she could tell he was dead. Seth was jacked up on drugs at any given time—it was physically impossible for him to be as still as the feet Ramona saw motionless in front of her.

Ramona's eyes continued up the legs seated at the table. She couldn't see the top of the table, but the angle of Seth's body and the knife handle sticking up told her enough. Seth's head was awkwardly and unnaturally slumped to his left. Ramona slowly stood up.

"Seth?" she asked as she stood. "Oh my God!" Ramona could see into Seth's neck. It wasn't a cut. It was a gash, revealing bone and tissue.

Ramona ran out of the RV, still in her stilettos, with only her work clothes on her back. She ran until she broke both heels of her shoes. She yanked them off, threw them in the street, and ran some more.

Chapter 64
Kenney Reservoir

It was the middle of the night of June first — or maybe it was second by now, if midnight had come and gone; Ned didn't know for sure, and he was tired of looking at his watch. He was sprawled flat on his back, staring at the tent's ceiling, with Julie next to him. He couldn't tell if she was asleep, but hoped she was.

They had pitched camp at Kenney Reservoir late in the day on June first, anticipating the rendezvous for the next day. The nine-day trek had gone smoothly from Western Lakes. Ned was grateful they had taken three treks in preparation for the final trip. It prepared them not only for the supplies and gear they needed, but as Ned thought about it, he said to himself, *It prepared us to work as a team under stress.* Ned replayed their arrival at the reservoir, hoping his dreams would catch one of the storylines and put him to sleep.

When they'd pitched their tent at Kenney Reservoir earlier in the day, Ned had taken note of several things, most notably the abandoned boats at the dock. The dock was new, but the boats attached to it were in bad shape. *Those have been there all winter*, he thought. The collapse had reached Kenney Reservoir. *Boat owners couldn't get here to winterize their boats.*

Ned approached the office at the marina. A laminated sign was duct taped to the door:

Marina closed indefinitely. Call for boat information.
Swimming area closed to the public until further notice.

Ned chuckled a bit under his breath. *Call from where? Cell phones don't work, and pay phones have been gone for a decade*, he thought. He'd looked over at Julie, who was standing under a tree near their packs, glancing out at the water. He knew what she was thinking. She was scanning the shoreline as far as she could, hoping to detect the sea plane. Ned wasn't going to guess if the plane was here already or not. The instructions given by Steve didn't say.

"I have only seen this kind of thing in movies," Ned told himself often.

He made his way to Julie and scanned the shoreline as far as he could see. He knew there were inlets and areas he couldn't see, but from what he could tell, the reservoir was void of any people except them. His eyes rested on Julie. He watched her continue to assess the shoreline. The sun was starting its descent to the horizon. She stood with her feet squared, and her shoulders and her arms relaxed, but crossed. Ned just watched her as her head slowly turned right.

She swiveled her torso slightly in his direction, keeping her arms crossed, and turned to look at him. "Did I catch you staring?" she called out.

Ned smiled and answered, "Maybe. I don't think the plane will be seen from here. This is covert. If they are here, the plane is hidden from the line of sight of this location. They wouldn't want to risk being seen by anyone."

Julie smiled her nervous smile. He knew she was a bundle of anxiety. He'd felt it intensify the closer they got to Kenney Reservoir. Her conversation was focused and anxious, or nonexistent. It reminded Ned of Julie when she first arrived at Western Lakes almost a year before: quiet, tense, and worried about where they had just evacuated from and what the future would hold at Western Lakes. Her home burning. School for Joel. The winter ahead. Should she stay in Colorado or try to rebuild in Eugene? The memories of those first few months came back to Ned as Julie slowly walked toward him, her anxiety etched on her face.

"What are you thinking, Ned?"

"I'm watching your anxiety, and it reminds me of when you first came after evacuating the fires."

"Interesting observation. I would say you're accurate. It feels the same as well." Julie nodded, then changed the subject. "Let's get a meal going and settle in. This might be our last peaceful night's sleep for, I don't know, the next eighteen years."

They moved their packs back to their campsite, away from the marina and out of sight of anyone who might happen to arrive. They ended up about a quarter of a mile away.

The evening was quiet. He wanted to talk to her, but they had talked about the plan so many times, Ned reasoned that it would just add to the anxiety at this point. He knew the only way to keep her calm was to remain calm himself.

Ned started a fire and boiled water for their freeze-dried meal. He mixed up one pack and handed it to Julie as she sat down. He dropped a tea bag into each of the two camp mugs then poured water over them, handing one to Julie. Julie set the food down and hugged the mug with her hands. She scooted her knees to her chest, leaning against a rock, and turned her head to the sunset.

"Cheers, Julie," Ned held up his mug to Julie. "To the adventure we're about to embark on."

Julie smiled and held up her mug to Ned. He noticed that Julie was not eating her meal and hesitated to make one for himself. Food consumption was a big deal. He and Julie had talked about it as they planned the treks. Meals were planned down to the calorie, carb, and protein content. It was agreed no food would be wasted. It was also agreed all meals would be consumed, since they would need the nutrients and energy. So, it concerned Ned to see Julie set aside her meal this way.

"Julie?" Ned said.

Julie looked at Ned, and he motioned to her meal. "I know. I am not hungry," Julie answered with a sigh. "I'm waiting a few moments to see if I can relax enough to eat it."

"Let me eat this one so it doesn't get cold. You tell me later when you're ready to eat. I'll heat up water to make another one," Ned offered. "For now, let's enjoy some warm tea."

Julie half-smiled. "Thank you."

***

Julie curled up in her sleeping bag with her back to Ned. *I hope he thinks I'm asleep*, she thought. She tried to breathe slowly, not only to help her relax, but to give the appearance that she was asleep. Julie's skin was tingly. She could feel her temples pulse slightly. Sometimes she felt her face flush with sweat as though she were sick. She knew these were physical symptoms of stress.

There was the regular stress of life, like Joel's school ending while she was gone, and hoping Floyd didn't miss any details wrapping up Joel's first year of school in Colorado. The latest batch of chicks were about half grown, and she worried about whether Joel was taking care of them. Last year he did a great job. Julie felt certain he would do well this summer. However, if something went wrong and they lost a catastrophic number of birds, the upcoming winter would be difficult.

Then there was the stress of Addison. Steve had said nothing about the required baby supplies she had imposed upon him. How would they arrive? Where would they be delivered? Western Lakes? Pierce Point was impractical, but who knew?

And then there was Addison herself. She would be six months old. When Joel was six months old, he positively did not like anyone but Julie or Steve to hold him. Julie knew that Addison would be scared and traumatized a bit by being handed over to her. The flight home and trek back to Western Lakes could be a nightmare simply because Addison might be extremely upset. Julie hadn't told Ned this concern. She made a note to tell him the next day.

Then there was Steve. She would be seeing Steve. It had been almost a year since she had seen him last, though she couldn't recall precisely when that was.

Was it when I picked Joel up after his time with Steve? Or maybe after? Julie struggled to remember a time that was only a year past, but also felt like a lifetime ago.

Steve. Julie wondered how much time she would have to spend with her ex-husband, and found herself wanting to talk to him. She wanted to know about Addison and her routine. Julie wanted to know the details about the collapse in Portland, and what Steve had experienced. *I wonder what he is going to do after Pierce Point? I can't imagine he would go back to Portland. Maybe his family back east will send for him?*

As she thought about Steve, the familiar frustration and anger returned. His leaving the family. The divorce. The rejection. The deep seed of self-doubt he planted in her by leaving her for another woman.

I should thank Steve when I see him, though. Julie surprised herself with the thought. As she revisited her memories of Steve, she remembered the years she'd spent since then, developing self-defense skills, obtaining her concealed handgun license, firearms training, prepping, preparing for and moving to Colorado. Independence.

If he hadn't left me, I would still be in Eugene, trying to piece something together, and living in a collapse much like Portland, Julie concluded. *I only have to see what happened to him in Portland to realize the future I dodged when he left me. Oh my word!* Julie's breath caught as she realized the gravity of the matter.

I can't believe I'm admitting this, but I'm thankful he left, Julie realized. The voice in her head was the one she had become familiar with since Steve left. It was confident and unwavering. She knew without a doubt — and with no one's confirmation — that she was right.

***

Ned and Julie stood at the Kenney Reservoir boat ramp on June second, as directed. It was six o'clock in the morning, and the pair were the only people around.

"Steve said the pilot would be here early in the morning," Julie muttered. She picked at a hangnail on her index finger. "I should have asked what time that was."

"He also said we would leave no later than noon. Julie, it's okay. It's only six."

Ned was nervous as well. *She's going to pop a vein somewhere if she doesn't relax*, Ned thought to himself as he watched Julie practically hum from nervous energy.

"Here," Ned said, grabbing her hand and placing it on his elbow. "Let's just walk around this area for a bit. You need to relax, lady."

Julie didn't pull her hand back, but she also didn't move forward. "Ned, this isn't funny. I want to make sure we don't miss the person. I wish I had asked so many other questions. What does he look like? What will he be wearing? Or even 'what the hell does "early morning" mean?'" Julie's frustration was palpable.

Ned reached over and hugged Julie's shoulders. He was certain she hadn't slept well last night. He felt her get out of the tent long before dawn to pack and repack her backpack. Ned would have joined her, except he was trying to sleep, too.

"It's okay. I mean it. We are both nervous. This is what we've planned for for so long. He is not late. If anything, we are early. Let's take a mental break from all the 'what ifs' we've played out, and simply sit here and enjoy the reservoir. Look around." Ned stepped back and swept his arm across the scenery in front of him.

The sun was above the horizon, but not by much. The sky was deep blue and everything was still. Their packs were leaned up against the tree near the dock, where they had been parked last night.

"Let's walk around and keep an eye out," Ned suggested. Julie reluctantly linked her arm in Ned's elbow.

"Ned, we can't miss this," Julie said as they started to walk.

"We won't," Ned answered.

Several minutes went by.

"Did you hear that? Was that aircraft?" Julie piped up.

"I didn't hear anything, no," Ned answered, not sure what Julie heard.

Several more minutes passed in silence before Julie spoke again.

"Look at the reservoir. It's huge. You see anything that looks like an aircraft?" Julie asked as she pointed toward the water.

"No, I don't," Ned answered.

More time went by. Ned could feel the steel-trap-grip of Julie's hand on his elbow. If he wasn't wearing a coat, her strong fingers may have left marks.

"What time is it?" Julie asked.

"Six forty-five," Ned answered. "Still early."

Julie's eyes darted across the water line of the reservoir hurriedly.

"Ned! What if Addison is super fussy because she isn't familiar with us?"

"Then we journey on with a fussy baby. It's not as if the flight will have other passengers who might complain to the flight attendant," Ned answered with a laugh, trying to lighten the mood.

So the morning went: nervous Julie asking question after question, and Ned answering them calmly and lightly.

The sun rose higher in the cloudless sky, turning the day hot and intense quickly.

In between Julie's worried questions and comments, Ned ran through his own line of concerns.

Does she have her pistol handy? Is it loaded? Did I check it today? Is my pistol loaded and ready? Did I check it today? Do we each have loaded magazines? Are we each so nervous that our security measures are compromised? Are the caches safe and secure from predators? Do I have the map for the caches?

Ned and Julie sat on the ground under the shade of the tree where they had propped their packs. The sun was now high in the sky.

"Ned, there is no one here. *No one.* Steve was clear. No later than noon," Julie said, the panic in her voice intensifying.

Ned had considered the possibility that their escort would not show. He had considered staying extra days at Kenney Reservoir in hopes the escort did appear. However, the best way to know anything would be to contact Steve. The only way that could possibly happen was if Ned could get within radio range of Western Lakes and have Floyd try to call Steve. If Steve were where he needed to be, he shouldn't be near a phone. The lack of a clear communication chain for the operation felt suddenly important, and Ned had to stop himself from getting frustrated. Nothing about this situation was normal, so why should he expect it to function that way?

Ned also considered what the trek back to Western Lakes would be like if the escort didn't show up. Julie would be crushed. He would be crushed. So much planning, effort, heart, and soul had gone into this day. Julie's heart would be broken—Addison had become her daughter already.

Julie was right. It's like being pregnant and preparing for the baby's arrival, Ned thought to himself. *And if we leave here having not even left the state, we'll both be heartbroken.*

"No one is here," Julie repeated. "It is so quiet here that if anyone *was* here, you would be able to hear them approaching." Julie's eyes never left the distance, as she scanned for any movement on the water, or a person walking along the water's edge.

"Hello, folks."

Ned was jolted by a deep, unfamiliar voice that called out. He saw some movement from the corner of his eye, and then saw a man with a drab baseball cap, aviator glasses, and a trimmed beard.

Where the hell did he come from? Ned thought to himself, feeling angry. He should have heard the guy approaching. His confusion quickly turned to feeling threatened. He turned and squared himself with his hand on his holster.

"Who are you?" Ned asked assertively.

"If you are Ned and Julie, I'm your ride. Didn't mean to startle you. I'm Kyle." The man extended his right hand and held his left hand up away from his belt. Still unsure, Ned did not reach out to shake his hand.

"The aircraft is about three miles down this path — far out of view. The trip is here to Pierce Point, then back. We are picking up a small child, and I am your armed escort and pilot. What else can I tell you?"

"Nothing. That's all I need. Julie?" Ned nodded to Julie. He hadn't noticed until this moment that she was also squared with her right hand on her holster.

"Let's go." Julie leaned over with her left hand and started to sling her pack on. Her look was stern and piercing toward Kyle.

Apparently she didn't appreciate being startled, either, Ned realized.

Chapter 65
City Hall

Kandi looked up and around inside the atrium of Portland's City Hall. On any given day, this building was impressive. Three stories high, it had striking open atriums that would awe visitors as they walked in. A glass ceiling illuminated the entire height of the lobby, and there was a glass elevator that had marble stairs wrapped around the elevator shaft.

Kandi hadn't been to City Hall in some time—the last election season, in fact. The change from then to this moment was shocking. Several of the elevator's glass panels were cracked. It was apparent they had been in that condition for some time. Beleaguered strips of duct tape were zig-zagged over the cracks to buy some time before the glass fully disintegrated.

Several risers of the marble stairs were broken or were missing large chunks. There was a distinct smell of human waste in the air. Displays showcasing various historical aspects of City Hall were vandalized. Broken glass or broken wood seemed to be the theme for any display pieces.

Kandi tsk-tsked under her breath at the sight—and smell—that surrounded her. "My tax dollars at work," she muttered as she gingerly walked up the cracked stairs to the third floor, because, of course the elevator was out of service.

To Kandi, this day was no different than any other day she would make an appointment with the mayor. Kandi had met with the current mayor, as well as many of his predecessors, many times over the decades. At these meetings, Kandi put aside the drag persona she was known for. Today she wore a pair of khaki slacks, and a brightly colored, button-down cotton dress shirt, with an open collar. Covering all of it was a basic raincoat. She had a portfolio in her left hand. She looked like the man she was born as.

By the time Kandi reached the top riser of the third floor, she was out of breath. As she ascended the stairs, she noticed that the damage lessened. Most of it was contained to the lobby and first floor. Kandi continued on.

***

Mayor Fred Whitlock was keenly aware of Kandi's appointment to "chat." Fred and Kandi's history as political allies went back long before Fred became Portland's mayor. Fred had been elected as mayor at the same time the new president was elected, and Kandi's public endorsement of Fred was an integral part of Fred's election.

Newly elected, the first crisis Fred had to address was the violent protests of the presidential election. Fred was everyone's hero because he found the fine line between allowing the rioters to riot, while also coming across as strong to local citizens who were alarmed at the uprising. His words said "no more lawlessness," yet those arrested were quietly released from police–custody — with no charges filed — after the violent dust-up had calmed in the media spotlight.

Fred enjoyed talking a tough talk at press conferences while also placating rioters who were supported financially and ideologically by hard left progressives — who also funded his campaign. Fred managed to gain the popular vote along with the key financial support of dark, progressive groups.

Teeze was a good example. Teeze never wrote checks to campaigns or candidates. He was functionally homeless. His name or — Dignity Domes — could always be found listed as an endorser to any far-left campaign. Teeze bartered his influence through intimidation. He made his money through human trafficking, which was hidden in plain sight at Dignity Domes. He wielded his influence to high-level political officials because of his perceived social justice advocacy for the homeless. Portland's ever-increasing homeless population kept Teeze in business. Teeze sent his thugs to riot occasionally to keep up the appearance of being a "community advocate" for the homeless. It was a façade and everyone in marbled City Hall knew it. In fact, Teeze's thugs did most of the damage to City Hall's lobby. There were a few tense phone calls between Fred and Teeze over the damage.

"I said you could riot, but I didn't say you could break shit," Fred had hissed into his cell phone during one of those heated calls.

"Fred. Shut the fuck up. The election day riots broke glass and started fires. The press would call me a pansy if we walked in chanting and waving signs," Teeze answered.

"My staff is scared. And I didn't agree to a broken fucking elevator!"

"Fred, Fred, Fred," Teeze said with a laugh. "Let me remind ya, man. You were the only one quoted by the local paper… 'we live in a culture of rioting, and we all need to get used to it,' right? Dude, you need to eat your own words. Get used to it."

Fred didn't hate dealing with Teeze, and knew if he turned up the heat on Teeze for property damage, his life would become intolerable. Not only would Teeze's riots be at his front door, but he would lose his endorsements from numerous homeless advocacy groups for the next election. More importantly, though, Fred wouldn't receive six figure campaign donations from harmless sounding donors such as "Friends of Affordable Living" that have direct lines of communication... with Teeze.

Fred's thoughts wandered as he remembered his anger during that phone exchange with Teeze. "Huh... I haven't heard from Teeze in a while. I should text him later."

Fred was weary. He had watched his city reach a level of degraded filth that he never expected. Homelessness, crime, property damage, and economic depression—Fred hoped that the worst was behind him, and his message of "rebuilding" could get underway. He needed the business community to invest in infrastructure—what little was left of the struggling private business community. He needed homeless people to find a home. Most evacuated citizens eventually needed to find a reason to return. Fred was exhausted by how to problem solve Portland out of the crisis it was entrenched in.

***

Kandi knocked on the mayor's door and announced herself to the secretary, Lindsay, who immediately led Kandi to the mayor's office. Stepping in, Kandi shook the mayor's hand with a flirty smile.

"Good morning, Fred."

"Good morning to you, Kandi." Fred smiled and motioned to a chair. They sat down, facing one another.

Kandi noticed how tired Fred looked. His eyes had new shadowy lines and wrinkles that Kandi hadn't seen before. Fred normally wore a crisp shirt and tie. Today, he wore an open shirt, stained on the collar. *He needs to comb his hair*, Kandi thought.

"It's been awhile. What brings you in today?"

"Fred, have you heard what has been happening to my customers?"

"Kandi, I apologize. I have had a lot on my plate in recent months. Tell me what's going on," Fred answered, leaning forward on his elbows, using his most falsely sincere voice.

Kandi told him the stories about Jon, Bruce, Matt and a handful of others who had been regulars at Kandi's Place.

"Fred, I'm losing regulars to murder!" Kandi exclaimed, extending her palms in front of her dramatically.

"Have you talked to the police?" Fred asked, wrinkling his eyebrows in what Kandy identified as a false attempt to appear concerned.

"Oh, Fred, that is a joke. Your police force is so overwhelmed with everything right now. When I called and asked for a detective, I was put on hold for three hours," Kandi answered, exasperated. "But, I did get a copy of the initial police reports from the responding officers." Kandi set a manila envelope on the small round table in front of Fred.

"The police are investigating an incredible amount of crime right now," Fred said. "Sounds like the murders have case numbers assigned to them. The police will do their best with what they've got. It sure didn't help when the Feds withdrew funding for public safety. We can't hire more officers... in fact, we've encouraged early retirement for many." Fred opened the folder and began slowly turning pages, as if he were reading details with great concern. Kandi knew that he wasn't.

"What? You're kidding me!" Kandi exclaimed.

"I wish I were," Fred said with a sigh.

"You do realize this is the president's agenda. He is such a hater of the LGBTQ community," Kandi said, frustration building.

"He pulled the funding because Portland is a designated Sanctuary City," Fred clarified. "Portland is one of many cities that were conveniently skipped over for funding." Kandi rolled her eyes and tsk tsk-ed as Fred pretended to look at the police reports. "You know what is happening here, don't' you?" Kandi asked after a long pause.

"Tell me," Fred answered, continuing his act of being interested in the police reports.

"I think the gay men you see in those reports are being targeted for being gay," Kandi hissed, as though telling a dark secret.

"What makes you think so?" Fred asked.

Personal assault crimes were nothing new in downtown Portland. Even before the riots. Portland had had an eclectic and eccentric nightlife, with bars, breweries and eateries. Kandi's was one of many places. The simple odds of a gay person — or any person — experiencing an assault was high, regardless. The victims and perpetrators made for interesting news stories.

"Matt and Bruce. Look at the report! They fell off a building. That is what happens to gay men in the Middle East, not Portland. It's no coincidence that two men should fall at almost the same time," Kandi said, trying to maintain composure.

"Looking here, it says the cause of death was a fall from a building, but it was uncertain if it was a suicide pact," Fred said. "Not sure the police are ready to conclude it was an intentional murder of two men."

"Matt and Bruce were running a great business. The last time I saw

48

them, they were celebrating. They were not suicidal. Jon, on the other hand, certainly might have been suicidal, but he was found murdered," Kandi responded. "Most definitely murdered. Keep looking." Kandi stabbed her index finger onto the table, demanding that Fred come to same conclusion.

After a few moments of looking at the reports, Fred asked, "What do you want me to see?"

"I think this is the act of haters using tactics of terrorists, such as throwing gay men from buildings — that is what I think. And I also think whoever is doing this is finding their victims in my bar. I tell you, Fred, I think you should send some undercover detectives to my place and…"

"Hold it, hold it!" Fred waved his hand. "I am horrified, just as much as you are, by these police reports. But I am not going to use the word 'terrorist' in any investigation coming out of my police force."

"Why?" Kandi spat. "As mayor, you oversee the police force. This is your chance to show real leadership and stand up for the basic rights of Portland's LGBTQ community. You know I've got your back on this. I always have."

Fred took a long inhale and leaned back in his chair.

"Kandi, I need to point out a few things that you just said." Fred looked Kandi directly in the eyes as Kandi nodded.

"You remember last fall, after the election riots, this city had a Unity March. That march had over a hundred thousand people in it, here in Portland. You were there, so I'm sure you remember," Fred said. "You remember the main theme of that march was against the hate of the current president, or, more specifically, his stance on immigration."

Kandi nodded. "Of course."

"You will also remember that in that march were hundreds of illegal immigrants, correct?" Kandi nodded, wondering where Fred was going with this.

"Many of those people you were walking next to, waving signs with, and cheering with, are criminals. Certainly not all of them, but many of them. Many have multiple deportations with the federal government, violent arrest records, and no regard for the law," Fred explained.

"Then arrest them! What is wrong with you?"

"We can't. Even if we did arrest them, we can't do anything with them but let them go again, to go out and commit more crimes. We can't deport them or hand them over to the Feds. This is a Sanctuary City, remember? Oregon is a Sanctuary State," Fred said.

Kandi leaned forward, her eyes growing large.

Fred continued. "I also know from my conversations with federal agents that many in that same crowd are not just violent criminals, but also foreign terrorists."

"What?" Kandi exclaimed again. "Deport them!"

"Kandi, we can't. We are a Sanctuary City, remember?"

"Jesus."

"I am going to be extremely candid," Fred said as he started straightening the police reports to put back in the folder. He looked directly at Kandi. "If I could venture an educated guess, I would say it is foreign terrorists targeting your community."

Kandi's eyes grew even larger. "Oh my God!"

"Think of the mass shootings that happened in gay nightclubs. Terrorists don't stop, Kandi, they just get better at what they are doing in places that allow them to do it. As a Sanctuary City, we allow anyone from another country to be here illegally and commit crimes. It is codified in state statute. I have to allow these people to stay here, let them go if they're arrested — even for violent crimes — not turn them over to the Feds, and hope they aren't too mean."

"My God, Fred! This needs to stop!"

"Then you need to decide what you support, Kandi. Do you support the LGBTQ community? Or do you support the deportation of illegal immigrants? You were in a march that supported both. You need to choose. You ready to stand at a podium at a press conference and announce that those here illegally should be deported? You ready to do that?"

"I support my community, of course. I don't support the deportation of immigrants."

"You can't have both, Kandi. And if anyone asks, this conversation never happened, and I support everyone. Equality. Fairness. Love, and so on," Fred said as his eyes slightly rolled.

"I just want those who perpetuated these murders arrested and put in prison, Fred, not deported," Kandi said, still hoping to offer a solution.

"So what? You're now in charge of the judicial system and how justice is dispensed?" Fred appeared tired with the conversation. "These are the policies you — and your community — have put in place. The policies the voters of this city have put in place. I have the fun job of enforcing conflicting laws and policies. You cannot support the gay community *and* support lax immigration laws at the same time, if what you allege is true. You obviously read the headlines and see what is happening to gay men in the Middle East. With lax immigration laws, it was only a matter of time before we started seeing similar crimes here. Terrorist-based hate-crimes targeting your community are commonplace in Europe. I knew it would only be a matter of time before they happened here."

Kandi was speechless. "You have got to be kidding, right? Because I don't support the president's hateful immigration policies, I'm to blame?"

"Let me ask you this," Fred said. "Name a city or state in the Great States region that has a problem with gay people 'falling' off high rises."

Kandi looked at Fred, intently trying to think of a city or state that fit Fred's criteria.

"You keep thinking," Fred challenged as Kandi stared. "I have an election to win. You are asking me to be labeled a 'bigot' or a 'racist,' and neither get people re-elected. I choose to be silent on this issue. In the meantime, I will talk to the police chief and ask him to look closely at these two cases for you."

***

After several moments, Fred stood up and looked at Kandi, who appeared morose and crestfallen. Fred reached his hand out to shake hands at the same time as he headed toward his office door. He was done with this meeting. There was nothing left to discuss.

Fred watched Kandi's profile as she walked toward the stairwell. He picked up his cell phone and started to type a text.

Teeze, how are you these days? Haven't seen you at City Hall. Want to do lunch?

Fred stepped behind his desk to look out the window. He watched Kandi's form on the street below as he pressed "send" on the text.

***

Patrick had been enjoying the spoils of Trevor and Adam's wealth, living in their home and accessing their bank accounts. After quickly sifting through their paperwork, he realized that they had multiple properties around town, so he bounced between locations, to avoid being seen too often by nosy neighbors. He made sure to arrive at a location late at night and leave early in the morning. Patrick knew his scam wouldn't last for very long, but he would enjoy it while he could.

He continued to spend time in the KOIN tower lobby making sure to handshake and greet building staffers. Hanging out at various eateries, coffee shops, and stores in the general vicinity kept his face familiar to regulars. Dipping into Trevor and Adam's closet, he found a fresh wardrobe that legitimized his look as a professional.

Many nights Patrick went to Kandi's, not to scope out his next conquest so much as to continue building relationships and enjoying a nice meal and entertainment. He watched people come and go. He watched those who stayed because they had no place to go, as far as he could tell. He listened to conversations.

Patrick was amazed at what he learned just by simply observing. He learned that Kandi's was a place for hustlers, and not just him. Others came to Kandi's hustling relationships, hookups, drugs, drinks, places to stay, and food. During breaks between lavish shows, conversations buzzed. Kandi's place had become somewhere to barter for needs among a community hard hit by the riots and Portland's decline. Patrick realized he wasn't the only one leveraging for needs. After a few nights, he knew the hustlers right away. Some nights there were several there, and other nights it was quieter.

He observed a transgender woman, Brie, who hustled sex. She would offer her services in exchange for a place to "put her pretty feet up" for a week or so. She targeted middle-aged men, and appeared to be in her late thirties. Once or twice a couple of young men tried to hustle her. Patrick watched one of those exchanges as Brie winked at her prey and motioned for him to follow her outside. Brie returned fifteen minutes later with a fierce look on her face that almost made her appear like the man she once was. Brie's soft, feminine face reappeared after taking a few sips from her drink, followed by some deep breaths.

A couple of times, Patrick considered another hustle more for Qaatel than for himself. He felt like he had more resources than he could handle with access to Adam's and Trevor's wealth.

One night, as he sat drinking water and enjoying happy hour appetizers, Patrick's thoughts wandered to Qaatel.

During a show, under the cover of the dimmed lights, he watched as Brie came in wearing a professional, but glitzy, skirt and blouse. She sat down with a flourish as her waiter asked for her drink order.

Qaatel walked in at that moment and caught Patrick's glance. They nodded to each other as Qaatel was greeted by a host. Patrick watched with interest as he realized Qaatel was not being shown to a table. Instead, Qaatel motioned toward Brie, who raised her hand to acknowledge Qaatel, accompanied by a bright, warm smile.

Patrick struggled not to stare at the pair as they began their pleasantries. *Brie does not like being hustled by young men like Qaatel.* Patrick wondered if he should text Qaatel to warn him that Brie had her own thing going. He decided to keep a discreet watch before sounding any alarms.

Interestingly, Brie leaned in toward Qaatel more. Instead of her bright, flirty smile, Patrick saw Brie's interest in Qaatel increasing, but not like other hookups he had seen Brie conduct. This looked like business interest. Brie was not negotiating for her next location. She was interested in what Qaatel had to offer... Patrick knew what Qaatel offered.

As the night wore on, dinner and drinks were ordered, and Qaatel paid the bill. Patrick watched as the pair stood up together during another show, when the lights were low and all eyes were on the stage. Usually Brie made a production out of her hookup standing up first, then holding out her hand to help her stand. Not with Qaatel. They stood as equals, partners. They made a discreet exit.

Patrick relaxed and yet became tense at the same time. He was relieved that Brie was not affronted by Qaatel's proposal. However, it sent chills up Patrick's spine as he wondered about the agreement he had just witnessed.

Patrick looked out the window as Brie and Qaatel continued to speak on the sidewalk. Patrick expected to see Brie leave with Qaatel, but again he was surprised to watch them shake hands again and wave goodbye as they each walked away into the night.

***

A few days later, Patrick sat in the KOIN building lobby, sipping a cup of coffee, in his snappy new slacks and the casual shirt he'd found in Trevor's closet. He looked up from the newspaper that he had found to see Brie and Kandi walking by the large glass windows. They had their arms linked and seemed to be flirting equally with each other in a pleasant manner.

Patrick took note of the exchange, and then continued to read his newspaper. He read about how so many illegal immigrants were making their way to Sanctuary States to avoid deportation while they made their way through the immigration process. Some quoted that the process, during normal times, could be years-long. In these unstable times, officials believed it would take even longer, especially since Sanctuary States were not welcoming to federal officials conducting business in their states. The federal government made a point to extend resources only to the Great States. Stuck in the middle were illegal immigrants, trying to either escape deportation, or finalize their immigration status.

Patrick looked up to see a national news show on public TV with the closed-captioning running. The story was the same as the one he'd just been reading; however, it was obvious the news was opposed to the president's policies.

"The president states his administration will continue to follow federal laws regarding immigration and national security. Those individuals, and now states, who choose not to follow them simply divide our country further. As the president chooses to accuse his opponents of inciting a Civil War, those in the opposing party declare victory in recent elections." The next clip showed an enraged opponent of the president yelling into a microphone, "We will stop this madman and his racist policies from harming our country!"

Patrick was mesmerized and had no idea what to think. He hadn't paid attention to politics — ever. He was registered as a nonaffiliated voter, but had never actually voted. When his ballot arrived in the mail, he would throw it away with his junk mail.

My one vote doesn't matter, he had always concluded.

Chapter 66
Taking Flight

Standing at the aircraft, Kyle laid out the plan.

"There will be two stops for fuel. All are water landings. While we are supposed to be landing at 'friendly' areas, it is assumed anytime we are in a Sanctuary State that we are in a dangerous area. At each landing, you each need to lay down under those canvas tarps, along with any gear you have with you. No one is to know you are in the aircraft. This is a cargo flight to anyone who asks me. For your comfort, I suggest that you stow all your gear in the back behind the seats."

The plane had a cockpit with two seats, and two rows of two seats each behind the cockpit. Kyle pointed at the empty space behind the back row of seats for where to place the gear. It had a customized door that seemed like a hatch, which he called an Alaskan door. The seats had cracks in the vinyl upholstery and seemed to be about a 1970s vintage.

As Kyle spoke, Julie noticed his leg rig with a Glock 17, a sheathed knife on his belt, and a neck knife. Under the neck knife was an empty chest holster.

"Alright, everyone in. If you feel sick, there are empty baggies back there somewhere," Kyle said as he held the door open, motioning for Ned and Julie to get in. They immediately stowed all their gear in the area behind the seats. Julie noticed several large cardboard boxes in the cargo area. She climbed into the seat row closest to the pilot. Ned followed and sat next to her.

"Do you think it might be more comfortable if we each had a row?" Julie asked. "Then we each have a full row to hide under when we land and need to go under cover."

Ned agreed and moved to the back seat.

Kyle closed the doors and walked around to the open pilot's door. Before entering, he unholstered the 9mm on his leg rig and put it in his chest holster, then climbed in and began flipping switches. He reached up and grabbed two headsets, handing one to Julie, and motioning for her to pass the other to Ned.

"Can you hear me? I don't plan on conversing much. If you have a question, simply ask. If you feel sick, don't throw up on or in anything other than the plastic bags I've stuffed back there. That includes your headset. There are no bathrooms. Let me know if you have any bathroom needs, and I'll make it happen at a landing. I suggest not drinking or eating for the next twelve hours until we get to the final destination. There is no flight attendant, free Wi-Fi, or packs of nuts. Any questions?" Kyle inquired.

Ned and Julie shook their heads, and Julie wondered if this guy could have a worse bedside manner.

Julie turned around as the engine warmed up and smiled at Ned; he returned the smile.

"We got this," Ned mouthed while giving a thumbs up to Julie.

Julie smiled again, shrugged, and swiveled forward. She watched intently as Kyle pressed buttons, cranked what she thought might be a throttle but wasn't sure, and noticed the propeller blades stopping — then starting — as they glided on the reservoir. He reached up and adjusted knobs. Julie was intent on watching his intuitive movements as they slowly lifted off the reservoir. The ground hovered below as Kyle slowly built up altitude. Just like a commercial flight, the earth below appeared to swiftly drift away.

Julie watched as mountains, peaks, valleys and thousands of pine trees rolled by. The hum of the plane and rolling motion made her sleepy. Her thoughts wandered. She wondered whether Addison would handle this noisy flight without too much bother. Julie worried about whether she would keep quiet under a tarp long enough to fuel. *How long does a fuel stop take anyway?* She had so many nagging questions and concerns. Kyle had said he would answer questions, but he certainly didn't strike Julie as a conversationalist.

Ned seemed to read Julie's thoughts as he interrupted her ruminations.

"Kyle, how long will the flight be?"

"Normally, around six hours. I anticipate eight or more with fuel stops. That will put us in Pierce Point right after sunset. I'm hoping we still have some daylight when we arrive."

"Is there anything we need to be aware of at fuel stops?" Ned asked.

"Yes. Be careful," Kyle said. "Stay out of sight."

Julie didn't remember much after Kyle's answer, as she drifted off into much-welcomed sleep.

***

Ned watched Julie's head begin to slump. He saw her attempt to fight off sleep by sitting up straight and rubbing her eyes. But moments later, she would begin to slide in her seat and her head would nod again.

Ned leaned forward and put his hand on her right shoulder and his face near her left ear. Using both hands, he slowly slid her headset off and motioned for her to lay down across the two seats. Julie looked up sleepily and gently laid down. Ned placed her headset near her head, and watched as her eyes slowly closed and her body fully relaxed.

Ned leaned back and wondered if he would be so lucky and get some shut eye. After a few moments, he realized he was wide awake and sleep would not happen any time soon.

"Kyle, how long have you been flying?" Ned asked, testing Kyle's conversational skills.

"Got my small craft pilot's license as soon as I legally could," Kyle answered.

"Is it a hobby or what you do for a living?"

"When I was young, it was a hobby I did with my father. When I went to college, the local municipal small craft airport hired me to do charters on the weekends. It paid for a lot of my college," Kyle explained.

"You haven't done anything else?"

"That is a tricky question," Kyle answered. "I've always run charters, but I do contract work as well."

"Contract work? What do you mean?"

"I have always worked for a charter company, flying charters over God-knows-what scenic locations. I've been all over the Americas, the South Pacific, and portions of the North Pole," Kyle continued. "Sometimes I'm contacted by a person or entity to fly, or transport cargo or passengers, from one place to another for a specific reason."

Ned nodded, taking in the information. "You married? Kids?" he asked.

"Not currently. Two marriages, both done. The first one was the longest. Have a kid from that one. She's in college somewhere. I don't talk to her much. I'm gone so much we never really connected, you know," Kyle said.

Ned was intrigued by Kyle. "Flying charters takes you away from home that much?"

"Not really. Those are regular hours. It's the contract work that takes me away a lot," Kyle said. "Contract work is where the money is, and raising a kid requires money."

Ned suddenly realized what Kyle was talking about—he was an occasional mule, smuggling for the drug trade. Ned also knew to dance around the subject and not speak to it directly.

"Interesting," Ned said. "I'm sure you've seen some exotic places and interesting characters."

Kyle glanced back at Ned. In one exchange of glances, Ned could tell that Kyle realized Ned had figured out his gig. Kyle nodded.

"More than I care to count," he said with an edge in his tone.

"We must be a cargo flight for you today," Ned surmised.

"Again, tricky question in the current state of affairs we find ourselves. In some places, flying citizens from one restricted area to another is illegal, and we could all be subject to arrest — technically. In other places, we're heroes. This whole upheaval we're in has made for some interesting work."

"What do you mean by 'technically'?"

"Technically, if we flew from a Great State and landed in a Sanctuary State, or vice versa, without domestic immigration forms in-hand, we could be arrested, depending on how strict the state is. We certainly could be arrested at any of the stops we are landing at. That being said, none of these states have the personnel to meet us in the middle of a body of water, check our papers, and cart us off to jail," Kyle answered. "It makes this kind of work much easier."

"Easier? But the two of us need to hide when we land, and you are armed."

"Those measures are not because of local law enforcement… it's for the gangs and thugs out there looking to pirate small aircraft like this," Kyle answered. "I know of a couple of pilots who have been assaulted, their cargo stolen, and aircraft burned in the last year."

The story reminded Ned about what the truck driver had told him when he arrived at Patsy's months ago. Anyone carrying cargo, of any kind, was a target for criminal opportunists — violent ones, too.

"I'm used to it. Times change, but moving cargo always has an element of danger, no matter the location, times, or people," Kyle said.

"How are things different now, versus, say… twenty years ago?" Ned asked.

"Twenty years ago, running cargo was incredibly dangerous. That was during the height of the drug trade and drug war. Certainly, you could be caught by federal law enforcement, and that had consequences — trust me, I know. But you lived. If any of the competing 'contractors,' let's call them, got wind of your movement, you could easily be targeted and not live to see another day. I am glad I didn't do it much. Just enough to make sure the kid had braces and the house payments were made. It was still good money. Sometimes I made more in two cargo flights than I did in six months of chartering, but I was gone for days, sometimes a couple of weeks."

"You get caught?" Ned asked.

"About fifteen years ago, I got caught in a customs sting by the

Feds. The bastards. My contractor gave me up to get leniency after being caught himself. My license was suspended, and I wasn't making any money. The wife was angry over that. I told her not to sweat it, that the license would be reinstated, and everything would be fine. Hell, we had six figures in the bank account. I don't know what her problem was," Kyle said with a huff. "And I was right, the charges were reduced, fines paid, and my license was restored. The damage was done. It rattled her. I think she saw too much of that side of the business I did, because she filed for divorce within a year after that, and took the kid with her."

Ned was fascinated by Kyle's story.

"To your question, things are really different now for this country. But the game is the same for me, I just need to stay under the radar of a different enterprise. This whole thing that is happening here is normal for other countries I've flown into, where the government is unstable. It feels the same, you know?" As Kyle said this, he slightly clenched his fist, as if to infuse the feeling to Ned.

"I never thought of it that way, but yes," Ned answered. "So, what happened to the second marriage?"

"Ah, well that was recent. I met a gal in Miami who understood what I did. I thought that might prevent what happened in my first marriage. We were together for about five years before the states started dividing. Last year, a coalition of folks offered me solid money to move cargo such as yourself. I couldn't turn it down. Folks aren't hiring charter flights over the Bahamas these days, if you know what I mean. I took it. At first, I moved cargo for a few weeks, then went back to Florida for a few days. That worked until domestic immigration really set in. I had to have a base in a Great State, and Florida is still deciding which one they are. I had to move, or lose everything. Plus, this is steady, good work. Not many can say that these days. And, she didn't want to move..."

***

Julie sensed something was changing. The hum of the engine. Air pressure. She found herself sprawled across the two seats with the headset off her head and in front of her. She quickly sat up and put on her headset. She heard Kyle and Ned in the middle of a conversation. Ned rubbed her shoulder as she awoke.

"...the divorce was final, and I've been moving cargo out here ever since," Kyle said with a sigh.

"Interesting," Ned responded with a nod.

"I'm going to turn off the radio. You'll hear the engine as we make our first descent. Make yourself scarce under the tarp. It will get hot, so make sure you can breathe fresh air," Kyle directed.

Julie and Ned quickly spread their tarps out beneath their seats and crawled under. She felt the bump of the aircraft landing, and heard the splash of water and the engine winding down before eventually turning off.

It didn't take long for the air under the tarp to grow stiflingly hot. Several minutes passed as Julie concentrated on breathing slowly and being still. The doors of the aircraft opened, and Kyle started to talk again.

"You'll hear voices. Ignore them. I'm going to put other cargo on top of you so you're obscured. No need for concern," Kyle said as Julie felt the weight of light boxes being tucked around the seats and on top of them. She heard something from underneath the aircraft as well.

"Yes, just the front tank. Thank you, Jim!" Kyle called out. "Just moving cargo today." A voice barely discernable could be heard far away. It sounded like Kyle was making small talk with this other person. Her breathing was becoming increasingly heavy, drowning out what little of the conversation she could hear. Eventually Kyle's voice grew louder again.

"Shut up. Everything I do is legit, Jim," he said. "I'm a fucking Boy Scout."

Julie heard Kyle flick a butane lighter and take a deep inhale.

Chapter 67
It Gets Worse

As Shawn drove across the I-205 bridge over the Columbia River, Steve watched Portland's skyline slowly fade away. He turned to face forward. Glancing up he saw "FUCK YOU!" spray painted over the Glenn Jackson Bridge freeway sign. The bridge surface looked damaged with spray paint, and was covered in scorch marks where there had recently been fires.

Steve saw two cars burned down to the metal frames surrounded by garbage. Down below, the shoreline was full of homeless tents as far as Steve could see.

Government Island, the island on the Columbia River that ran under the bridge, was now void of its once rich vegetation and trees. The lush forest Steve remembered was gone. There was nothing to see but the tents. Steve cringed at the putrid odor that made its way into the vehicle.

"What a nightmare," Steve muttered as he took in the sight of the Columbia River he hadn't seen since before the collapse.

Shawn nodded. "Listen. There are three checkpoints coming up. Two are hostile, one is friendly. The forward team will have intel shortly. Keep quiet. Do not talk. No eye contact to anyone who approaches this vehicle. Understood?"

Steve nodded. "Got it."

"You do whatever is asked of you. The less you hesitate and the faster you comply, the better. I will stay as close to you as possible."

"What could I be asked to do?"

"You could be asked to exit the vehicle and be searched. You might be asked to remove the baby from the carrier. I will stay close to her and execute any demands they have related to her. You won't."

"What?" Steve was surprised at the thought of Shawn having control of Addison and speaking for her.

Shawn let Steve's words go unanswered. "The first two checkpoints will be the most dangerous. The third should be in friendly territory, and should go as smoothly as the 205 checkpoint. Put on your badass face and keep your eyes forward," Shawn continued, and glanced at Steve's terrified expression in the rearview mirror.

"Oh, fuck," Shawn muttered, sounding exasperated. He grabbed at a zipper in a bag on the passenger seat and pulled out a set of sunglasses, tossing them back to Steve. "Put these on and look forward. Try again. Put on your poker face and keep your eyes forward," Shawn repeated firmly.

Steve complied, though his hands shook as he slipped the glasses on.

Shawn steadily drove north. A voice cut through the silence on his radio.

"Three-four to eight-zero-eight, you copy?"

"Eight-zero-eight, copy," Shawn replied.

"Three-four has visual. Be advised, roadblock with full stop. Combatants," came the voice.

"Eight-zero-eight, copy," Shawn replied as he released the key on the handset and placed his palm back on the steering wheel.

"Like I said before, you will be asked to exit the vehicle, as will I. I will take the baby. Keep your eyes on me. Answer any questions quickly, and keep your eyes straight ahead. And don't forget—poker face," Shawn instructed.

"Copy," Steve muttered.

Steve watched as the familiar I-205 freeway whizzed by. Everything seemed like a normal drive north, except for the scenery. Burned out cars were scattered along the shoulders. The Vancouver Mall complex could be seen from the highway, as always, but the parking lot was full of rickety RVs and tents. The building had scorch marks on it, much like the buildings in downtown Portland. The large illuminated letters normally on the sides of buildings were mostly gone, leaving silhouettes of the business names that Steve assumed no longer existed.

"Oh, wow," he said under his breath as they passed by the mall. As the burned-out businesses turned into open grassy farmland, an eerie hush came over the car. Steve noticed that what was once a normally humming freeway was empty. The only cars moving north were Shawn's and three others that were waved through at the same time back at the I-205 bridge. There were no cars headed south.

As the farmland continued, Steve saw more homeless tents and RVs parked in fields. Cows no longer grazed on the land as they headed farther north.

A sign approached that normally indicated the exit for the University of Washington campus. The sign had been ripped off the posts and replaced with a spray-painted plywood sheet that read "FUCK the President! Fuck you!"

As they passed by the university, Steve peered straight ahead. He knew the next upcoming juncture was where I-205 merged into I-5. There were over a dozen cars blocking the expansive lanes of freeway, with several people standing in front of a barricade. The people wore black face masks and black hoodies. About half of those guarding the blockade were armed with rifles. Shawn gradually slowed his speed and came to a stop at a break in the vehicles, but was blocked by several people.

Steve instinctively put his arm over Addison, who had been sleeping since her fright at the previous checkpoint.

Shawn rolled down his window and looked at the first person who approached.

"Get out," the guard ordered. "All of you."

Steve quickly unbuckled Addison from her car seat and handed her to Shawn as he exited the vehicle. Immediately, his upper arm was yanked and he was pushed, face first, against the back of the SUV. He felt his sunglasses crunch against his face, and a palm pressing hard against his against head.

Another set of hands started frisking his body roughly.

"What's your name, pussy?" hissed the man who was behind him.

"Steve Atwood," he said quickly.

"Who's your driver?"

"Shawn."

Steve realized he didn't know where Shawn or Addison had gone. With his face pressed against the vehicle and his sunglasses crushed, he had limited vision.

Steve hung on to what he could see. He kept his mind focused on looking forward, just as Shawn had instructed. *Stay calm, stay calm, stay calm*, Steve repeated in his head—though it wasn't working.

The aggressive frisking finally subsided, and two hands roughly grabbed Steve's shoulders and thrust him to the ground. This he was not expecting. His arms were still being held so the full brunt of the impact was his right cheek. He heard his face smack on the hot pavement and felt the jarring pain radiate through his jaw and head. As he collected his thoughts and took a mental assessment of whether or not he was injured, he felt a shoe heel press on his neck.

"*I'm not resisting!*" he wanted to scream, but he couldn't formulate words. As the shoe bore down on his neck, he slowly found it harder to breath. He concentrated on controlling his breathing as items from the SUV dropped onto the pavement near his head. Addison's supplies and his jacket were what he could see directly in front of him.

"Hey, asshole, keep your foot there much longer, you'll kill him," Shawn said. The shoe lifted from Steve's neck. He inhaled deeply, desperate for a lungful of air.

After what Steve estimated to be about twenty minutes, he felt a hand take a tight grip of his upper arm and yank him up.

"Get up, pussy!" someone hissed from behind him as he rose to his feet.

He was faced toward the front of the vehicle. Shawn started picking up items to put back in the SUV. It didn't take long for Steve to realize that Addison was not in his arms! He locked eyes with Shawn, his eyebrows raised in dramatic fashion. Wordless, Shawn slightly twisted his head and directed his eyes to the backseat. Steve exhaled, assuming Addison was safe back there.

"We done here?" Shawn asked. He came across as slightly angry, yet still respectful to the hooded guards around them.

Steve glanced at all the masked faces and realized none of these men were over thirty. He saw young, angry eyes. *Stop looking at them,* Steve warned himself.

"Get out of here," one of the men barked.

"Gladly," Shawn replied, sounding edgy. He climbed into the vehicle and motioned for Steve to follow. Once Shawn was inside, he reached under the driver's seat and pulled out two cartons of cigarettes. He smacked the cartons into the chest of the guard closest to him. Shawn wore sunglasses but Steve knew there was a steel glare directed at the recipient of the cartons.

Steve settled into the back seat. He was relieved to see Addison in her car seat, unstrapped. "Oh, thank God," he whispered as he snapped the buckles.

Shawn started the car and pulled away from the stop. Steve leaned back and gazed at the passing landscape. He scanned the horizon, and even glanced back to the checkpoint. He squinted his eyes and saw what looked like two bodies, face down in the ditch near the checkpoint. Squinting made the swelling in his right cheek more noticeable.

Turning forward, he began to ask Shawn a question, but Shawn spoke first. "Look at me. You took a hit."

Steve reached up to his right cheek and felt gravel and wetness. Craning his neck, he looked at the rearview mirror and saw deep road rash scrapes and swelling.

"I'm okay." He leaned his head back against the headrest.

"Next stop will be rough. It will be longer, so be prepared," Shawn said.

"Swell," Steve whispered. He realized he needed to get a bottle for Addison and feed her, or else she would be a crying mess. He leaned down to the floor and began locating baby supplies from the disheveled items. He expected some things to be missing, but was glad to see the bag had only been ransacked.

"What are you doing?" Shawn asked.

"She needs to be fed. I'm getting her a bottle."

"Eight-zero-eight to three-four," Shawn said in his radio.

"Three-four, copy."

"Stopping north of Battle Ground rest stop. ETA delayed thirty minutes," Shawn said.

"Three-four, copy."

Another voice came on the radio. "Seven-nine to eight-zero-eight, do you require cover?"

"Eight-zero-eight, affirmative," Shawn answered.

"Seven-nine, received."

"Eight-zero-eight, copy," Shawn responded.

Steve poured bottled water into a baby bottle and began opening a tube of powdered formula to add to the water, but found himself distracted by the radio chatter and what Shawn would be doing next. He carefully poured the powder, placed the cap on the bottle, and then began to shake it. Addison knew what was coming next, and started to reach with her tiny hands and whimper for what Steve had that she didn't.

"Shh… here you go, baby girl," Steve cooed as he held the bottle to Addison with one hand, and stroked her head with his other.

Shawn slowed down and flipped the SUV into four-wheel drive, then pulled off the road about one hundred yards after passing the rest stop, just as he had said. He slowly backed the vehicle into some brush — Steve assumed for concealment.

"Eight-zero-eight to seven-nine, in position," Shawn stated.

"Seven-nine, copy. I have visual."

Again, just like at the 205 bridge checkpoint, Steve didn't see anyone, yet someone had a visual on them? It was comforting, yet eerie. Steve had no clue what kind of people he was dealing with. He scanned the bushes — nothing. He looked father around the horizon, but didn't see a person or another vehicle.

Shawn reached under the front passenger seat and pulled out an envelope-sized pouch. He squeezed it, causing a crunching sound. "For your cheek. It might swell enough to block your vision. You need all your senses," Shawn said, and handed the pack to Steve.

The ice pack soothed Steve's aching head. He mentally braced himself for the next checkpoint as Addison enjoyed her meal.

***

Julie estimated she had been cowering under the tarp for about thirty minutes. It was stifling. She watched her sweat drip and pool on the fiberglass floor in front of her. It took everything she had not to reach out for Ned, who was only inches away. She didn't want to make the slightest noise or cause any noticeable movement. She could hear movement under the aircraft, which she assumed was the fueling process.

"Jim, we done?" Kyle called out.

"Done. Get out of here," Jim called back. "Check the network, locations are being rotated again. Heads up."

"So soon, huh?" Kyle answered. "What happened?"

"Compromised."

"Shit! That isn't good," Kyle said sounding surprised.

"It isn't. It's being dealt with from what I understand," Jim said.

"Good. I'll check and catch you next time, my friend," Kyle said.

Julie could hear him hoist himself into the aircraft, and caught a shadow of movement from the small ray of light coming through the crack between the tarp and floor.

The door closed and the motor started up. Julie wanted to get up, yet she dreaded what she might see.

She decided to wait until Kyle beckoned to her, and it appeared Ned was doing the same. He was only inches from her; if he moved, she would know it.

Fifteen minutes must have gone by when she felt the aircraft begin to move. Again, Julie willed herself to wait for what seemed like an eternity. She listened hard to every noise, looking for any clue about what was happening — but it was just so loud. Kyle's voice would be impossible to hear over the running motor. *Wait, just wait...* she kept saying to herself.

Then she felt it: a tug on the tarp. She slowly peeked out and saw Kyle stretching his arm over the copilot seat to tap her. When he saw her head emerge from the tarp, he gave a thumbs up. Julie made her way up, and Ned quickly followed. He must have felt her moving. They both quickly got their headsets on so they could hear what Kyle had to say.

"That went well," Kyle said.

Julie took some breaths of air and looked at the body of water below them. It was large, like Kenney Reservoir, but surrounded by many more evergreen trees. Julie knew there were hundreds, if not thousands, of bodies of water between Washington State and the Rocky Mountains. It would be fruitless to try and guess which one it was. It wasn't so much where they were, but to Julie, she wanted to know how close they were to their destination.

"Next stop is in a couple of hours," Kyle said, interrupting her thoughts.

"Kyle, I heard something about a location being compromised.

What is that all about?" Ned asked.

"It's not a concern to you two. That fueling location will be relocated for security purposes. He was letting me know, is all," Kyle answered.

"What does he mean by 'being dealt with'?" Julie asked.

She saw Ned nod in agreement and open his mouth, about to say something, but Kyle spoke first.

"Those responsible for the compromise will be dealt with," Kyle answered, offering little detail except that a person had created the breach in security.

Julie and Ned looked at each other. Ned shrugged, silently acknowledging he was also wondering what on earth was going on.

***

Steve found himself face down on the ground again. He counted himself lucky—this time, he wasn't slammed to the ground. He was ordered to lay face down, and he complied. In doing so, he found himself with his hands zip tied together while the car was searched. Shawn stood by the engine block holding Addison in one arm like a football.

Everything was removed from the car. *Everything*. Items that were accessories to the car were removed. Not only were they removed, but they were taken apart. Addison's items were removed from bags. Her car seat was taken apart. Seats in the vehicle were flipped open with attempts to remove them.

This checkpoint was at the Woodland, Washington exit, at the Clark County border. After passing the exit, they would be in Cowlitz County. The black masked thugs were there, just like the previous checkpoint. There were many more of them this time. Everyone had a rifle. The cars were not lined up across the freeway this time—they were piled. As Shawn slowly approached, Steve counted about thirty cars crossing the freeway, three vehicles high. Interestingly, they were burned, too. Steve figured they must have been driven up on each other somehow, then lit on fire. The scorch marks on the pavement under the vehicles confirmed his thoughts.

Steve saw a large passenger van in a gas station parking lot. About a dozen people sat on the sidewalk outside the opened door, with their hands zip tied behind them. In normal times, it would look like a police raid of some kind—except there were no police around; it was the masked checkpoint guards detaining the van.

"Oh my God," Steve had muttered.

Now, merely moments later, Steve found himself in the almost identical situation as the van passengers. He was thankful to be spared having another shoe pressed into his neck. He was thankful he wasn't thrown to the ground. *How quickly one's standards change*, he thought to himself.

The zip ties were worrisome. He could be beaten with no way to defend or shield himself. He could easily be picked up and carted off without the ability to resist. Shawn stood at the front of the vehicle—not zip tied. Steve assumed it was because he had Addison. Steve knew that his father had instructed Shawn to put Addison first—no matter what. That reassured Steve, despite that it meant he would not be a priority if they found themselves in a truly dangerous situation.

As he lay on the cement listening to the crass conversation among the checkpoint guards about the contents of the vehicle, he wondered if he should ask Shawn about his directive to prioritize Addison's safety over his. Did he want to know, really? It seemed like a stupid question to ask, the more he thought about it.

Steve found it difficult to keep his mind alert. He knew that, at any moment, the tense mood could shift to a more dangerous one, and he could easily receive a swift kick to the ribs or face. He wondered what Shawn would do if that happened. Did he have any sense of loyalty to Steve? Would he attempt to save him, or was his laser focus only on Addison?

He tried a different mind exercise, to stay alert and learn from what was going on around him. He knew he should take in details and memorize them, try to catch names. Essentially, he needed to be like Shawn, who was always assessing his environment even in moments that didn't require it.

It was fascinating to Steve the more he concentrated on details. He counted eight pairs of feet going in and out of the vehicle. Two of them wore a name brand black tennis shoe. Two wore black basketball style high tops. Four wore black goth-esque leather lace-up boots. From what he could tell, they were all men, but he could hear a female voice in the distance, not part of the car-ransacking detail. One person did most of the talking and seemed to be the leader. Someone called him "Finn," and he answered back.

Steve also noticed that they were all encumbered by their rifles. He remembered the many times he had seen members of the military or police carry rifles. Usually their guns were attached to their bodies with a strap or sling around their shoulders. Most of these people, however, didn't have slings, and they picked up and set down their rifles by their barrel ends, as if they were broomsticks. Steve had seen this setup for rifles often among Portland police at the dozens of riots he had attended. It looked odd to see so many people walking around with firearms, and it seemed obvious — even to Steve — that they had little to no experience with what they were handling. Steve mused to himself, *I know next to nothing about rifles, and even I know this is bad.*

During the car ransacking, no one addressed Shawn or Steve. Shawn seemed his normal, even self. Steve watched as Shawn followed his own orders, keeping his eyes forward while wearing a poker face. In fact, Shawn *always* had the same stern, firm look on his face.

Steve felt a small amount of comfort knowing Shawn was fully aware of their current surroundings, as dangerous and unnerving as they were. However, it was more comforting to know that Shawn was ready for anything if things went south.

Steve changed his thinking in *that moment*: he was no longer afraid of what the checkpoint guards might do. *The voices I hear on Shawn's radio probably have a visual right now. Shawn has Addison. I have been beaten before. I'm sure I will be again. If I die in this moment, all loose strings in my life are taken care of. I will finish this. And I might die doing it,* thought Steve.

Shawn and his detail had this checkpoint planned out, and the car ransacking appeared to be more of an inconvenience to him than anything dangerous.

I wonder if Shawn feels like we're in danger? Steve found his mind wandering again, but he answered the question immediately in his head. *Yes, it's dangerous. Idiots carrying rifles they don't know how to handle is a recipe for danger. But he's not frightened of the danger, he's ready for it.*

Steve was no longer afraid. He relaxed his mind, knowing that Shawn was truly the one with control of the situation. He also wanted to be an asset to Shawn instead of a liability. He wanted to make a point of trying to be one step ahead of Shawn.

Suddenly, Steve's left arm was yanked up and he was lifted off the ground. He instinctively put his feet under him to get his footing.

"Who are you?" a man, whose voice he recognized as Finn's, hissed.

Here we go again, thought Steve. "Steve Atwood," he replied while staring forward at Shawn.

"Who's your driver?" Finn shot.

"Shawn."

"Who is she?" Finn demanded, pointing to Addison.

"My kid," Steve said with an equally even tone, all the while keeping his gaze on Shawn. His heart jumped at the prospect of Addison being the center of attention, even if only momentarily. In the back of his mind, he couldn't escape worrying about all the horrors of human trafficking he'd been hearing about since the collapse. Now they were asking about her. *Why is he interested in her?* He felt himself start to panic. *Stay calm. Shawn has her. He'll protect her before you. Keep your eyes forward and your poker face on.*

"Why does he have her?" Finn demanded. "What kind of a father are you?"

"The kind who has his hands zip tied behind his back," retorted Steve with an edge.

Steve saw the corner of Shawn's mouth twitch up a bit.

"Where are you going?" Finn continued.

"Pierce Point," Steve answered again.

"You leaving this place? Let me tell you something, you skinny little fuck — don't ever let me see you here again. Take your spawn and leave. I'll remember you. You come down this freeway again, I'll cut you to pieces," he growled.

Steve felt his wrists being pulled up, and he instinctively leaned forward. The cold edge of a blade slid between his thumbs and lifted, releasing the zip ties. As his hands were freed, Finn pushed Steve forward. He took a large step and caught his balance before falling. He immediately straightened up, then walked toward Shawn and took Addison. After taking the baby, Steve quickly entered the back of the SUV and buckled her into the car seat, then joined Shawn in tossing everything back into the vehicle.

Steve gathered up the last few items, and Shawn fired up the engine and put it into gear. Steve hefted himself into the SUV, and Shawn immediately pulled away.

He pulled the SUV into a long line of vehicles waiting to pass the pile of burned out cars. Steve kept his eyes forward.

Chapter 68
Newsflash

Patrick sat comfortably in an employee's lounge in the KOIN tower. He had managed to smile his way through the key swipe door, taking advantage of a familiar person also entering the building. Patrick, in his upgraded business attire, simply fell in step behind the person. Smiling, he'd said, "After you," and held the door as if he belonged there.

In the cafeteria, Patrick had found a used clamshell meal container to set on his table, making it appear as though he were finishing a meal. He'd displayed the clamshell when no one was looking. While the room was at its busiest during the lunch hour, he made a point to purchase a beverage from the vending machine. He spent his "lunch break" drinking his beverage while looking over Adam's bank statements he had found in a filing cabinet. Patrick had found canceled checks in that same cabinet — checks that had Adam's signature on them to help Patrick with his forgery efforts. To another employee on their lunch break, Patrick appeared to be hard at work, deserving of nothing more than a glance.

As people milled in an out of the cafeteria, Patrick spoke warm pleasantries to people with familiar faces. As the lunch hour wore down, and he was eventually alone in the room, he moved to the sofa where old magazines and a couple days'-worth of newspapers were strewn on a side table.

Spotting the TV remote, he clicked on the TV mounted in a ceiling corner above the vending machines. It immediately turned on to a regional cable news show. Patrick set the remote down and started looking through the papers.

"The bodies of two local homeless advocates were discovered yesterday. Police are investigating it as a 'hate-crime'..."

Patrick's eyes shot to the screen, and his ears perked up to the news being broadcast on the TV.

"The bodies of a man known in the homeless community as 'Teeze', and his associate, were found in the bathhouse of a local homeless community. Let's go to Kelly Birch, who is live on scene."

Patrick's jaw dropped, and he quickly tried to regain an appearance of mild interest in case anyone wandered into the room.

"Thank you. As you can see behind me, police have taped off the entire shower house as they investigate the gruesome discovery of the bodies of Mr. Telhas, known as 'Teeze' among his community, and his associate, who is currently unidentified. We asked those who live in this community what their thoughts were. None wanted to join us on camera, but the resounding sentiment was shock. Police say evidence at the scene indicates this could be a hate crime, and they are investigating as such."

Patrick was riveted. He knew of Teeze mainly through all the social services he had tried to access over the last few years. Teeze's face was distinctive, and his Muslim attire made him memorable. *Was it an anti-Muslim, racist thing?* Patrick wondered.

The story then went to an interview with Police Chief Paul Sampson. A microphone was in front of his mouth, and he looked directly at an interviewer. "Our officers are shocked at Teeze's murder," he said with an ominous tone.

The reporter with the microphone asked, "What makes you think it's a hate crime?"

"We are still processing evidence, and will be for the next day or two. However, the position of the two men's bodies indicate we can't eliminate that as a possibility."

The reporter pressed, "What sort of hate crime?"

Chief Sampson took a short pause to consider his words, "At this point we are considering the evidence, and pursuing this as an anti-LBGTQ crime."

The faceless interviewer perked up at this bit of information — and so did Patrick. "Are there any suspects? Should Portland's LGBTQ community be concerned they are being targeted?"

"It is extremely early in the investigation at this point. I am not going to comment on anyone associated with this crime. For those in the community, we always ask citizens to be cognizant of their surroundings and to be on the lookout. If they see anything suspicious, they should call police. If you have any information regarding anyone associated with this heinous crime, please call police. Thank you," Chief Sampson said. He smiled and nodded, stepping out of the view of the camera.

Patrick's mind absorbed the information; he wanted more. He skimmed through the stack of newspapers, locating the morning paper that had the double murder as the front-page headline. His eyes focused on the details. Bodies found. Violent scene. Homeless village.

Patrick kept reading. *How was this a hate crime?* he wondered. The newspapers were just as vague.

Patrick let the paper lay on his lap as he looked out the window at Portland's streets. His mind went in one direction. *The gay community has always been a target. Most of them time it's downtown. Why a homeless camp? And Teeze? I didn't know Teeze was gay. He was such a public figure. How did I miss that detail? And who is this associate of his, and how did I miss that? Why would someone kill gay people in a homeless camp? Homeless people motivated to kill a gay man and his associate? I do not get it. Maybe drugs? But no one has money for drugs these days.* Patrick was bothered by the double homicide as he tried to connect why a hate crime would happen to a prominent advocate in a homeless village.

As he continued watching out the window, Qaatel and Kandi walked by on the sidewalk across the street.

Oh my God, Patrick thought, as his mind connected with Qaatel's motivations. "*Could he be behind it? Could Kandi? Kandi has the same connections with the city that Teeze had. Kandi wouldn't hurt anyone, though. Shit, she'd protect a gay person before she'd hurt them.*"

Patrick's thoughts went in another direction. He remembered Qaatel's threat that if Patrick didn't accept his proposal, Qaatel would go to the police with evidence of Patrick's deadly scam. *Would he pin this on someone? Me?*

Patrick gasped.

***

Patrick knew his time squatting in Trevor and Adam's house was over. Like previous scams before, he hadn't stayed long. With the backlog of police investigations and delay in procedures, the notification of family members — and their subsequent journey to the house — would take some time. Patrick was able to find out that both men had family members on the East Coast. While they lived in Sanctuary States, it would take a tremendous amount of effort for them to get to Oregon. However, Patrick had to assume that a friend could be called to "check on the house" at any point in time, and he didn't want to risk it.

Trevor's cell phone had several texts come in asking about loan documents, property showings, and many requests for him to return calls. Patrick could only see the preview of the texts, but knew it was only a matter of a day or so before someone came to the door to make a welfare check. While he certainly wouldn't answer the door, he needed to not be there when someone arrived unexpectedly with a key. In the case of Trevor and Adam, Patrick made up a phony lease agreement to one of the couple's managed properties, forging Adam's signature.

Patrick spent an afternoon packing up a suitcase with two changes of professional clothes. He packed one box of food items, medications, and key paperwork from their home. He cleaned the home of any evidence of his presence, including a thorough wipe down of all surfaces for fingerprints.

The following Friday, after he had transitioned to his new apartment, Patrick made his way to Kandi's. He wanted a good meal, and to keep up on pleasantries with fellow patrons. More importantly, he wanted to hear any news about the double homicide. He knew the bar would be steady, and people would talk more freely there about their opinions or knowledge than anywhere else. Patrick made a point to sit at the bar instead of a table for that reason.

He watched as several couples and small parties came and went throughout the evening. A few new performers were making their debut, and had supporters in the audience, cheering loudly. Patrick eavesdropped intently, trying to catch any word about the murders. Nothing. The night's discussions were set aside for drinks and partying.

After the final performance, the bar got busy again. Patrick stayed in his seat as the bartender served the busy crowd. Looking to one side, Patrick saw Kandi enter the bar area in her full costume of feathers and beads.

"Hello, Zane! Busy night! I will get out of your way. Just need you to make a couple of goodies for me. I'll be in the office if you need me," Kandi crooned to Zane.

Kandi was in a great mood. To Patrick, it looked like everyone was in a great mood that night.

"Patrick! Good to see you! Zane, you know Patrick is one of my best customers. Make sure you give him some extra attention. Good night everyone!" Kandi reached over and patted Patrick's forearm, then waved to everyone at the bar as she grabbed her drinks and left with a flourish.

Patrick's heart leapt at the sight of her moving toward the exit. Qaatel held the swinging door open for her and she exited the bar area. They made their way — together — to the hallway that lead to the stairwell and up to Kandi's offices. Patrick craned his neck, watching the final glimpse of them disappear in the darkened hallway.

Patrick retraced thoughts he'd had earlier. He ran through facts he knew to keep his mind from racing. He *knew* Qaatel approached him to target Adam and Trevor, specifically because they were a gay couple. Next fact: Kandi ran a successful business catering to the LGBTQ community. Fact: Qaatel did not have a friendly relationship with Kandi when Patrick struck his agreement with Qaatel. Yet, they appeared to have one now, to the point that Kandi was inviting Qaatel to her private office. Finally, Teeze and his associate were recently murdered in an alleged "hate crime" against the LGBTQ community. The crime had the feel of Qaatel all over it. It reeked of Qaatel. The only fact Patrick couldn't discern was whether Qaatel was responsible. Lacking a key fact, Patrick couldn't tell if Kandi was the next target, or simply a new partnership being formed in a bar where relationships and hookups are established daily.

***

Patrick sat at a dingy coffeehouse near Portland State University, watching through the cracked glass storefront as people walked down the street. Duct tape traced the cracks in the glass from the floor to the ceiling. One pane was boarded up completely. The coffeehouse was a few hundred feet from the entrance to the university, which was dangerously close to the ongoing riots. The coffeehouse was caught in the middle. Many of the few remaining students attending the university participated in the riots regularly. The shop owners had tent cards placed around the shop on tables stating, "Free speech is recognized and appreciated here. Everyone is welcome. Don't break anything."

Patrick scanned the few people who came into his line of sight. His right leg bounced nervously, frantically. He was meeting Qaatel. Patrick felt a tap on his shoulder and jumped at the unexpected gesture.

"Calm down," Qaatel gently instructed as he pulled up a barstool. "Nice view."

"Hey," Patrick replied, attempting to keep his cool.

"This is a strange place. What made you choose this dump?" Qaatel asked.

"They… uh… have good coffee," Patrick said, aware of how lame he sounded.

"Ah, well. Next time, I choose. What's on your mind?"

Patrick had rehearsed in his mind how to get to the answers he was looking for. Upon seeing Qaatel's intense face, he felt what little confidence he had start to dissipate.

"I've seen you around Kandi's lately. I keep thinking, since we have an agreement, that I should get to know you more. It seems odd to see you and not say hello," Patrick said.

"It's smart to not say hello. It's because we have an agreement that we don't," Qaatel replied.

"See, I thought so, which is why I chose this place since it's far away from Kandi's." Patrick was doing his best to sound casual and conversational.

"It smells like shit," Qaatel said.

75

"Downtown smells like shit," Patrick shot back.

"Let me try this again. What's on your mind besides the smell of downtown?" Qaatel said, already sounding a bit exasperated.

Patrick tried a different angle. "Did you know Teeze?" He looked Qaatel in the eyes.

Qaatel took a moment to return Patrick's gaze. He began to chuckle and answered Patrick's question with a question. "Why would I know Teeze?"

"That is exactly what I am asking you," Patrick said.

"This is absurd. You ask me to meet you for an important discussion on the other side of downtown to ask me if I know someone… who is this person? Teleeze? What did you say?"

Patrick knew Qaatel's avoidance of the question, and dodging questions with questions, was deception. He also played that game.

"I know the nature of our agreement," Patrick said. "I am covering my bases and being circumspect. Are there other serious agreements out there?"

"Why are you asking this?" Qaatel responded.

Patrick didn't answer. Instead, he continued to look Qaatel in the eye. Curiosity was not an option. Patrick gave no answer and Qaatel was clearly not amused.

"Who is the person you mentioned earlier?"

"Teeze. It was in the news. He and another person were found murdered in a homeless village," Patrick said, feeling his frustration mount. "A murder that is being investigated as a hate crime."

"Hate crime? Murders happen all the time. Murder generally happens because of hate," Qaatel said. "What does this have to do with anything?"

"When I heard the news, it was the kind of murder — and murder investigation — that could have come out of an agreement… if you know what I mean," Patrick said.

"Oh! You're wondering if I did it," Qaatel said, switching to a mocking tone again.

"I am concerned when something like that makes the news, and the police are taking it seriously and not just adding it to a stack of papers," Patrick said.

"Agreements that I make with you, or anyone else, are confidential," Qaatel continued. "Do you want future work with me?"

"Not sure. Not if what I do makes the five o'clock news, I don't," Patrick said with an edge.

"I keep my agreements, and those I make agreements with are

confidential, so you have nothing to worry about," Qaatel said.

"What sort of agreement are you making with Kandi?" Patrick asked. "You don't seem to be making a point to keep *that* confidential."

"You're assuming I'm working with her. Why would I negotiate with her about anything? She is useless to me," Qaatel said with a small wave of his hand.

Qaatel's English was perfect. But in talking to him, Patrick picked up on small inflections in his speech and mannerisms that hinted of his Middle Eastern descent. The ambiguous use of the word *useless* was one of them.

"What do you mean by useless?" Patrick asked.

"She is useless to me," Qaatel repeated.

"For someone who is useless, you seem to be wasting a lot of your time with her," Patrick pointed out.

Qaatel leaned forward and said in a lowered tone, "You mention that you're concerned about things you know about ending up on the news? Then stop asking questions that are none of your concern."

"Did you know Teeze?" Patrick pressed.

"Do not ask questions you do not want to know the answers to," Qaatel said.

"I wouldn't ask them if I didn't." Patrick didn't flinch, and was tiring of Qaatel's word games and evasiveness. "Did you know Teeze?"

"I hope you and I have other meetings in the future where we can put together agreements that are mutually beneficial to each of us. I think you'll agree that this isn't one of them. I need to make my next appointment," Qaatel said as he stood and tapped on the table.

Patrick watched as Qaatel swiftly exited the coffeehouse and made his way down the street outside.

"Well shit," Patrick muttered. "That didn't go well."

***

Patrick was unsettled. He sat on the floor of his new apartment, feeling less and less like going downtown. It was unsafe. If he played his cards right, this new place could be his for a long time. The new management would come in, take inventory of current tenants, and not think twice of his presence as long as the rent was paid. Until the "new management" showed up, he could get away with not paying, which was fine with him.

He was considering his options for how he was going to manage to pay rent. He could keep hustling or playing dangerous games. That would just increase the risk of law enforcement discovering his deadly gig. Getting a real job was appealing. Knowing that people like Qaatel were slithering through Portland and targeting the LGBTQ community — Patrick included — unnerved him.

His desire to hustle downtown this particular evening was low. Kandi's place drew him in, but for different reasons tonight. Normally it was to keep up relationships, much like a store owner likes to maintain good will with customers. Tonight was different, though. Patrick felt like he needed to keep an eye on Kandi herself.

Patrick picked up on the subtle warning in the few details Qaatel gave away during their meeting days before. Qaatel was spending generous amounts of time with someone he deemed "useless." Patrick couldn't understand why he would do that. He realized he may never know if Qaatel had anything to do with Teeze's demise, but he knew Qaatel was targeting Kandi.

His decision was made: he would stay in this evening, and let his thoughts continue to consume him. He would hope for restful sleep — something he hadn't had in a very long time.

Chapter 69
Asset Delivered

Julie and Ned tucked themselves under the small passenger seats for the next stop, after a two and a half-hour flight over the Rocky Mountains that gradually turned into dry flatland, which Julie assumed was western Wyoming or Utah. *Maybe Idaho?* Julie wondered.

She made a point to arrange the tarp so she could breathe fresh air more easily, which also improved her ability to hear. Just like before, Kyle chatted with someone she assumed had a similar role as Jim at the previous stop.

"Kyle, how goes it?" she heard a man ask.

"Living dangerously, you know me," Kyle answered back casually. "You?"

"Screw that, you're flying the friendly skies these days. I'm doing my thing. You get the latest?"

"On?" Kyle asked.

"Compromise of the network."

"Yep. I'll check coms when I land. I'll adjust," Kyle replied.

"Good."

"Hey, Jesse, got a light?" Kyle asked after a pause.

"I do, but get a dozen-or-so more yards between us before you light it up!"

Julie heard rustling, and assumed Kyle was walking away from the aircraft to smoke. She listened to the swooshing sound of fuel entering the fuel tank, and found herself relaxing on the hard, dirty floor while the aircraft fueled. Just like before, Julie heard Kyle climb into the cockpit, and she waited for his signal to come out from the tarp.

As the aircraft lifted, Kyle gave his instructions. "I checked the intel for our next stop. It will be a water landing, just like all the others. Once we reach the dock, grab all gear. You will be met and led to quarters where you will sleep tonight. Some judge is supposed to meet you in the morning. I don't have much more info on those details. I'll meet you back at the dock the day after next at oh-six-hundred."

"You won't be at Pierce Point?" Ned asked.

"I have a quick transport I can do, and will want to catch some shut-eye before I pick you up. When I'm not flying, I'm not making money," Kyle replied.

Ned nodded.

***

Shawn slowed down as the signs for exit 79, Chamber Way, approached. Steve fought back the urge to ask, and chose to observe instead.

"Eight-zero-eight to seven-nine, status," Shawn said into his radio.

"Seven-nine to eight-zero-eight, clear."

"Eight-zero-eight, copy," Shawn replied.

Steve watched his surroundings closely as Shawn took the exit and slowed to a stop at the top of the ramp. This area was not as disheveled as the previous checkpoints. There were no piles of cars blocking the roadway, or bodies on the side of the road, or black masked checkpoint guards. There was certainly damage everywhere. Several scorched and abandoned buildings surrounded the overpass.

The sign for a discount hotel was damaged extensively. Burn marks were on the building, but there were cars in the parking lot, and he could see a maid's cart on the second-story balcony floor.

A large box store to the northwest of the intersection reminded Steve of Vancouver Mall, with shadowy silhouettes all that remained of the store names. A fast food restaurant shared a parking lot with the box store. There were multiple law enforcement vehicles parked in the lot.

Steve knew things were not normal, but they weren't as dangerous, either. He trusted Shawn's words, that two of the checkpoints were dangerous and one wasn't.

"Sir," Shawn said as he rolled down the window.

"Hello," greeted a man in a khaki shirt and blue jeans. He had a large handgun holstered to his belt. No black mask. No rifle. He didn't appear angry. There were six people along each side of the freeway. Everyone had handguns in holsters, and wore mostly matching clothing. All were talking to the few cars at the top of the onramps. Steve didn't recognize any of the cars, and guessed they were locals from the area.

Shawn handed the checkpoint guard a small manila envelope. Steve expected cash to be inside, but instead, the man unfolded papers. He took several minutes to read each. Shawn put on his poker face and looked forward. Steve unbuckled Addison, who was quiet but restless, and held her.

"Good. Everything is in order. If you head over to the parking lot over there, you'll be able to fuel up, grab some food, and stretch your legs," the man said as he pointed to the parking lot of the box store.

"Copy," Shawn replied, and lifted a few fingers off the steering wheel in a half wave as he slowly pulled forward.

Steve kept his eyes forward as they approached a parking space.

80

"Food carts over there, porta potties over there," Shawn pointed. "Do what you need to do. Leaving in sixty minutes."

"Copy," Steve said.

Steve and Shawn both stepped out of the vehicle and stretched their legs. Steve held Addison in his left arm, grabbed the car seat in his right, and headed for the porta potties. He spent a quick moment in the plastic box with Addison strapped in the car seat on the ground just outside the door — he cracked the door open very slightly so he could keep her in his sight. He exited, picked her up in the carrier, and headed back to the vehicle.

After changing Addison's extremely fragrant diaper, Steve placed her in a shaded area created by the car door and began the long process of reassembling the ransacked items. He wadded up her clean clothes and crammed them in one pocket of her bag, found all the unused diapers and tried to stack them into another compartment, and searched around for the small pack of wipes. Next, he sorted through all the items to find every little packet of baby formula. He wanted to make sure he had every single one. He realized he was probably missing one, and it concerned him. He found three out of four pacifiers. He located his few clothes, and stuffed them in his nylon pack.

Steve glanced at his watch and realized he had about thirty minutes to get a bite. He quickly installed Addison's car seat, tucked her in his left arm, swung his nylon pack on his back, and headed to the food carts.

As he approached, he inhaled deeply at the smell of grilled meat. *I haven't smelled good food in so long*, he said to himself. There were two food carts and four picnic tables at the edge of the parking lot. About eight people were in the area, either ordering or consuming a meal. Shawn stood at one of the food carts with a bottle of water, and was talking to a man dressed like an overpass guard with khaki shirt, jeans, and sidearm.

Steve wasn't sure what to do as he approached the carts and realized had no money. *I can't imagine what the prices could be for a hot, fresh meal*, he thought as he sat down at a picnic table opting to not approach a cart.

Shawn noticed, excused himself from his conversation, walked up to Steve and tapped the table. "Hey, get some food," Shawn said.

"No money," Steve replied.

"It's taken care of, get some food," Shawn repeated.

Steve was taken aback and pleasantly surprised. He nodded slightly and headed to a cart with Addison. Standing at the cart, hearing and smelling the sizzling food, watching pleasantries around him... Steve got a knot in his throat.

"Hey, how are you?" came a voice from inside the cart. He saw a young man come to the counter perched a few feet above Steve.

Exhaling, Steve answered, "I'm okay."

"What can I get you?" the cook asked.

"Oh wow, umm… how about teriyaki chicken, extra rice, and a bottle of water," Steve said as his eyes got slightly misty. He had been eating meals out of boxes, protein bars, junk and canned soda for months.

"You got it. I'll bring it out to you. Grab a seat."

"Sure thing," Steve mumbled as he walked to an unoccupied picnic table. *Shit, Steve, pull it together. It's teriyaki chicken, for Pete's sake, not your fucking wedding day.*

Steve cradled Addison in his left arm, and she pulled on his t-shirt sleeve as if to look under it. He looked down at her and smiled as they played a little game of peek-a-boo with his stretched-out sleeve. He gazed down at her as a surge of fatherly love coursed through his veins.

The cook approached with a heaping plate of chicken and rice, and two bottles of water.

"It's hot today, thought you could use an extra bottle of water," he said, setting down the meal.

"Thank you," Steve replied, trying to conceal his emotional moment in his voice.

The cook stopped and bent a little, looking at Steve. "Hey, man… you okay?" he inquired, motioning to Steve's right cheek. "Looks like you took a hit."

"I think I'm fine. I'll find a mirror in a bit and look after I eat," Steve said. "I feel fine. I'd actually forgotten all about it."

"Let me grab a bag of ice," the cook said as he went back to the food cart.

Steve was hungry and wanted to eat. He knew he needed to eat quickly. He felt incredibly grateful and overwhelmed. He took a bite of chicken, and offered some to Addison, who gummed it and pointed to the chicken.

***

Shawn drank from his water bottle, watching the cook, and ticked off the sixty minutes until departure.

"I'm not in the mood for this today, dude," said the cook as he approached Shawn. "I'm being paid to be nice, and that is all."

"Then shut up and do your job," Shawn said.

"You bring these dirty fucks through here. We spent months

retaking this location from the Limas. Those Limas were fueled by the likes of this kind," said the cook, tossing a glance towards Steve. "Even after we got rid of them, rioters from Portland kept coming here trying to retake it. They traveled up and down the I-5, and we met them each time, and dealt with them each time. There isn't enough money anymore. I'm done being nice to them. I'm done licking their wounds and wanting to inflict more. Next time, find another food place to take your passengers when you're passing through. I am sick of this shit."

Shawn nodded.

***

Steve took a bite of food and then gave Addison another bite. He also offered her drinks of cold water. He was aware that Shawn was nearby, watching him, and that he and the cook were exchanging pleasantries.

The waiter brought a sandwich bag with a handful of ice in it to Steve.

"Here, try this," he said, and sat down. "I'm Bobby." He extended his hand to shake Steve's.

Steve shook with him and said, "I'm Steve. Thank you for a great meal. It's been awhile since I've had good, hot food." Steve took another bite then stabbed the fork into some chicken to give to Addison.

"Who is this little one?" Bobby asked.

"My daughter," Steve answered.

"We don't see small babies around here much. Where are you from?" Bobby asked sternly.

Steve looked up from Addison to answer, and saw Shawn by the food cart slightly swinging his head from left to right. He put his fingers to his lips and made the motion as though he were zipping his lips shut.

"Just passing through," Steve answered vaguely.

"Ah, so you're from south of here." Bobby' voice took a more serious edge. The persistence of his question struck a chord with Steve. The seriousness also tarnished Steve's desire to eat. His defenses went up.

Steve just looked at Bobby, not wanting to answer — refusing to answer. He concentrated on locking eyes and keeping a poker face with Bobby.

"Well I'll say this, Steve — you are from south of here. Just based on what you smell like, I know where you come from," Bobby said very firmly. "I just want to make sure you have a good meal, feed your kid, and leave in peace. Don't bring back any of your friends from Portland. We like it here, like this. Not smeared in shit, like you smell. Got it?"

"Hey, Bobby," came Shawn's voice from somewhere out of Steve's line of sight, "lighten up."

Bobby kept his gaze on Steve, stood up, and walked away.

Shawn sat down across from Steve.

"What did I do this time to piss off a complete stranger?" Steve asked.

"Nothing. This overpass experienced significant bloodshed a year or so ago. It was a battle between those types you used to riot with in Portland, and those who live here who want peace. He is making sure you aren't inviting your friends. He is tired of fighting," Shawn said. "Ten minutes, we go."

Steve nodded. *Friends*, Steve thought. *Wow.* He closed the cover of his food and headed to the vehicle, dropping the ice pack in the garbage on his way.

***

"Approaching Pierce Point," Kyle said.

Julie's heart jumped. They had made it!

"Thank God," Ned said softly.

"Stay put until we are lashed to the dock," Kyle instructed.

Julie looked out onto the water she knew was one of thousands of waterways in Washington. She was amazed at the rich greenery. She had always thought of Colorado as green and lush, but now it seemed desert-like compared to this. Trees with beautiful orange and red bark swooped from the water's edge and dipped into it. Robust ferns filled in gaps between trees, providing a continuous palette of green over the water. Buildings dotted the shoreline as far as she could see. Some appeared to be industrial in nature, but most seemed like homes. The sun was starting to kiss the mountaintops in the distance.

Ned tapped her shoulder. "Time to go."

Julie nodded and jumped out. Ned reached into the back of the aircraft and pulled out their backpacks one at a time. Julie grabbed them and caught Ned's smile. She could tell he was excited, too.

He hopped down from the fuselage onto the short dock. "We're here," Ned said giving Julie a side hug. "I guess we wait here for instructions, right, Kyle?" Ned called out.

"You know what I know," Kyle said, poking his head out of the cockpit. "I keep a tight schedule. Day after tomorrow, here. Oh-six-hundred... don't miss your flight."

"See you in two days. Be safe," Ned waved. He grabbed his pack

84

and slung it on one arm, grabbed Julie's bag, and backed away from the plane towards shore. Julie waved as she followed Ned.

***

Steve settled in the back and buckled Addison into her car seat. He had so many questions about what just happened. He wanted to ask Shawn, but decided not to. He wasn't hungry anymore, and that was all that mattered. Shawn started the engine and began to pull away from the parking lot.

As the car pulled onto the freeway, Addison's eyes began to droop. Steve was feeling sleepy, too. He was aggravated, thankful, beat up, and exhausted. *I haven't slept a full night of restful sleep in months,* Steve recalled, *and that's not because I have a small baby.*

Steve directed his gaze to Addison. *I have a baby. In less than a day, I won't have her anymore.*

Suddenly, Steve felt the depth of his situation and what was about to happen. He gently unbuckled her from the seat, turned her towards himself, and let her snuggle down onto his chest. *Screw car seat laws right now.*

Steve breathed in the smell of Addison's hair. Touched her fingers. Rubbed her tiny back. Felt her deep, sleepy breaths as she dozed. He caught a glimpse of himself in the rearview mirror. He cheek had swelled up and was dark purple. In that mirror, he saw himself clearly for the first time in months. He was a broken, beaten, bloodied man who had nothing but the shirt on his back. In his arms, he held a perfect, tow-headed little baby girl, with soft porcelain skin, who was blissfully unaware of all the evil around her. He saw her perfect head in stark contrast to his battered and bruised face. Steve's eyes watered again. Thoughts raced through his mind. *When I hand her over, I will have lost everything.*

Steve squeezed Addison a little harder and rocked her slightly as he felt tears trickle down his cheeks. He looked to his left out the window. He wanted to commit this moment to memory for the rest of his life. He never wanted to forget one of the last moments he had with his beautiful girl, Addison.

***

Steve's eyes slowly fluttered open. The familiar weight of Addison on his chest made him instinctively hug her as he awoke. Looking out the window, the sun was just setting behind the mountains. The road was winding and densely lined with trees.

"How long was I asleep?" Steve asked Shawn.

"Couple of hours. Almost there," Shawn replied.

"Eight-zero-eight to seven-nine, status," Shawn said into the radio.

"Seven-nine to eight-zero-eight, status clear."

"Eight-zero-eight, copy. ETA 30," Shawn responded.

"Seven-nine, copy."

"Eight-zero-eight to three-four, what's your position?" Shawn spoke into the radio.

"Three-four to eight-zero-eight, visual. Fifty meters," a different person answered through the radio.

"Eight-zero-eight, copy," Shawn answered.

Steve squeezed Addison as she continued to sleep. *Thirty minutes,* he pondered. *Thirty minutes until I am in a safe place. At the same time, that safe place is also where I hand her away for good.* Steve was mourning the loss of his daughter. As he thought about saying goodbye to her, his mind wandered to Joel. He'd never said goodbye to Joel. He assumed for so long that once everything blew over, he would see him again. *If this is what it takes to travel,* Steve thought, *there is no way any of that is going to be possible.* There was no extended visit planned for this summer, nor would there be in the future. Weekend visits would never happen again. *I wonder what he looks like now. I haven't seen him in almost a year.*

He was slowly realizing the likelihood that he'd never see his son or daughter again. His stomach lurched and his throat tightened at that prospect. How had he been reduced to this?

It was almost completely dark. Shawn pulled the SUV up to a gate across a road with a guard shack. A dim light came from within. Shawn stepped out of the vehicle. A man stepped out of the shack as he approached. Shawn appeared to hand him the same envelope of papers he'd handed to the man at the last checkpoint. He stepped into the shack, under the light, to read them closely.

The man pointed to one part of the paper and appeared to ask Shawn a question. Shawn stepped into the shack and spoke to the man. The man listened and then nodded his head. They exchanged a few more sentences, and then shook hands. Shawn stepped out of the shack and the man followed behind him. Shawn entered the SUV and turned over the engine.

"Hello," the man said to Steve through the driver's window. "I'm Dan Morgan. Shawn will be taking you to your quarters for the night. Get some sleep. If you have any questions, come find me."

"Thank you," Steve answered.

"Eight-zero-eight to seven-nine and three-four," Shawn muttered into the radio as he drove a short distance through the trees.

"Seven-nine, copy."

"Three-four, copy."

After the sound of the last radio voice, Shawn stopped the vehicle and said, "Asset delivered."

"Copy."

"Copy."

Shawn looked in the rearview mirror and said, "Arrived."

Chapter 70
Treasury Department

Grant Matson sat at his huge wooden antique desk in the capitol building on a warm July afternoon. *One thing those Loyalist bastards did right*, he thought, *was have nice offices.* He had a magnificent view of the capitol campus, the Olympic Mountains, and Puget Sound. Well, he had half of a good view—one of the two windows was boarded up. It had been shot out during the assault on the capitol about six months ago when the Patriots like him took over. The bullet holes were still in the wall.

He was going to leave them there to remind himself and visitors how hard-fought the seat of power in the new state of New Washington had been. It didn't come easy, and he wasn't about to let anything threaten the Patriots' victory. The bullet holes reminded him of this every day.

He couldn't help but stare out the one good window at the sunny, warm, and beautiful summer day. The birds were singing with that familiar sound Grant had been hearing since he was a kid. He heard those birds all over western Washington state. Their familiar chirps reminded him that as much as things had changed from a little over a year ago when the Collapse started, some things stayed the same. The birds were still the birds, civil war and all. The birds hadn't taken sides, and just wanted to keep chirping. Just like most of the people in New Washington—they just wanted to get on with life while the Restoration was underway.

Grant tried to refocus on the files on his desk. He had important work to do—lives literally depended on it—but, he had to admit, he was thinking more about the weekend. He felt guilty, then he realized that he couldn't be all business *all* the time. He needed to live as normal a life as possible. And a barbeque at the cabin with his Pierce Point friends on a stunning western Washington weekend was living normally. In fact, it was living pretty darned good.

"Colonel," his executive assistant, Samantha, said.

She didn't need to knock—she walked right in, which was how he wanted it. Grant's door was always open when he wasn't in a meeting or trying to write something. He thought it was important for his door to literally be open. It kept him connected with people. He took that very seriously. It was far too easy to become isolated here in his stately office. He refused to become like the people he and the Patriots had ousted and replaced. They had practically viewed themselves as royalty, and feared the regular people. That wasn't going to happen again. Grant needed to remain just another person—even if he was the chairman of the Reconciliation Commission, which decided which former Loyalists would be pardoned or tried for their crimes. Trials almost always ended in hanging. So, his job was a matter of life and death.

"Hey, Samantha, what's up?" he asked, suddenly returning to reality, instead of the sun and birds and thoughts of grilling a juicy steak at the cabin.

"Anthony Casbar at Treasury would like to talk to you about something," she said.

Grant knew Tony fairly well. He was the Assistant Treasurer, the number two person in the Treasurer's Office. He was a good guy. He had been a banker—one of the few decent ones—and the leader of a Patriot cell during the Collapse and subsequent war.

New Washington consisted of the former state of Washington minus the Seattle metropolitan area, which was still part of the former USA, or "FUSA," as everyone called it. New Washington was currently an independent republic, but most people still called it a new "state." New Washington was in talks to join a federation with the other Patriot republics and the Great States, but it hadn't happened yet.

When rebuilding a state from the Collapse and war damage, the question of how to pay for things constantly came up. The Treasury had to have an answer, or the project didn't happen. "We're not doing it if we can't pay for it," Governor Trenton would always say.

It could have been much worse. The fledgling republic of New Washington pulled off something rare: fighting a war without any debt— and even more rare: winning it. That was mainly because the war had gone so quickly, and to be honest, no one would loan New Washington any money. So New Washington never had a chance to go into debt. The war was self-funded with the weapons the Patriots had on hand—which was a lot—and by military units defecting and bringing their stuff with them. Low-intensity conflict is low-cost—if done right.

Being debt-free was what would make the Restoration successful, Grant often thought. Without debt, New Washington could focus on what needed to be done, like restoring order and repairing critical infrastructure, instead of worrying about how to make payments to creditors.

Restoring order was going remarkably well. The people had had enough of violence and theft; they craved the "good ol' days" of being able to sleep at night without worrying about dying or their food being stolen. There were still criminals, but the Patriots were mopping them up very effectively. Actually, average citizens — armed to the teeth — were doing most of the mopping up.

Repairing critical infrastructure like bridges, power lines, and roads was harder. A lot harder. Once again, due to the relatively short war, the damage to infrastructure was spotty. The Loyalists (or Limas, as they were known) didn't burn too many bridges, so to speak, in the areas that would become New Washington. This wasn't because they were nice people, but because they were so busy trying to suppress the quickly unfolding popular uprising — and because the Patriots' military efforts had been so effective, that they hadn't had time to destroy infrastructure. Besides, the Limas had always assumed the pesky little hillbilly Patriots would be easily defeated, so they didn't want to destroy the infrastructure that they, the Limas, would quickly retake. The Limas were much better at politics and social division than at military affairs.

But still, lots of damage had been done. Right after the war, infrastructure like the electrical grid didn't work, for the most part. Slowly, spare parts on hand were used to get some things back up and running. However, those locally available spare parts started to run out. There were only so many intact electrical transformers, for example, sitting around. To get more required buying them from other Patriot areas and transporting them to New Washington. That's when things got hard, as the new President's domestic immigration policies stunted interstate travel and delivery routes.

New Washington naturally sided with the Great States. The Seattle area, and Lima areas of Washington, naturally sided with Sanctuary States. Washington was one of many states split up into two or more parts.

There were only a few sources of revenue for the new government. The largest source of assets, but one that didn't help the New Washington government, was repatriating Lima resources. That meant taking stuff back from the enemy who had previously stolen it from the people. The general population had been doing this on a localized, ad hoc basis. Euphemistically called "reverse taxation," average people were taking things from the Limas, who had previously taken it from them, usually in the form of taxation. Now the people, who felt like they'd paid enough for the Limas' past fancy lifestyles, took stuff back. Sometimes they took things directly from Limas, but as the Limas fled New Washington and scurried into Seattle and the Sanctuary States, people just started taking the Limas' abandoned property. This fed and housed many citizens after the war. Grant, for example, lived in a "guest house" that had been abandoned by a fleeing Lima. But houses and food were just daily necessities; they weren't the funds to repair an electrical system. Many states were looking at New Washington as an example of how to rebuild.

The largest source of revenue to the Treasury was gold mining. Colonel Randy Heintz, the "Midnight Miner," and his people in Okanagon County, mined newly-discovered gold and turned it over to the New Washington Treasury. This was not only money, it was hard money: gold. New Washington could buy a tremendous amount of building materials and pay workers with highly sought-after gold.

Another source of money was selling Lima assets. This was tricky because the biggest source of assets were bank and retirement accounts. Most Limas took their money out of accounts in New Washington before they fled to Loyalist areas. New Washington couldn't access these funds, for the most part, because the banks and other financial institutions were usually in the FUSA, in places like New York. However, some banks and financial institutions with Lima money were in the Patriot-friendly Great States. Those states usually cooperated with requests from New Washington to seize accounts. The problem, however, was that the Great States, in varying degrees, were similarly using reverse taxation to seize Lima assets. This meant that usually all or most of a Lima's accounts had already been seized by a Great State. New Washington and other Patriot governments only got the leftovers.

The few hard assets that Limas left in New Washington, but which hadn't been seized by reverse taxation, were available for seizure by the Patriots, but there was a limiting factor on this, too. Not too many New Washingtonians had money to buy things. This was getting better by the day as the free market in New Washington roared to life. New Washington had a solid currency — gold-backed, of course — so there was "real" money in circulation, and a growing economy producing wealth. But still, it wasn't enough money to rebuild the damaged infrastructure just months after the war.

The usual sources of revenue — state taxes and borrowing — were very limited. New Washington imposed almost no taxes, in order to let the free market fuel the Restoration. New Washington refused to borrow money, because that was how the FUSA got into so much trouble. Besides, no one was lining up to loan money to a brand-new republic that had only won the war a few months earlier — and still didn't control the major metropolitan area, Seattle. The money was in Seattle, where all the rich and connected people lived, not the "hick" hinterlands.

A final source of revenue was gifts. Maybe "gifts" wasn't the right word. These "gifts" were monies that other entities paid New Washington for whatever it might become. Others saw that New Washington had a solid local militia, locally run government, and infrastructure. Grant thought of it almost like consulting work. He would give Pierce Point's model for government, advice, or information to help other communities rebuild and restore. It wasn't just putting rules on paper. It began with basic trust. Grant had also been contacted for other services that might bring gifts to New Washington.

That's why Tony from the Treasury was visiting Grant.

"To what do I owe this honor?" Grant asked.

Tony closed the door behind him as he took a seat in front of Grant's desk. Grant knew this topic would be interesting if the door was closed. It was rare for the Treasury to have business with the Reconciliation Commission. Something that did not produce revenue for New Washington, despite numerous offers, was Grant selling pardons. It was not done. Period. It couldn't be, or the Patriots would end up like the corrupt Limas they just defeated. The people needed to trust the new government, so Grant knew that Tony wasn't coming to see him to get someone's cousin out of the noose.

"We have a chance to earn a lot of money for the Treasury," Tony said. Seemingly anticipating what Grant was about to say, Tony continued before the other man could speak. "This has nothing to do with the Reconciliation Commission."

"Oh," Grant said, relieved that he didn't need to inform Tony that he could not be bought. That was always an awkward conversation.

"This has to do with you, Grant," Tony said, piquing Grant's interest.

"Is my state paycheck finally coming, and you need me to sign for it?" Grant said with a smile, knowing that he was working for free, like all other New Washington officials. His basic needs were taken care of, like the "guest house," the food in the cafeteria, and his security detail, but he wasn't taking a salary.

Tony laughed. "Nope," he said. "This is about Pierce Point."

Chapter 71
Shipping and Handling Charges

"Huh?" Grant asked.

"We have a chance to make a bunch of money—hard assets. Gold. But we need to borrow your place in Pierce Point," Tony explained.

Grant could not imagine how Pierce Point would produce gold for the Treasury. He stared blankly at Tony, who beamed with enthusiasm.

"This is so cool," he said.

"Okay," Grant finally said. "Tell me."

"Shipping and handling charges," Tony replied. He paused and smiled.

"You enjoy this, don't you?" Grant asked, jokingly. "You're killing me, man. Tell me."

"A very wealthy individual in New York," Tony continued, "needs to retrieve something from Portland and hand it off."

"Hand it off to whom?" Grant asked.

"Some people who need to arrive by sea plane," Tony said. "The sea plane will then fly to one of the Great States."

"Ah," Grant said with a grin. "A sea plane landing on the water in a very secure area—an area frequented by a state official who can make sure this gets done discretely?" Grant asked, hopeful that he could get back into the game of covert operations. It had only been a few months, but he missed that type of activity—and the adrenaline rush it provided— very much.

"You got it," Tony said. "You in?"

"Of course," Grant said without hesitation. Then he thought about it. "Well, probably I'm in," he hedged. "This delivery isn't for some bad purpose, is it?" Grant figured it wasn't, but didn't want to participate in drug running, or something like that. That was the kind of stuff the Limas did as the former state was falling apart.

Tony smiled again and leaned toward Grant. "Here's the cool part," he said, clearly sweetening the deal. "It's an adoption."

An adoption? This was not business as usual. "This must be a heck of a special baby," Grant said.

"Yep. Her grandpa is making sure that she's treated well," Tony said with a grin. "And, well, we could use the money," he said with a shrug.

"I see," Grant said, mulling it over.

Pierce Point—the home of the famous 17th Irregulars—was a very strong Patriot community. Many people who lived there had either been in the 17th Irregulars, or were related to those who had. The residents were very discrete. They were used to covert operations in their area, and they knew that blabbing was dangerous. They knew that just six months ago, if someone had started rumors about the build-up of troops at Pierce Point, the result could easily have been Lima helicopters lighting the place up. They understood the benefits of secrecy, which was why the New Washington military often used Pierce Point for delicate operations.

But Grant couldn't help but wonder: why was it "delicate" to deliver a baby for adoption? Who would be opposed to that? He knew it wasn't the operation's purpose that concerned the New Washington military. They generally did operations like this—for "gifts." Politically they didn't like emphasizing to the general population that the new state basically accepted donations and would use the military to make money.

"No risk to Pierce Point?" Grant asked. He cared about his people, and really wanted to be sure that there was no more to the story than what he was being told.

"Nope," Tony said. "Nothing more than a simple drop-off by land and departure by air."

"Anyone want to harm this baby?" Grant asked.

He knew it was unlikely here, but he couldn't help but worry—even momentarily—what if the baby was a gang leader's child? Then, perhaps a competing gang would want to hit Pierce Point to either stop the transfer or take the kid. Revenge and retaliation were common in the Lima world. Grant didn't want any of that to come to Pierce Point. Let the gang wars rage in Seattle, but not here. He knew he was probably just being overly cautious.

"Not at all," Tony said. "It's just some rich guy's granddaughter. He's getting her out of Portland. You know what a shithole that place is. You can't blame this guy." Grant knew of the riots and mayhem in Portland. The Patriots in Oregon were not nearly as organized as they had been at Pierce Point when Oregon collapsed. In Grant's mind, Oregon—as a state—was Lima-controlled.

Grant sat back in his chair and thought about it. Some dude was going pay the New Washington treasury a bunch of gold to land a sea plane and hand off a baby that's getting out of hell-on-earth Portland? He chuckled.

"What's not to love," Grant said. "Let me know what I can do."

Tony opened a folder and produced a handwritten note, which he handed to Grant. "Here's the info you and your guys will need."

Grant looked at the note. It had a date and time—the operation would happen tomorrow, Saturday—along with some authentication codes for the party handing the baby off, and for the pilot taking the baby. Pretty simple. Grant realized that this had been planned a long time ago, and he was being told at the last minute. He subordinated his ego often, in an attempt to be a team player. What mattered was that this operation succeeded—and the gold being deposited into the Treasury.

Tony removed an official-looking sheet of paper from his folder and said, "One more thing. Here's the certificate of adoption form. It's 'official,' though we just kind of made it up. We put the new state seal on it. Looks cool, huh?"

The government of New Washington, with all the rebuilding and mopping up, hadn't focused on mundane government things like adoption records. The plan was for the counties to do that, but, in the meantime, they would just make up this document and worry about the legalities later. Whichever Great State this baby was going to would obviously recognize an adoption from a Patriot state like New Washington. And if they didn't… what courthouse would someone go to? They were still closed in most places.

"Addison," Grant said after reading the name from the adoption certificate, "you are one lucky little girl."

Chapter 72
The Pope and Kid Rock

"Sgt. Vasquez," Grant said as he walked out of his office and poked his head in the neighboring one. "We ready to roll to that super-secret location?"

Vasquez was a member of the SPU — the Special Protection Unit — of the newly formed New Washington State Police, and was the leader of Grant's personal security detail.

"Of course, sir," Vasquez said, knowing that on a Friday afternoon, especially a sunny one, the cabin in Pierce Point was the "super-secret location" Grant was joking about. Everyone in Grant's office knew his Friday afternoon routine, but it seemed unprofessional to yell out where he'd be for the next few days. While almost all the Lima terrorists had been killed, captured, or had just given up and left for Seattle, there were still some out there. And the Chairman of the Reconciliation Commission was a prime target.

The other SPU trooper on the detail, Trooper Timmons, came into Grant's office, with some hangers and a duffle bag full of Grant's "real clothes."

"Thanks," Grant said as he closed his office door and changed out of the suit he hated so much, yet felt obligated to wear when taking on the solemn duty of deciding on behalf of the state who lived or died. He changed into a t-shirt, shorts, light hiking shoes, and his Glock 27 that fit in his cargo pocket. This was the same gun Manda had used to kill Doctor Greene when he was attacking her back at Pierce Point. He didn't want a perfectly good gun go to waste. Besides, he knew it worked. Ask Doctor Greene.

Putting on real clothes — and especially that pistol — refreshed him. It made him feel "normal" again. He left his suit in his office on the hangers Timmons had brought in. There was something symbolic about leaving his suit in his office and putting on his shorts for the weekend.

"Hold my calls," Grant jokingly said to Samantha. "Unless it's the Pope, or something. Or Kid Rock. You know — the usual."

Samantha laughed. "The Pope and Kid Rock. Duly noted," she said.

Every time he left the office, Grant rattled off absurd names of the people he would take calls for. It had become a game at this point; it kept things light.

Timmons took the lead, Grant was behind him, and Vasquez took up the rear as they walked to a nice, recently seized, unmarked state police car. Grant got into the back seat with Vasquez, and Timmons got behind the wheel. Soon they left the capitol campus in Olympia and headed to Pierce Point. Every time Grant made this trip, he remembered how, in early January a few months before, he had gone in a military convoy in the opposite direction, and fought to take Olympia — losing Wes in the process. That loss was ever-present: a reminder of times before and the sacrifices people made in order to create a better world.

Over time, Grant was able to think less about the war and Wes and all the others who had died. It was getting easier to have a normal life, but he would never completely forget — nor did he want to.

"Cole will be out there, right?" Grant asked Vasquez. Cole was Grant's mildly autistic son who lived at the cabin. Cole was best friends with the neighbor girl, Missy, who'd lost her dad in the war, and whose grandfather, Mark Colson, had gone insane at the loss of his son. The trauma was devastating — Missy had stopped speaking. She and Cole were therapy for each other; they both understood the power of silence.

"Yes, sir," Vasquez replied.

Grant had tried to get Vasquez to stop speaking to him so formally, but gave up when Vasquez and everyone else continued to call him sir.

"You guys know about the guests Saturday?" Grant asked. He figured they did, but better to talk about it now, as they drove, than later.

"Yes, sir," Timmons said.

"Rich know about it, too?" Grant asked, referring to Rich Gentry, Pierce Point's de facto mayor.

"Yes, sir," Vasquez said. "Everyone's been briefed. It's handled."

"All I need to do is shake some hands, take custody of a baby, hand it off, and give someone an adoption certificate?" Grant asked.

"Yes, sir," Vasquez said. "And have a relaxing weekend."

"Copy that, Sergeant," Grant said with a big smile. He had grown so accustomed to being the leader and ensuring all the details were taken care of — from his time building up the 17th Irregulars at Pierce Point, and then fighting the war — that it was a big relief to just be a participant in something, instead of the organizer.

"What's for dinner tonight and tomorrow night?" Grant asked.

"Steaks from the Holaday family farm tonight," Vasquez said, referring to a family at Pierce Point with a small ranch. "With Cole and the Morrels," he finished, now referring to Grant's son and the neighbor family, the Morrels, who would be at the dinner.

There was one name that never came up out at the cabin: Lisa. That was Grant's ex-wife. They divorced after Inauguration Day, when Grant joined the government of New Washington. She had never recovered from the bitterness she'd built up against him during the war. She so desperately wanted her old life back—her life before the war—that she just couldn't adjust to the new reality of post-war New Washington. She saw Grant as a totally different person, and no longer loved the stranger Grant had become.

Grant didn't think about her much anymore. His kids were OK, which was all he cared about.

Grant was officially single, but was too focused on his work to even think about dating. Besides, given that his job was to decide who lived and died, he expected a lot of women to be interested in him to gain influence over him. Grant thought it was sad that he even needed to think about that, but the aftermath of the war had so many unforeseen terrible consequences. Having to second-guess the motives of women you might want to date was one of them for Grant.

"Saturday night will be a workday," Grant said, thinking of the impending baby-handoff. "So, burgers on Saturday? Rolling production?" That meant cooking and eating the burgers whenever people were ready for them, as opposed to a sit-down meal.

"Yes, sir," Vasquez said.

Vasquez and Timmons always ate with Grant and his guests. "Risk your life to protect mine, and you're welcome at my table," Grant would always say. Grant would do anything for those two young men.

"How's the family?" Grant asked Timmons as they sped to the cabin.

After catching up on Timmons' life, Grant asked the same of Vasquez.

They had all become like family.

***

After a magnificent dinner Friday night, Grant spent Saturday doing one of his favorite things: walking the beach at Pierce Point. Vasquez and Timmons stayed somewhat nearby, but almost out of sight. This was as close to alone as Grant ever got. He thought about the cases on his desk— the lives he unfortunately had control over—and Lisa, and the war, and the Restoration, and a dozen other topics.

As he was walking, he heard a soft hum. It quickly grew louder. It was an airplane. He watched as a sea plane landed a few hundred yards from him and taxied to the landing dock. Sea planes used to be somewhat common at Pierce Point before the Collapse, but now that fuel was scarce, such sightings were unusual.

He started to head back to the cabin. As he rounded the point on the beach — the land that jutted into the bay and gave Pierce Point its name — he saw Rich Gentry on the deck stairs that went from the cabin to the water.

When he got close enough to the deck stairs, Grant yelled to Rich, "Mr. Mayor!"

Rich answered, "Colonel."

They both chuckled. Two old friends had fancy titles — or at least the outside world thought so. Neither one of them thought the titles mattered.

"Are the folks here?" Grant asked.

"The receiving party will be in their quarters soon," Rich said. "They're disembarking."

"Is the other party here?"

"Yep," Rich answered. "In his quarters now. We'll meet at the cabin tomorrow for the handoff." Apparently, the Saturday handoff had been moved to Sunday. That was fine; details often changed in these kinds of operations.

By this time, Vasquez and Timmons had caught up to him and were in their usual positions nearby.

"Good," Grant said. "I'll enjoy my evening with Cole and the Morrels."

Chapter 73
Adoption Proceedings

Julie walked through the door of Grant's cabin. She looked back at Ned, who hadn't followed her. He looked at her and nodded toward a figure sitting on a chair in what looked like a comfortable living room. "That must be Steve. Julie, I'll be right out here. Call for me if you need me." Ned reached out to squeeze Julie's hand. "You got this."

Julie nodded, knowing Ned was fully aware of her trepidation. She stepped inside and her eyes adjusted from sunlight to the dimness of the room. The person on the chair across the room turned his head. It was Steve.

As soon as he saw her, he stood up. "Julie! You're here," he gasped.

"Hello, Steve," Julie said as she approached him. When he turned toward her, she could see a sleeping baby draped over his chest. She also saw a black eye and facial injuries.

"Oh my word, Steve! What happened to you?"

"Let's just say that it was a rough trip to get here," Steve answered. Julie saw tears start to well up in his eyes.

"I am sorry," Julie said. Deep inside, she wanted to reach out to him and comfort him somehow. He looked awful. His clothes were dirty, and he smelled like an outhouse.

Is this the man I met on a college campus so many years ago? The man who broke through my hardened heart with his kindness and softened me? Julie wondered, as she stood in front of this broken and battered man.

"Well, this must be Addison," Julie said, trying to change the subject.

Steve cleared his throat. "Yes, it is." A tear streamed down Steve's bruised face.

"I'm sorry. I was hoping to… uh… talk with you. Chat. Before the judge, or whoever, comes here to make this legal," Steve said clearly trying to keep his composure. "I am having a hard time letting her go."

Julie nodded. Steve sat down and cradled Addison, who stirred slightly as he changed his position. He put a hand to his eyes and began to sob without restraint.

Julie went down to one knee in front of Steve. "Steve, are you okay?"

Julie didn't know what else to ask, despite it being obvious that Steve certainly was *not* okay.

"No, but I can do this," Steve answered and straightened up, wiping his nose gingerly with the back of his arm. "Don't worry. Please forgive me. Seriously. The last few months have been nothing short of hell getting Addison here, and more than once in the last two weeks I didn't think we would make it safely. I'm a bit emotional. I feel like I've run two marathons. Yay, me! I made it!" Steve gave a tear-stained, feeble smile.

"You made it. You did it," Julie assured him.

"You told me once that I needed to dig deep and make this happen. You told me to do the 'right thing,' and that it wouldn't feel good. It would be sacrificial and painful. You told me I had a lot to lose," Steve said as tears welled up in his eyes again.

Julie nodded, recalling the words she'd said to him only a few short months ago.

"You were right," Steve whispered.

Julie's heart broke for Steve. At that time, in their heated exchange, she'd only meant to push Steve to do the right thing, not for him to beat himself up after actually being beaten.

"Steve, I am sorry if I was cruel when I said that."

"Oh no! You were right. To save her, I needed to make major sacrifices, and I have. Handing her to you will be the last one, and it will hurt the most. I am a little beat up and broken as I do it. Do you mind if I hang on to her until it's official?"

"Of course not," Julie said with a warm smile. Steve nodded as tears dropped from his eyes.

"Tell me about Joel. How is he?" Steve asked after a moment.

"He is great, Steve. I wish you could see him."

Steve listened as Julie told several stories about Joel and their new life at Smoky Flats. She told him about Joel raising chickens, learning to use an ax safely, butchering wild game, fishing, enrolling in online school, helping at the trading post, and so many more things. Steve smiled as he heard the stories, and Julie thought she might be successfully boosting his mood a bit.

"Your dad sounds like he's doing well," Steve commented.

"He is. I'll tell him you inquired," Julie answered.

"Ned sounds like an important person to you."

"You're asking about him in a much kinder way than you did a few weeks back," Julie commented, recalling Steve's snarky questions during a recent phone conversation. "Yes, he is important to me. Without his help and insights, I wouldn't be here."

"I hope he continues to take care of you," Steve said. Julie thought she detected a tone of regret in his voice. "You deserve it."

"How is Mandy?" Julie asked, changing the subject.

"I have no idea."

He went on to describe the dynamics of his relationship with Mandy and her sister, Jody, over the last few months. "It was contentious at best. We stuck together because we knew there was safety in numbers, and even that was a little dicey at times," Steve said shaking his head. "What a nightmare. But, to answer your question, I have no idea where she and Jody went after Dignity Domes. They hinted at a plan they hatched. They weren't going to tell me about it, and it wasn't worth asking. I wish her the best, wherever she is. I do hope she is safe. I have mixed feelings that she's cut all ties with Addison, but Addison deserves more than Mandy."

"What are you going to do now?" Julie asked.

"I don't know," Steve said, his eyes becoming serious. An aura of sadness fell over Steve.

***

Trooper Timmons went into the cabin first, then Grant, followed by Vasquez. It was their habit. A few minutes earlier, Timmons had checked the cabin and confirmed that it was safe. He'd let the female and male in because he was told they might have some personal business to discuss before Grant entered.

As the men entered the cabin, Grant saw the couple, who were clearly having a heart-to-heart. Grant, who always wanted to make people feel comfortable if he could, said, "Hello Mr. and Ms. Atwood." He had read the briefing packet a few minutes earlier, which would make this process go more quickly.

"Hello," Julie and Steve said at the same time.

"I'm Grant Matson, and I'm here to welcome you to the state of New Washington, and to sign your adoption certificate."

The couple nodded.

"This is Sgt. Vasquez and Trooper Timmons," Grant said as he gestured to the two men. Vasquez was watching the door, Timmons the windows. "They will make sure we're very safe here." Grant looked at Steve and noticed the black eye. "It's much safer here than in Portland, or hiking through Colorado," he said, once again referring to the information in his briefing packet.

"Please," Grant said, "sit."

They sat, and so did Grant.

"Thank you, sir," Steve said, his voice a bit shaky.

"Well, hello, little Miss Addison," Grant said to the baby in Steve's arms. "She's adorable."

"Yes, she is," Steve answered with a warm smile.

"This will be brief," Grant said, "and then you guys can be on your way."

He could sense the tension in the room.

"Before I hand Ms. Atwood the adoption certificate," Grant said as he took it out of the folder, "I want to thank you, Mr. Atwood, for getting Addison here safely. I understand it's pretty awful in Portland."

Steve nodded, clearly disinterested in chitchatting, but Grant wanted information.

"Would you please tell me what it's like there?" Grant asked Steve. This was not polite chatting; Grant was always gathering intelligence, and a recent arrival from Portland would have lots of good information on the conditions there.

"It's pretty bad," Steve said as he looked at Addison. "Lots of homelessness, that kind of thing." Grant didn't appreciate Steve downplaying the severity of Oregon's collapse amplified by lawless riots.

"The riots are a problem. The criminals in the homeless camps are secondary. We're trying to start a new state here and move on. The domestic immigration policy by the President has been a Godsend. It keeps that political violence away from here most of the time. It isn't welcome here. Do you understand?" Grant glared at Steve.

"Understood," Steve said.

Grant saw Julie gazing curiously between himself and Steve, as he held the other man's gaze for an uncomfortably extended period of time. Finally, realizing Steve was much more focused on the emotional exchange he was in the middle of, he broke the stare with a sigh of resignation.

"I'll have someone here in a few minutes, and you can tell them what's going on in Portland, and about the drive up here," Grant said. He would have Rich come and take Steve's report, and then Rich would get it to the Patriot intelligence people.

Steve didn't respond, and Grant noticed that he was starting to have a faraway, despondent look in his eye.

"You, too, ma'am," Grant said, turning to Julie. "We'll have someone reach you later at your quarters, and you can tell them what's going on in Colorado."

Julie nodded.

"Well, Mr. Atwood," Grant said. "You're lucky you got out of Portland. The Sanctuary States aren't doing so well—just ask Seattle, which is now surrounded by New Washington. If I had to bet, Portland will soon be like Seattle: surrounded by a Patriot state."

Grant didn't elaborate, but he had been briefed that the Patriots in rural Oregon were a few months away from pushing the Oregon Limas back into Portland — to let them rot, just as the New Washington Patriots were doing to Seattle.

"Portland better not expect any help from California," Grant continued. "That state will be falling soon. I can hope the rural Patriots there follow suit, and push back Limas to the major cities, but it may be too late."

Grant didn't tell them that the Mexican gangs ran southern California, and that Chinese "humanitarian" ships were landing in Long Beach. The Great States' military wasn't even bothering to "liberate" California. No one wanted that state back.

"But, rural Colorado, on the other hand..." Grant said. "I understand that except for Denver, you guys are doing great."

"That's true," Julie said, elaborating no further.

"We're hopeful here," Grant said. "Hopeful that New Washington will establish recognized statehood soon, and be counted among the Great States. It would be an honor to trailblaze such a process for other states to follow." Grant knew that is was a definite possibility, but also knew to let the conversation die down — this was not a time to talk politics.

"Well, let's get down to it," Grant said as he pulled a pen from his pocket. "Mr. Atwood, would you sign right here?" He pointed toward the designated area on the form.

Steve paused and Grant sensed hesitation. After a few seconds, and a long sigh, Steve handed the baby to Julie and then stood over the adoption certificate that Grant had set on the dining table.

Steve signed it quickly. "There," he said. "I've thought about this moment a hundred times, but I guess I still wasn't entirely ready for it. But, it's the right thing to do..."

Grant motioned for Julie to come over to the table. She got up and handed Addison back to Steve, who looked happy to have the baby in his arms one last time.

Julie signed on the appropriate line, and her eyes lingered on the certificate. "New Washington, huh?" she said. "I guess this country really will never be the same."

"Now for the witnesses," Grant said, motioning for Vasquez and Timmons.

Steve started to hand Addison back to Julie, but she motioned to Steve for him to hold onto Addison.

"Nah," Steve said, as he smiled and gently handed Addison to Julie.

"She's yours now." Grant saw Steve struggle to keep tears from streaming down his face. As a distraction, he pulled papers from his back pocket. Handing them to Grant, he said, "This is the signed and notarized relinquishment from the birth-mother."

Grant accepted the document, nodding.

Chapter 74
Walks on Beaches

Ned felt tingly and a little lightheaded. He walked toward the RV that he and Julie were assigned upon arrival at Pierce Point the night before. "Guest's quarters" was the term the gate guard had used. It was tucked away in the woods a few yards from the front gate, along with other RVs. When he and Julie arrived, he wondered if Steve was stashed away in another RV in his "guest quarters." He had listened for sounds of a baby, but heard none. *Maybe he's in another location,* he wondered.

Now, twenty-four hours later, he approached the quarters with Julie—and Addison. Julie held Addison, softly comforting her as she cried. The handoff from Steve to Julie had been emotional and heart-wrenching, not so much for Steve, but for Addison. Upon being handed to Julie, Addison immediately wanted to be back in Steve's arms. She reached for him, pumping her little fists and crying "Da-da!" as she began to scream. Ned watched tears stream down Steve's face as he backed away from Julie and Addison.

"I love you," Steve had blurted out.

In that moment, Julie had looked at Ned and said, "We should go back to the RV."

Ned had grabbed all the baby gear he could identify and lead the way. Now, as he opened the RV door for Julie, he felt a little weak in the knees. The baby was here. All they had worked for was here, and it was surreal. Julie walked toward the far end of the RV so Ned could bring in the baby gear. She stayed standing, holding Addison tightly with her cheek next to her head, softly saying, "Shh… shh… shh…," and slightly bouncing Addison to comfort her.

Addison was huffing, as a child does after an upsetting cry. She clung to Julie's shirt, and tears welled up in the woman's eyes.

After several minutes, Julie and Addison had calmed, and Ned started looking at the baby gear. One large backpack, like what a high school student would use, held supplies. Then there was the car seat. He stared at the car seat, trying to figure out what happened to it. He knew something was wrong the moment he'd picked it up and felt how weighted down it was. Looking behind the cuts in the lining, he saw the body plates. *Good grief,* Ned thought. *Where are we? Fallujah?* Despite its weight, Ned decided that the car seat would be good for Addison on the plane. They would ditch it upon arrival at Kenney Reservoir.

Opening the backpack, Ned found four changes of clothes, two water bottles, and six disposable diapers. Three tubes of powdered baby formula were in a side pocket. Each were good for one bottle feeding.

This is it?! Ned exclaimed to himself. *This isn't enough to get us through the night, let alone the next two weeks!*

Ned didn't want to startle or concern Julie right now, but he was concerned. His mind raced as he tried to find a solution to Addison's lack of supplies. *This is exactly the sort of thing I was worried about,* he fumed. He knew they had powdered milk and water at their caches, but the closest one required a long plane trip and two days of backpacking at a fast pace.

There was a soft tap at the door. Ned quietly opened it, and stepped out when he saw the familiar face of Dan Morgan, the gate guard who had met them the night before.

"Mr. Collins, this box was delivered a couple of days ago for you and Miss Atwood. I wanted to keep it secure in the guard house," Dan said as he handed Ned a medium sized box.

"Delivered? Is the U.S. Postal Service working?" Ned asked, reaching out for the box.

"Not really. Not dependably. This was delivered by private courier," Dan explained.

"Okay, thank you. Much appreciated," Ned said, extending his hand to shake Dan's.

Ned stepped back into the RV, hoping this box had the much-needed baby supplies. Julie watched silently as Ned took out his knife and quietly sliced open the top of the box. The first thing Ned found was two packs of a dozen cloth diapers wrapped in plastic. Below those were two packs of antibacterial wipes, plus a bar of antibacterial soap. Underneath that were small boxes of baby formula packaged in single serving tubes, for a total of fifty-six tubes.

"Perfect!" Ned said.

There were also a dozen disposable diapers, a sunhat, sunscreen, and a set of noise canceling headphones. *Wow!* Ned thought. *Fancy!*

Immediately Ned's mind went to two places. First, he mentally rationed the baby formula as best as he could. With fifty-nine baby meals in hand, and Addison taking four or five bottles in a twenty-four-hour period, that gave them just about a fourteen-day supply of formula. *She's seven months old – I wonder how much she eats that isn't formula? I wonder if she could eat something else, if needed?*

Until they attempted to give her some adult food, he needed to plan for her to take only baby formula. Her main nutrition for the next two weeks would be those tubes of powder.

Ned also started to map out how they would repack their bags to accommodate Addison's supplies. He had done this so many times already in his mind, but until he saw the supplies, it was only an exercise in good guessing. Now he knew what the weight and space constrictions were. The challenge would be for Ned to take a portion of the weight Julie had carried, and repack her bag with the baby items. The bulk of the baby items were lightweight, but would take up a lot of space. He would need to compact them as much as possible to make them fit. Julie would still need to carry some of their supplies as well, plus Addison.

The redistribution of their packs had been a concern for Ned since the initial planning. He knew they could feasibly end up with weighted down packs that could affect their endurance and pace on their way home. If their pace was affected too much, they could run out of supplies before reaching caches, or home.

***

Julie watched Ned open the box. It was touching to see that someone had not only been generous, but incredibly thoughtful. Sunscreen? For tender baby skin in the high country in July, that would be invaluable. Noise canceling headphones? For a baby riding a noisy aircraft, that would make for a much calmer flight. Someone had thought not only of the supplies they would need, but their journey ahead.

Julie had managed to calm Addison down. As the baby slowly relaxed, Julie wondered if she was falling asleep. Julie sat down on the bed and adjusted Addison so she could glance at her face. Addison was starting to nod off.

Just as Julie got Addison adjusted to a horizontal position to sleep, her eyes opened and she saw Julie. Immediately, her face turned red and scrunched up for another cry.

"Oh, baby girl! Shh… shh…," Julie cooed. She laid down next to Addison and continued to hold her as she slowly relaxed again.

***

Ned had taken the packs outside of the RV after watching Julie fall asleep next to Addison on the bed. He decided to do what he had done so many times when preparing for this trip — he unpacked the backpacks and laid out their contents so he could strategically repack them. He found himself missing Julie's input in this shakedown.

Carefully, he repacked, taking weight and its distribution into consideration, and the ease of access to the most important items. It was a balancing act to get the packs redistributed.

After leaning the packs up against the RV, he quietly pulled the latch on the door, hoping to make as little noise as possible. He looked toward the bed at the back of the RV and saw Julie and Addison curled up tightly — asleep. Immediately, Ned remembered all the nights he fell asleep holding Johnny.

"The best sleep is that which is curled up next to a baby," he remembered his mother saying when Johnny was a toddler. Watching Julie and Addison asleep together, Ned knew he was witnessing the early stages of a mother and daughter relationship. This was the beginning of their lives together. He felt overcome by a tenderness toward the two of them. Slowly, he sat down at the tiny table, caught up in his thoughts.

After a long while, Julie stirred, opening her eyes slowly. Ned watched as her eyes scanned to room as she woke up. She went from focusing to searching, and her eyes landed on Ned.

"Hello," Ned whispered.

Julie waved to Ned and smiled.

"You okay? Need anything?" Ned whispered.

"I need to pee," Julie whispered.

"I'll take her," Ned offered.

"Okay."

Ned stepped close to Julie, and easily picked up Addison and took her to his chest. Addison stirred a bit, blinked her eyes, snuggled to Ned's chest, and went back to sleep.

"Phew," Julie whispered with a smile. She stood up and stepped aside so Ned could sit on the bed.

"Take your time. Walk around and stretch your legs if you need to. No hurry," Ned said as Julie made her way to the door.

"Thank you, I think I will. There is a bottle right there for you if she wakes up. I think she'll be ready for one when she does."

"Got it." Ned smiled. "We got this."

***

After the urgent trip to the outhouse, Julie enjoyed a stroll around Pierce Point. It was lush greenery, feathery ferns, thick moss, and evergreen trees. The smell of dampness, even in warm July, was intoxicating. She looked out over the glassy waterway and wondered if she was looking at saltwater or freshwater. Where exactly was she? Pierce Point, that was all she knew.

She found a path that lead to the beach and decided to explore. She felt enveloped by the forest as branches of bushes hugged her during her descent down the path, which popped her out on a short beach. The beach was not like the Oregon beaches she was accustomed to — where you can take your kid, step on soft sand, and find a sand dollar every hundred feet or so. This was rocky. Oyster and clam shells were everywhere. The water was still and peaceful. Even the lake at Western Lakes had ripples on it from the wind. This waterway was as calm and reflective as glass.

Looking at the beach, Julie marveled at the trees leaning out over the water almost horizontally. They were grand, with red bark. Someone had told her they were madrone trees, and native to the Pacific Northwest. *They must be native to Washington, because I've never seen these in Oregon*, Julie mused.

She sat down on a log and relaxed. One train of thought took her to Western Lakes, wondering how her father and Joel were doing. It had been about ten days since she'd seen them, although she couldn't remember precisely. The trek to Kenney Reservoir had been long, but manageable. The dry run trips they'd made prior to the real trek were invaluable.

Julie's thoughts trailed to the trek back. It would be much different. They had Addison now, as well as her gear. She had seen the repacked packs leaning against the RV, and knew the trek back weighed heavy on Ned's mind. *People backpack all the time with babies*, she told herself. *It can't be that hard — I hope.*

Looking down at the rocky beach, Julie marveled at the broken shells. There were so many!

In Oregon, there were broken clam and mussel shells, but not so many oysters. They certainly weren't as plentiful as they were here. One side of a shell was ugly and resembled a muddy rock covered in barnacles. Flipping it over revealed the pearly white inside that was smooth and soft. Julie reached to flip over a shell and realized it was intact — an actual live oyster!

She felt like a kid discovering a bug for the first time. Placing it back on the rocks near her feet (after considering whether to throw it back in the water), her eyes purposely looked at all the other shells around her, and she wondered how many others were alive, rather than empty, abandoned shells.

Let's take a walk, she decided and stood up. It was an easy stroll. Her eyes wandered from the rocky beach full of life to the dramatic madrone trees. She found one shell she particularly liked for how swirly and long it was, and decided to try to bring it back to Smoky Flats to give to Joel.

"Hey!"

Julie quickly turned around to see one of the patrol guards waving at her. She waved back and started walking toward him. When they were within earshot of each other, he called back again, "Don't stay out too long—the tide is coming in. The water will get up to there in about thirty minutes." He pointed to a spot on the bank at about Julie's shoulder height.

"Thank you! Will do!" Julie called back and waved. The guard turned around and waved over his shoulder as he disappeared up the embankment. *I guess that answered the question about fresh versus salt water: Julie didn't know of many lakes that had tides.*

This little vacation on the beach is over, Julie mused as she turned around to head back to her trailhead. *I'm also being monitored*, she realized looking up into the trees, remembering where she was.

This is Pierce Point, a secured location. Someone was watching out for her as she walked. Grant Matson had been brutal in his honesty about what was happening outside of this pristine place.

Earlier, when Julie and Ned walked back to the RV with Addison, their heads spun—not only from having Addison, but because of the nation's current state of affairs that he had laid out. It was a sobering, and sad.

Things will never be the same again. Our country can't recover from this. There will be a new normal. This collapse will be memorialized in my grandkids' history books. This isn't even a full collapse. Things could actually get worse, Julie concluded solemnly.

As she looked out over the water, she wished Ned was with her. This walk reminded her of their walks around Western Lakes where they would discuss whatever was on their minds. Julie wanted to hear Ned's thoughts about Grant's foreboding news.

Thinking of Grant's report of what was happening around the country brought Julie's mind back to Addison and Joel—her children. They would live in this new normal long after she was gone. It brought tears to her eyes to imagine the tenuous years ahead. Opportunities for them to have a prosperous and full future were diminished.

If things were this bad right now, what would it be like in five or ten years? Would Joel be able to get a high school job? He needed one in just a few years. Would he be able to go to college or get a job that could support his independence after he graduated? Would he want to move away for lack of opportunities in Smoky Flats and, if so, where would he go? The nation was so torn right now, she wondered if he would go so far away that she wouldn't be able to see him easily. The same difficult questions applied to Addison's future as well. These were all concerns that would not just simply go away; the future was unchartered for Julie's kids. No generation had come of age in the United States as it currently was. Her kids would be pioneers, or they would perish. Julie shuddered thinking of the challenges she would face as she tried to guide them — safely and successfully — toward the unknown.

Julie thought of tiny Addison. The baby had finally arrived, and it was surreal. *How do you simply walk into a building and walk out with a baby?* Julie marveled at the strange process. *Is this what adoption is like?* Settling Addison down and taking a nap with her had flooded Julie's mind with memories of young Joel — Addison's baby smell as her soft head rested on Julie's cheek, her soft breathing sounds, her velvet skin and her bright eyes.

I need to get back, she realized, swiftly walking toward the trailhead leading to the RV. *Addison needs me.*

***

Julie thought she heard baby giggles coming from the RV as she approached, but wasn't sure. She came to a halt, stopping the sound of her crunching feet to make sure she was hearing correctly. *I am definitely hearing a baby giggle.* She smiled.

She opened the RV door to see Ned sitting at the table, with Addison on the table in front of him, Ned's arms resting around her. He had a cloth diaper on his head, covering his face. Addison was shaking and waving her arms giggling.

"Where is Addison? Where is she?" Ned said playfully. "Where could she be?"

Addison grabbed at the diaper, managing to get a fistful, and then began shaking her arms to pull off the cloth. As soon as Ned's face appeared, he said, "Peek a boo!" with a smile on his face.

And Addison's deep belly laughter came tumbling out. Ned couldn't help himself from laughing, too.

"You're a silly girl!" he said to her. "Do it again?" he asked, putting the cloth on his head, and glancing at Julie before he disappeared behind it.

"Hello, there, I'm a little preoccupied," he said.

"You are! Please continue!"

Julie sat down and watched. She was reminded of Ned's constant and assuring words during the months of planning: "babies are a blessing." It was what she had to focus on as the dark thoughts of Addison's future laid heavy on Julie's mind.

Addison slowly tired of the game and cuddled up to Ned at the table.

"Let me grab you a bottle, she might be ready to wind down tonight," Julie offered.

"You need some mom-time. You want to switch places?" Ned asked.

"Sure," Julie answered thankfully. She was a little jealous of the fun Addison and Ned were having. She wanted to enjoy some baby giggles!

Ned handed Addison to Julie, and she quickly reached for Julie and snuggled into her arms, with her eyes fixed on the bottle. Addison sprawled into a laying position, nestled next to Julie's chest. As Julie leaned back against the sofa to relax, she felt Addison's hand make her way up Julie's t-shirt sleeve and rest on her skin by her shoulder.

Tears welled up in Julie's eyes. She recalled how Joel would reach into her hair and roll it around in his little hands. Julie remembered wondering if Addison had an endearing ritual to comfort herself with her parent. Julie wondered no more.

Julie and Addison's eyes met, and Addison smiled slightly with her mouth full of baby-bottle. Julie smiled back.

"Hello, baby girl," Julie cooed as her nose stung and eyes watered. "I love you."

Chapter 75
Carry a Stick

Ned looked at Julie as she held Addison. It was a moment they played out only a few days before. Now, they stood at Kenney Reservoir with their gear, except in this moment they were heading home with Addison. Julie felt a surge of nerves running through her body—excitement and apprehension about what they were soon about to face.

It was agreed they would set up camp after landing at Kenney and sleep, instead of immediately setting out for Smoky Flats.

"I want to see how Addy does in a tent, and reassess what we have and what we're capable of," Ned said, using a nickname he had given her sometime in the previous twenty-four hours. Julie liked it.

"I'll fill up some water bottles and get them filtering," Julie offered as she pulled the bottles out of her pack.

"Good, it's hot," Ned agreed. "And, once we're all set up, I think we should talk about the gear situation," he added.

"Sounds like a plan."

"I really tried to redistribute our packs for this trek to accommodate Addy and her gear. Can you put yours on while you're carrying her and make sure this will work?"

"Of course," Julie said, knowing this was weighing heavily on Ned's mind. And now that they'd gotten over one hurdle, this was their first chance to really consider the trek ahead.

"Okay, here goes," Julie said as she hoisted the pack on with Ned's help and immediately realized the extent of the additional weight. "Oof," she gasped.

"Too heavy?"

"It's heavier than I'm used to," Julie admitted. "Let me put Addison on and walk around."

With that statement, Julie realized she had no ability to simply put a baby in a front carrier while she was also wearing a heavy pack. Ned had to help her connect the buckles, and then hand Addison to her. If she bent down at the waist or the knees, she would strain her back to get to a standing position. A back injury would end their trek in disaster. With Addison in the carrier, she also could not see directly in front of her. She had to swing Addison to the right or left and look over her to see ground in front of her. On a rocky or uneven trail, this would slow her down.

"We have to stick together, Ned," Julie said solemnly. "If I have to carry a pack and Addison all by myself, we are in trouble."

Ned smiled warmly as he gently lowered Addison into the baby carrier. "Plan on it," he replied. "I have."

Julie walked around carrying the full pack and Addison. It was much heavier than she anticipated.

"I'm going up the trail and back," Julie said, wanting to see how her legs and feet did on the trail's uneven surface.

As Julie made her way up a slight incline on the shady trail, she felt how off balance the pack and baby made her. Instinctively, she reached out to tree trunks to steady her balance and make sure her footing was solid. Addison bobbed her legs and giggled, enjoying her new scenery. Turning around after about ten minutes to descend the trail, Julie saw that Ned had followed her while keeping several yards' distance.

"I think you might need a walking stick to help steady you," Ned called out.

"That is a great idea!" Julie called back.

Ned watched as Julie slowly descended the uneven trail, walking partially sideways to see the steps she took.

"Can I try?" Ned asked, motioning to Addison.

Julie nodded, and began to unbuckle the carrier.

"What did you think?" Ned asked.

"It reminds me of carrying a mountain lion on unsteady terrain," Julie answered with a grin, recalling that tremendous experience that now seemed like so long ago.

The load they would need to carry for several days was being realized. Ned took a turn up the trail and back. He was able to move at a faster pace, but the uneven trail — with exposed tree roots, rocks, and gravel, coupled with the inhibited view of the ground with Addison in front — made him consider each step.

"I'll see what I can remove from your pack and put in mine. I'll also find a walking stick for both of us. Having her on our front really throws off balance," Ned said.

"This really slows us down," Julie responded, feeling concerned.

"It does. Let me think this through. We need to make a minimum pace to get us to our cache with radios. I can call in some help at that point," Ned said. "Let's get back to camp."

Julie put her pack on with Ned's help, and they headed back to their camp tucked in the woods out of sight.

Julie could tell Ned was calculating what they could do with what they had. She was, too. She knew they had food to get them to each cache in so many days. If it took them just a little longer than planned, they would need to stretch out their food. If it took them days longer to get to their caches, they would need to stretch food to a dangerous degree. *Recreational backpacking in the high country is a calorie burner, doing it for survival at a hurried pace will be compounded*, Julie worried as she took off her pack at camp. She turned to help Ned unbuckle Addison and get his pack off.

"Okay. We can do this," Ned said, sounding determined. "It's just not going to be easy."

Julie took a deep breath. Addison began playing with Julie's hair.

"I had planned to be back at Smoky Flats in ten days, you'll remember," Ned started to explain. "Clearly, that isn't going to happen. From what I can see, our pace is cut in half easily."

Julie's heart sank and a sense of doom started to grow.

"So, we reschedule our trek, that is all this is. Our first cache was originally supposed to be two days away, but it's now four or five. That is fine, don't worry. We have plenty of food right now to get us there in four and a half. The next one after that was originally scheduled to be another two days, but that is now four. We must make that one. That is when we have the final stretch home, and where the radios are if we need help."

Julie nodded as Ned spelled out the new schedule. "What about Addison and her supplies?"

"That is somewhat of an unknown. If she only bottle feeds, based on what we have here, I think we have about a fourteen-day supply of formula for her. She is seven months old, so she can pick at some of our food, which will stretch out her supply, but also take needed energy from us," Ned answered.

Julie nodded as she took in the new plan.

"We also only have a few disposable diapers," Ned continued. "I would prefer not to use those, since disposing of them will be difficult. I think it will get a bit messy, but we should use the cloth ones, bury her waste, and boil them to sanitize them. That will be a time-consuming process each night."

Julie's eyes widened as she nodded. She hadn't considered any of that.

"What are your thoughts?" Ned asked.

"I like the plan. I want to make sure we slather her with that sunscreen, and maybe drape something over her for sun protection. If she gets a severe sunburn, we could have a medical situation on our hands," Julie pointed out.

"Good point."

"Ned, I also don't know how she'll sleep at night. Steve said she slept through the night, so that's a plus."

116

During their months of planning, they had discussed sleepless nights, and on one of their dry runs, they made a point to stay up late and get up early to simulate lack of sleep. "It's something to consider as we shuffle the pace."

"Yep. Nice thing, though, is that all the unknowns we had are now known. We know what is ahead, and we have a plan. Let's hit the sack here soon to see what the sleeping will be like," Ned replied.

"I'll start working on that first diaper boiling," Julie said with a grimace.

***

The sun was at its peak of the day. Julie figured they had been hiking for about four hours.

For our first day, I'm okay. Not great, but okay, she assured herself.

She had started to notice little things, like how hot her feet were. She knew hot spots were developing because of the extra weight on them. She and Ned had figured each person was carrying about thirty pounds more than they carried on the trip to Kenney Reservoir. Between new gear, and Addison and her supplies, it added up quickly.

She also noticed how much more fatigued she became. Normally by the end of a day, her muscles would begin to tighten, and exhaustion would set in. Her thigh muscles were now tightening by midday. She would need to continue for at least four — if not six — more hours.

Ned made sure every water bottle was filled. Julie made a conscious effort to sip continuously as they slowly walked along the path.

Addison had taken a bottle right before bed, and another when they woke up. Julie made a point to have one ready before going to sleep. Luckily, Addison wasn't fussy about how cold or warm the bottle was. After a night of sitting on the cold ground, the fluid in the bottle was not warm. Julie did her best to warm it by putting it in her sleeping bag for a few minutes to take the chill out.

Steve didn't have a microwave to warm bottles either. She's used to roughing it a bit, Julie had concluded. Addison held the bottle herself and leaned into Julie to snuggle while she drowsily drank. She fell back to sleep as the sky began to turn blue.

Ned watched Addison as he quietly rolled up sleeping bags. "She's got the disposition for this. If she were fussy, this would be miserable," he whispered.

"I agree. Only a few upset moments, but nothing out of the ordinary," Julie whispered back.

Julie thought back to the night before. She had laid Addison next to her in her sleeping bag, which is what she had planned to do. Ned laid on his side watching the pair try to settle in. Addison had wanted to rub the slick nylon of the sleeping bag, and seemed entertained by the sound it made. After an extended playtime, she'd slowly settled down. Julie could feel Addison relax in her arms as she slowly let her body go to sleep.

Julie had had trouble falling asleep, partially due to worrying that she was going to roll over on Addison. During the night, every time Julie had wanted to move, she had fully awakened to make sure she knew where Addison was in relation to her. When Julie had slept, she'd slept well. She just hadn't gotten much of it.

Which is one reason I am so tired today, Julie thought as she took a sip of water.

"There is shade up ahead. Let's find a spot to stop for a break," Ned called from behind.

"No argument here," Julie called, giving a thumbs up to Ned.

"How are you doing?" Ned asked as he helped Julie unbuckle Addison.

"Tired... between all this weight, and lack of sleep... it's a lot, but I'll get used to it," Julie assured.

"Let's take breaks often. Lots of water, and maybe a few snacks from our meals," Ned said.

Julie knew having a constant energy supply coursing through her would help keep her muscles energized. But would it be enough?

***

Patrick couldn't take the four walls of the apartment any longer. He found himself at Kandi's. A show was set to begin in about fifteen minutes, and there was a hum in the air. Patrons made sure they had fresh drinks before it started, and were crowding the bar. Patrick sat at a pub table near the bar, and felt the bumping of people all around him. It was a busier-than-normal night.

"Are these spots taken? Can we join you?" a well-groomed man asked. He looked to be about thirty.

"Yes, please. Have a seat." Patrick gave his striking smile and motioned for the men to sit. Patrick's mind considered the pair in front of him. Did he need anything? Did they have anything he needed? The conversation would tell him if he did. He would let the conversation flow before he decided.

"I'm Patrick. You are?" he gushed, extending his hand to shake it.

"Blaine. This is Evan," the well-groomed man answered, and then motioned to his companion. "This is our first time here. A friend recommended it. We just moved to the area."

"You moved *here*?" Patrick was taken slightly aback. *Why would anyone move here?* he wondered.

"Yes! It's exciting! We heard what an inclusive place Portland is. Loved that show... what was it called... Evan?" Blaine turned to Evan.

"It was *Portlandia*. Love that show! Food carts. Hippies. So funny! Then, when Blaine got a job offer from a tech company in Beaverton, of course we wanted to move here!" Evan oozed excitement. "We spent the day over at the food carts in midtown. Such a whimsical city!"

"You spent your day in downtown! How fun!" Patrick wondered if they could sense his mockery. *How in the world could anyone enjoy a meal downtown with the constant smell of human feces?*

"It was. A couple of my new colleagues joined us. It's been fun getting around and seeing the sights," Blaine said and smiled.

"The national news didn't bother you?"

"We researched it. We knew Oregon was an inclusive Sanctuary State that was taking a stand against the president's hateful policies. When that job offer came, we knew it was meant to be that we move here," Evan continued. "I'm hoping I can get my foot in the door at the same company where Blaine is working. I have an interview in a couple of weeks."

The house lights dimmed, and the stage lights came up suddenly. Everyone sat back, anticipating the show about to begin. Out of the corner of his eye, Patrick saw a familiar face over by the darkened bar. Trying to be inconspicuous, he craned his eyes without moving his head to see Kandi and Qaatel at the bar, talking to Zane. Zane handed Kandi two drinks while Kandi chatted flamboyantly. It was show night. She was dressed to the nines.

After a few minutes, Kandi handed Qaatel one of the drinks and walked past him, heading to the office. Patrick kept his eyes on Qaatel, only to see him drop something in Kandi's drink. Patrick blinked and squinted. *What did I just see?* It was dark over in the bar area, but Patrick was pretty sure he'd just witnessed Qaatel spiking Kandi's drink.

Oh my God, he thought. *Should I do something? What can I do?*

After a few moments spent paralyzed by indecision, Patrick made his way to the bar. "Hey, Zane, Kandi is looking great tonight."

Zane smiled. "It's show night, she always does."

"Who is that guy she is with?" Patrick asked, playing dumb.

"Not sure. Some new business deal she's putting together. I don't know him that well." Zane appeared disinterested.

Patrick leaned in. "He seems sketchy to me. I think I saw him put something in her drink. Can you check on them?"

"Oh." Zane seemed slightly surprised. He was known to have an eagle eye watching for drugged drinks in his bar, and was caught off guard by this claim. "Sure thing."

"I'm serious."

"On my break, I'll knock on the door. I always do. Don't worry," Zane assured as he rearranged glasses behind the bar.

He doesn't care. So, neither will I, Patrick dismissed, returning to his seat. He smiled at Blaine and Evan.

***

Patrick laid in bed replaying his evening with Blaine and Evan. They were exceptionally nice. It was refreshing to enjoy someone's company without thinking about a dangerous hustle. Blaine had suggested that Patrick should also apply at his new employer.

"They're hiring from the bottom up. They need a workforce since they just moved here. Entry-level positions are opening. You don't need a tech background."

"What made this company decide to move here?" Patrick finally had the nerve to ask, confused why a company would locate here just as others were quickly moving out. *Only a year or so ago, the governor taxed the shit out of all corporations across the board. Why would a tech company open here now?*

"Oregon's governor has this huge plan for green-energy companies to come here. They brokered green-energy credits in exchange for re-locating. The news said Oregon was offering green energy tax credits. So cool to be a part of being green!" Blaine had oozed.

She taxed everyone, and now she's handing out tax credits. Patrick shielded his embittered thoughts, putting on an interested face and listening to Blaine and Evan.

"Ah," Patrick said, pretending to understand. He also remembered from the news the controversy surrounding those very green-energy tax credits, and the corruption that was revealed in multiple state audits. Several companies had gone belly-up after brokering similar deals with the governor. Patrick didn't want to give Blaine and Evan that news. *Maybe their company's deal is different since the audit,* Patrick told himself. *No need to ruin their good news. This is a shit deal all around.*

"We like downtown Portland for its charm, but we're super glad we'll be living in Beaverton. After hearing about all the riots and fires, we hesitated at first," Evan explained.

"How so?"

"We love the food and shops, but it's gross and not well-kept. The human waste, burned out buildings, and graffiti are off-putting. We'll come for food and to visit Kandi's. Tomorrow we'll check out things closer to us out in the west hills," Evan gushed.

Patrick wondered if they knew that an urban fire had taken out quite a bit of the green spaces in the west hills. The area was at high risk for mudslides. The nearby zoo had been closed for months for "upgrades" following the initial collapse and fires. *Highway 26 to Beaverton from Portland is the only way for commuters to move from Beaverton to work in Portland. Does he know that the mudslides might not allow him to go to work?* Patrick wondered.

As the conversation carried on, he felt empathy for Blaine and Evan. They'd uprooted their lives and put all their hopes and dreams into moving to Oregon—based upon nothing more than upbeat word-of-mouth recommendations, glossy brochures, and false promises of "inclusiveness" and "tolerance."

They haven't met Qaatel yet, Patrick sighed.

Chapter 76
Ned's Whiskers

Julie lay on her back against her pack. They had just finished the second day of their voyage home. She fought to hold in her tears, which were threatening to burst.

Ned leaned over Julie's feet, which were propped up on a rock, so he could examine her blisters. The extra weight was taking its painful toll, and the balls of her feet were covered in hot spots and tender blisters. Ned said she needed to expose her skin to the air so they could cool off and dry out.

"We need to talk about popping them."

"Give me pros and cons," Julie muttered, continuing to look up at the sky, hoping the tears in her eyes would sit still.

"Pro, the pain of standing on them will stop. We can dress them with gauze or moleskin, and you'll have some immediate pain relief. Walking will be easier. Con, you risk infection. And that is not good. Next, if we don't dress it right, we'll get a blister on top of this one. Double the pain you feel now. Trust me, I'll do my damned best to prevent that," Ned answered.

"Those options suck, Ned."

"I agree."

Ned stepped away from Julie and started unpacking the tent.

Julie was fighting with herself about what to do. She didn't want to make the decision, yet she wanted to stand and help set up camp. Addison stomped her feet right next to Julie, using the pack to cling to for balance.

"You don't know how lucky you are, little lady," Julie muttered, supporting her as she tested out her baby legs.

Julie also knew she needed to hike the next several days. These blisters could hamper that significantly. If their pace slowed so that they couldn't make their caches, their journey would become dangerous. She needed to make the right decision, and quickly.

"Ned, I'll pop them. I think we need to do it sooner rather than later, so they can heal tonight," Julie called out.

"Okay," Ned said from behind the tent. "Let me get the med kit."

Ned finished the tent and walked toward Julie. "You know it won't hurt to pop them, right? It will probably feel good," Ned said.

"I do. I'm just worried about the days ahead of us."

"Me too. This could get ugly. Your feet are going to take a beating.

Every night we'll need to assess them and dress them," Ned offered.

"I never thought this would be a problem. We did fine on our dry runs — a hot spot here or there... but this is worse." Julie shook her head.

"It's the extra weight, and I think, the warmer temperatures. It's July, and it's hot," Ned offered. "Let me see if I can take Addison tomorrow for a few hours in the morning, to give you some relief and give your feet a chance to toughen up."

"Ned, that is an incredible load. Your pack is full of almost all the heavy gear as it is. I would worry about you and *your* feet." Julie didn't like the idea.

"Let me try," Ned said as he opened the med kit. "Just for a couple of hours."

"Okay," Julie said reluctantly. She leaned her head back and watched Ned take out a pin, knowing what he was going to do next.

Feeling the liquid ooze down the arch of her left foot, the immediate sting was followed by relief as the swollen skin shrank — then the other foot. Ned cleaned the exposed skin thoroughly with alcohol swabs.

"Let this dry. The skin needs to be exposed to air and dry, just like hot spots," Ned directed. "I'll take care of camp."

"Wait, what? I can't help? You said I could walk around. Give me something to do to help you. You'll be up all night with dinner and diapers alone," Julie objected.

"Start the fire and get the water boiling? I'll get the pots for food and sanitation for you. Could you get a couple bottles ready?"

"You got it." Julie was glad she could do something. *A couple of blisters had better not set this trek on a sideways path*, she thought to herself.

Julie leaned up, rolling her feet under her, and sat on her knees to unzip pack pouches and get ingredients for baby bottles. Addison played with the dangling zipper pulls. Ned gathered firewood.

***

This is the night I was afraid of, Julie thought to herself. Addison was not sleeping. Julie had tried to settle her down with soft singing, a bottle, and rocking. No matter what she tried, Addison cried. Loudly. If Julie stopped holding her, Addison began playing. With everything. She scooted in and out of the sleeping bag, poked her fingers at Ned's scruffy face, squealed at the sound of her hands on the nylon sleeping bags, and made several attempts at unzipping the tent.

"For a kid who doesn't crawl, she isn't limited in movement," Ned whispered as Julie stopped another escape attempt.

"We need to sleep!" Julie whispered loudly.

"Tell her that." Ned chuckled. "Reminds me of Rachel when she was just a baby," he said.

"Come here, you goofy girl." Julie scooped up Addison and kissed her cheek. "Shh… shh… shh," Julie whispered with her lips close to Addison's cheek. Addison squealed and giggled at the tickle, while her back was arched in protest of being taken away from her immediate plans.

"Let me try," Ned offered, holding out his hands.

"Sure," Julie answered, unsure how this would go. But everyone needed sleep, so she was willing to try anything.

Ned's large hands encompassed Addison's torso like a glove. Addison seemed to instantly realize their strength as she relaxed her back.

"Come here — who has a scratchy face?" Ned asked Addison as they locked eyes. "You don't, thankfully."

Ned placed Addison's hand on his chin, and she was mesmerized by his whiskers. He hadn't shaved since leaving Smoky Flats, so the whiskers were beyond the sharp stubble phase. They were slightly soft, yet scratchy. Addison sat on the space between Ned and Julie, with Ned on his side, gently rubbing his cheeks.

"I can see it now — I get an email from Steve asking what sorts of toys Addison plays with. I will answer 'whiskers,'" Julie whispered as a new relaxed mood came over the tent.

Julie laid on her side facing Ned and Addison, with her hand on Addison's rump to steady her and keep tabs on her. Her eyes began the gentle process of closing and relaxing as she felt Addison's body soften.

As Julie relaxed in the dark quiet, she let her thoughts trail…

Julie startled awake. *Where's Addison?* she thought frantically. The tent's interior was slightly aglow with the sunrise's very early-morning light. She could barely make out what she was seeing, but she knew she didn't see Addison. Julie's protective hand had long-since made its way back into her sleeping bag during the night.

Julie bolted up, unsure when she fell asleep, or for how long, and if Addison had managed to escape. The zippers were still zipped on the tent.

Looking over at Ned, he was still asleep on his side facing Julie, just as he had been the night before — but at that time, it was with Addison perched between them. This morning, his face was obscured by his sleeping bag, practically tucked inside. Addison was no longer there.

Julie reached over to touch Ned, but as she brushed the sleeping bag near his chest, she realized that Addison was curled up against Ned.

She pulled the sleeping bag back to take look. Addison's beautiful baby-white-skinned cheeks were pressed up against Ned's dirty t-shirt. His arms were wrapped around her. They were both breathing heavily, enjoying their restful doze.

"I'm glad someone got some decent sleep," Julie said to herself as she laid back down, willing her blood pressure to resume normal function.

***

At the end of the third day, the exhaustion was in full force. Ned had taken Addison, along with his pack load, for the last two mornings. Julie's blisters were stabilized and not growing, but she always had hot spots at the end of the day and needed to tend to her feet. Ned knew Julie was trying to be tough, but the relentless discomfort was getting to her.

Another snag: Addison wanted more than a bottle. Since leaving Kenney Reservoir, she had eaten the equivalent of two freeze dried meals that were rationed for Ned and Julie. She seemed to like the macaroni and cheese meals the most, and fussed loudly if she saw someone eating it and couldn't have a bite.

Julie and Addison sat at the entrance to the tent while Ned waited for the water to boil for their dinner. Addison was too curious to be close to the fire.

Normally, I'd make another batch of mac and cheese, Ned thought. *We both desperately need those calories. We have to make the first cache by tomorrow night.* He was resolute.

"Hey, Ned, have you ever drunk baby formula?" Julie asked out of the blue.

"No," Ned replied, wondering why on earth Julie was asking that question.

"If we have to, we'll drink it," Julie declared. "I don't think we are that dire yet. But if she keeps chowing on our food, I am happy to let you have meals, and I'll drink it."

"Let's hope we don't have to think about that as an option," Ned said as he poured the hot water into the pot to hydrate their meal.

"Agreed. What can I do to help you with camp so we can get to bed early? I know you're exhausted. The sooner we can get to bed, the sooner we can do the little games she plays to get to sleep."

"I know it's awful, but can you boil the diapers? I'll go hang the bear bag," Ned said. Both jobs were the worst of the evening. Diapers for obvious reasons. Hanging a bear bag effectively, without help, was

125

difficult. Ned would spend thirty minutes throwing a rope into the trees with a rock tied to the end, hoping it caught on a sturdy branch. If he was not successful, he could end up throwing rocks for a long time, and exhausting himself as dark settled. Being in camp with food after dark in the Rocky Mountains was inviting black bears.

Ned was already at the end of his reserves. He hoped his meal would give him a little burst of energy as he packed items into the bear bag.

"Good luck," Julie said.

"You too." He winked as he pointed to the pot and the bag full of dirty diapers.

"Hey, Ned," Julie started to ask, then paused before continuing. "Are we okay?"

"We are okay," Ned assured.

"No, I mean are *we* okay? You and I? I know that sounds strange, but we haven't talked much for the last few days," Julie said. "Hearing me say this makes me feel like an insecure teenager wondering if her boyfriend still likes her. This is different, obviously. I am not overly verbose, as you know. But just checking with you that we — this team — are okay."

"Yes, we are okay," Ned said, offering her his familiar warm smile. "This is not ideal, by any means. We are struggling, and curve balls have been thrown at us. My goal at this point is to make sure this trek remains a trek, and not a rescue mission. If we need to be rescued, it will be dire, and there isn't much out there these days that can swoop in and come to our aid."

Ned noticed fear bubble up in Julie's eyes.

"Ned, I have said it numerous times before, but it bears repeating right now. You have sacrificed for me beyond what any 'friend' would do. To accompany me on this trip and put your life in danger… I knew that going into this and was thankful. As we stretch the limits of what this trek is supposed to be, I have to say it again — thank you," Julie whispered.

Ned stood up and looked at the sky, which was growing dark. He had limited time to get the bear bag up, but couldn't just walk away from Julie at that moment. He stepped over next to her and slowly lowered himself to a kneeling position beside her and Addison.

Putting his arm around her shoulder, he squeezed her close to him. He put his lips next to her head as she leaned into him, and whispered, "Julie, you're welcome. We're in this together." He held her for a moment longer than a normal hug, and kissed her on the head. "I gotta get this done… back in a few."

***

Julie was startled by Ned's simple and tender loving gesture. She watched him pick up the filled bags and rope and head towards a tree clearing. The hug and kiss on the head were unfamiliar to Julie, and yet so comfortable and natural. In her mind, she had to process it. *That hasn't happened in years. Never expected it to happen here.* Julie smiled.

After a few moments, she began the tedious task ahead of her. The feeling of Ned's embrace stayed with Julie.

Chapter 77
Meet the Family

Patrick sat in a coffee shop tucked inside the grocery store near his apartment. He was avoiding downtown, and hoping to hear from the company Blaine and Evan had gushed about. *I sent a resume, and I have Blaine and Evan as references. Let's hope that gets me an interview,* Patrick ruminated as he gazed out the window at the parking lot.

Patrick's eyes spotted a familiar face, and he watched as Qaatel stepped out of the driver's side of a parked car. A woman came out of the passenger side and immediately opened the back-seat doors to help two young children out. *Qaatel has a family?!* He watched the foursome as they entered the store and disappeared down an aisle.

Grabbing a napkin from the neighboring table, Patrick made note of the vehicle's make, model, and license plate. A headline from a discarded newspaper caught his eye: "Local Business Owner Found Deceased" with "Mourners gather at downtown club for candlelight vigil" as the byline. Patrick grabbed the paper and quickly read.

Marvin Walters, owner of Kandi's, was found deceased in his office Friday. Walters is well known as his transgendered name and persona, 'Kandi.' Walters had been in good health, with no apparent cause of death.

The piece went on to quote those close to Kandi and their shock and dismay of the sudden passing.

"Kandi was an advocate for the LGBTQ community. Kandi's was a place of safety, acceptance, and refuge for our marginalized community," said one mourner.

Patrick's eyes quickly scanned the paper trying to get beyond the emotional outpouring. "What happened?!" he whispered under his panicked breath.

Turning the page as the story continued, Patrick caught up to a quote from the mayor.

"I am saddened and shocked, like so many, at Kandi's passing. She was a great supporter of mine, and I of her. Portland has lost a friend. I have lost a friend. Portland police are investigating. An autopsy is scheduled. Upon our initial investigation, there are no indications of foul play; however, as we

continue and conduct the autopsy, we'll have more answers," quoted Mayor Fred Whitlock.

Looking at the dates and times of when Kandi was found, Patrick's heart raced. She was found in her office in the early morning hours, after the bar closed the night Patrick witnessed Qaatel slip something in her drink, and accompany Kandi into her office.

Qaatel was one of the last people to see her alive! Patrick's heart pounded as he connected details from the story to what he knew happened that night. Patrick flipped back to the front page and began to read the piece again, hoping to catch information he might have missed. He leaned back in his chair to open the paper, and noticed Qaatel at the cash register. He held the paper in suspension and closely watched Qaatel, letting his thoughts take over. *Did he do something to her in the office? Did he kill her? Did he slip her something that made her look like she died of natural causes?*

Looking up, he realized Qaatel was approaching with the woman and her two children.

"Hello, Patrick," Qaatel greeted evenly.

"Hello, Qaatel," Patrick replied, realizing the headline of the paper was facing Qaatel.

"I see you heard the news," Qaatel said, pointing to the paper.

"I have. Sad. Wonder if the place will stay open?" Patrick replied casually, willing his voice to show none of the panic that was coursing through his veins.

Qaatel nodded. Patrick knew Qaatel would never give up information. He knew that from the recent coffee shop meeting. *I'm doing all the talking. Let your questions communicate,* Patrick told himself.

"I was at Kandi's the night before she was found. It's weird to think about, you know?" Patrick probed.

Qaatel's eyebrow twitched slightly, but he kept the stone-faced, confident demeanor that he always had. The eyebrow was the only crack in his stoicism.

"Is this your family?" Patrick asked, forcing a smile.

"Yes. This is my sister and her children." Qaatel motioned to them, not giving their names, never taking his eyes off Patrick.

"Hello, I'm Patrick."

The woman and her children nodded and said "hello," also not giving their names.

"I didn't know you lived in this part of the city," Patrick said.

"We need to be heading home. I'll be in touch," Qaatel said as he began to motion for his group to depart.

"Have a good morning," Patrick said, still smiling.

***

Patrick made his way to a brewery on the west side that streamed local news on one of their many televisions. He found a table near the news stream—an easy accomplishment, as most patrons were watching a sporting event. He held the section of that morning's newspaper he'd grabbed from the grocery store coffee shop.

Kandi's death was the top story of the local evening news. The studio news went to a street reporter standing ground in front of Kandi's, with the larger-than-life sign in the background. Police had cordoned off the front door with yellow caution tape. *Is it now a crime scene?* Patrick wondered.

Police state they are being proactive by asking management to close Kandi's and not enter until more information is obtained. What we know so far is that Marvin Walters, better known as Kandi, was found at 2:30 AM by the closing bartender. She was unresponsive and unconscious.

The report then went to an interview with Zane, whose face was red, and he appeared emotional and shaken when he was interviewed.

"I shook her and realized she wasn't responding. I called 9-1-1 right away. They talked me through CPR while I waited for the paramedics to arrive." Zane paused for a moment, and then gasped as he recounted Kandi's last moments. "They came and took over. I just can't believe it."

The footage included a reel of various businesses around Kandi's. The report transitioned from the meager details surrounding Kandi's death, to her history in the city, followed by file footage of the performances Kandi's was so well-known for.

The police don't know much. I am sure Zane told them about what I saw. I wonder if I should call the police and let them know. But if I call them, they might snoop into other things I know… Patrick's thoughts darted to a new direction he hadn't considered until that moment.

If Qaatel is involved in her death, what if the police figure out how I know Qaatel? What if they figure out the things we have done together? The things I did before I knew him? Patrick's heart raced as he realized the implications of being so close to Kandi's. Just the prospect of being questioned by the police made his stomach turn. The thought of a phone call from them made Patrick's mouth go dry. It wasn't worth it. If they did their job the right way, maybe they'd find out. But he didn't have to worry about that.

If Qaatel is involved in her death, then he could easily pin it on me! Patrick's thoughts took a horrifying turn. *I'm at Kandi's often. I was there that night. I drew attention to Zane by pointing out Qaatel spiked Kandi's drink. That could easily be twisted that I was trying to create a diversion. Unless someone was really paying attention, no one but me can say they saw Qaatel there that night. He always stays in the shadows.*

Patrick pondered Qaatel's motivations, especially now. *Why would he want to kill Kandi? When I asked about them that one day at the coffee shop, he gave me nothing. But now it's not a verbal game of cat and mouse. Why would he do it?* Patrick didn't have to think long before Qaatel's words rang through his head like a recording: *"Kandi is useless to me."*

Patrick's original agreement was to let Qaatel help him with his deadly identity theft scam. Patrick didn't like the deadly part of his scam. He only wanted the cars and money it garnered. Qaatel didn't want the money.

"You're good at what you do, and I want to learn," Qaatel had said. At the time, Qaatel's words hadn't clicked. Patrick didn't make the connection. He had been willing to agree to almost anything Qaatel would suggest in order to keep him from going to the police with the evidence. It had felt like a deal at the time — now Patrick knew it had been inescapable blackmail.

Before the collapse, Patrick would scam someone, use their identity for a while, and then move on. In Oregon, identity theft perpetrators received nothing more than a court date and a black mark on their record.

After the collapse, ATMs were unreliable — and they still were. No one cashed checks. Traveling was difficult after the car he owned broke down and he couldn't pay the enormous cost for the repair. *A repair that should have been cheap and easy before all this shit started to fly,* Patrick had fumed.

Patrick had had a job a local credit union. It was there that he'd learned how to steal identities and make money. He'd done it occasionally when money was tight, knowing that if he did it too often, he would most certainly be caught and prosecuted by his employer.

Patrick had saved his paycheck and used the "get back to class" incentive from the credit union to try to finish a degree at the local culinary school. The school had shuttered when the governor had raised taxes across the board after federal funding had been pulled from Oregon. The credit union downsized, and Patrick had quickly been left with little after he was laid off. The one skill he'd had left was identity theft.

***

Patrick's first homicide had been a few months before Jon's (the unfortunate kid who'd had the antibiotics Patrick had needed to sell).

He was at Ethan's house. While Ethan was showering, Patrick quickly rifled through his briefcase hoping to find cash. Instead, he found all the things that were no longer useful—credit cards, checks, bank statements… no cash.

Just as he closed the briefcase, Ethan came out of the bathroom and caught Patrick red-handed in the perceived theft.

"You fucking son of a bitch!" Ethan yelled as he stormed at Patrick, making an attempt to punch him.

A violent fight ensued. Patrick apologized—loudly—several times, hoping to quell Ethan's rage. It didn't work. It actually seemed to make Ethan angrier. Patrick fought back at the same time as he tried to escape the house, but Ethan came at Patrick relentlessly. Patrick got the upper hand and landed several dizzying punches to Ethan. Once Ethan was down, Patrick grabbed the briefcase and slammed it into Ethan's head repeatedly until it broke apart.

Patrick panted from exhaustion as he left the living room where Ethan was sprawled out on the floor. It scared him to think what could have happened to him had he not fought Ethan off. *Now what do I do? Call 9-1-1?* Patrick wondered. *Is he alive?* He went back to the living room and looked at Ethan, whose face was now barely recognizable. Patrick hadn't realized how brutally he'd beaten Ethan. *Oh my God*, Patrick thought, as he slowly realized he had just killed Ethan. *What do I do? Leave? Someone will see me!* Patrick panicked as he tried—unsuccessfully—to come up with some believable story about how this had happened. Would anyone believe that he was defending himself? He wasn't sure. After another moment of indecision, Patrick checked for Ethan's pulse. There was none.

"Fuck!" Patrick hollered.

That night, he was wired, and stayed awake for several hours ruminating over what he should do. A few times, he examined his own face in the mirror, bruised from taking many punches. It sure could look like self-defense. He splashed his face and hands with cold water. The cold jolt calmed Patrick. As the night wore on, Patrick galvanized his decision not to call the police. Next, he needed an exit plan from the house. *How do I get out of here without anyone seeing me? I can't just walk out and hop on the bus*, he worried.

The house. Ethan's house. Ethan had lived alone in a tastefully decorated cottage on the east side, which he'd bought for pennies-on-the-dollar from the bank, in a foreclosure after the 2008 housing crash.

Realizing he had full access to the house, Patrick took full advantage of the situation. He grabbed the largest suitcase he could find and packed it with items he hadn't been able to afford for months—prescription medicine, some clothing, food, toiletries, and cash (which he'd found stashed in Ethan's desk). There was over a thousand dollars in various denominations—just the jackpot Patrick needed to live for a few more months. *Just until I can find a fucking job!* Patrick justified. He went out under the cover of darkness, and stashed the huge suitcase in the back of Ethan's car. Patrick waited until the early morning hours before he decided to leave Ethan's house.

Slipping on Ethan's gym clothes, he grabbed Ethan's car keys and a gym bag and headed out the side door. His heart pounded as he pulled the hood over his head. Patrick casually walked to Ethan's vehicle, slid into the driver's seat, started the car, and drove away from the house.

Finding his way to the 205 freeway, he merged into traffic and drove south. *What if someone sees me in Ethan's car?* Patrick could taste fear. He felt like the murder was being advertised in neon lights from the car's headlights. He was sure someone would see him. He was convinced a police officer would know immediately who he was if he passed one. Patrick drove—almost hyperventilating—the fifty miles it took him to find a gas station at the Woodburn exit off the I-5 freeway.

He sat in a parking spot to the side of the gas station and gasped as he recounted Ethan's last moments. *He wouldn't stop hitting me!* Patrick screamed in his head, rubbing his temples hard. He calmed himself, rationalizing that he had been reacting to Ethan's violence; subsequently, Patrick recounted the multiple blows he'd delivered. *I should have called the police! But I didn't know if he would get up and hit me again...* he rationalized, over and over again. As the morning wore on, Patrick grew numb. He had been in the car for three hours, and a store clerk had peered around the building a few times.

The first time, Patrick was startled and immediately fearful that he had been identified. Thirty minutes later, the same clerk came out and sat on the curb with a bottle of water.

As Patrick felt the panic begin, he quickly grabbed a set of earbuds he found in a cup holder, placed them in his ears, and began to talk.

"Ron, missed your call yesterday," Patrick began, nodding his head to the imaginary person on the other end of the conversation. "You okay? Great... Glad to hear... Those numbers look good to you then...? Then let's meet... Next week is great. Can you put me through to Amy in project development, and I'll get her up to speed...? You bet. I'll hold." Patrick took a pen and pretended to write on a piece of paper in the passenger seat while being on "hold."

The clerk had stood up and tossed the empty water bottle in the dingy garbage can. Patrick caught the clerk's eye and gave a friendly wave. She waved back, turning around and disappearing into the gas station store.

Realizing — after a few more staged phone calls as clerks came out of the store — that he needed to leave, Patrick relocated to a large parking lot of a strip mall that had a small gym. *"It works with what I'm wearing,"* he reasoned.

The strip mall was sketchy and had few occupied spaces. *How does a gym stay open these days?* Patrick wondered, considering Oregon was in a depression-like funk, and few businesses — especially small businesses — had stayed afloat after the governor's mass tax.

Patrick wasn't about to start asking questions. He had a cover where he could park the car, pretend to make phone calls, and rest. And rest he did.

***

Patrick pulled himself out of his never-ending, obsessive thoughts. He shuddered recalling what he had become in the last year, since the fierce fires and continual riots ruined Portland. *I need to get out of here*, he bemoaned, circling back to the pressing question: did Qaatel have anything to do with Kandi's death, and why?

The answer was clear: Yes. Qaatel was clearly the last person to see Kandi — a person who had no use to him — and he had slipped her either something deadly, or something that rendered her defenseless. There was no other reason to covertly spike drinks. Why did he do it? For the same reasons he participated in the murders he committed with Patrick. He eliminated people who were "useless to him," and the one thing they all had in common was they frequented Kandi's. Who frequented Kandi's? Members of the LGBTQ community.

Why would Qaatel target the LGBTQ community? *People have hated the gay community for years, but this is different*, Patrick considered. *This is covert and targeted. There are no confrontations. There is no political rhetoric. This is systematic.* Chills went up Patrick's back. He sipped his beer as his line of thinking continued.

The beer was flat.

Chapter 78
Behind Schedule

At the beginning of the fifth day, Julie didn't know whether to be happy or sad. They had reached a food cache the day before — on the fourth day, having changed from their original timeline, to the timeline that Ned had laid out when they'd landed at Kenney Reservoir. The supply of food was like finding gold at the end of a rainbow.

Addison preferred to consume half of her meals as regular food, not formula. To give her formula when she was reaching for food was to prepare for a fussy baby. *If we were home, this would be easy, just give her the food! Babies should transition to food, right? Just — why now?* Julie pondered.

Giving Addison food meant that Ned and Julie were hungry. Julie prepared three freeze dried meals the night they arrived at the cache. This allowed Julie and Ned to have a portion plus some, and Addison enjoyed a small meal as well. It felt decadent — almost like a holiday meal — eating their large dinner. Julie was happy they had full stomachs and a full night of sleep. She was not happy about the newly added weight to their packs. Her feet were a blistered, bloody mess.

Ned spent a lot of time helping her get her feet out of her boots each night, and then he undressed, aired out, and assessed each wound. As she applied moleskin, she knew he would arrive soon to wrap each of her feet in a light layer of gauze to absorb the nonstop ooze her feet were producing.

It was excruciating to walk. Julie kept her attention on Addison as she hiked. For several days, she had been able to either ignore the pain, become numb to it, or a combination of the two.

Hiking with Addison had developed its own rhythm. Julie let Ned take her for the first couple of hours of the morning. The cooler temperatures helped ease Julie's feet into her day. Around their first stop for a water break, Julie would have a turn carrying Addison.

Addison liked being perched facing Ned in the morning. She was generally still sleepy, and she loved reaching up to touch Ned's face. Julie could hear her giggles and Ned's chuckles as they walked.

In one of the first couple of days with Addison, Ned tripped and barely caught himself from a nasty fall. "Dammit! I hate it when I do that!" Ned leaned a hand on a tree after the near miss. "I have a hard time seeing over her head, and can't see a thing in front of me. I am going to find another walking stick and have one in each hand," Ned had decided.

Julie watched him closely as he put weight on his ankles and knees to make sure he hadn't twisted anything.

"Let's take a water break early and I'll take her. You can walk the kinks out," Julie offered.

Ned stood up and nodded and unbuckled Addison, He handed her to Julie, Addison's arms outstretched to reach her, a big smile on her face.

Julie settled in with Addison, making sure her diaper was dry. Cloth diapers added a whole other element to the hike. They leaked a lot. Every night, Julie and Ned boiled their own t-shirts before the batch of cloth diapers were boiled, because of the messes that ended up on them otherwise. Julie would hang up the cloth diapers and t-shirts overnight, but they never dried. The morning dew would make sure they were still damp. She would hang them from the zipper pulls on their backpacks as they walked.

"We look like mummies shedding their skin," she mused, watching several diapers sway back and forth from Ned's pack. The sunlight and breeze in the high-elevation mountain airdried them quickly. The diaper use and cleaning plan they had was working.

Ned stopped, turned around, and handed Julie a flask of water.

"Thank you," she said, and immediately began to make a bottle for Addy, who was reaching for it.

As they walked, Julie found so many of her thoughts taking her to the cabin, and settling in with Addison, Joel, Floyd… and Ned.

Julie wrestled with her thoughts as she pictured life at the cabin, in Western Lakes, as a part of Smoky Flats. *Ned has never said he wants to be a part of Addy's life. But I don't see him staying away because of her — I see him as a part of her life,* Julie thought. It was perplexing, and even bothersome to Julie. Her feelings churned as she hiked. *If he is a part of her life, he's a part of our life. He a part of mine.* Julie's heart quickened. *And what does that look like?*

Julie knew how unlikely it was that they'd return home only for him to distance himself from her and her family. Everyone had become too close. *We have all come to enjoy each other since moving here, long before Addison was even a concept.* Julie remembered the first few weeks after arriving at Smoky Flats. She remembered when Ned would tap her on the shoulder, startling her at the worst time. There was also the mountain lion: Joel would talk about the night that he, Julie, Ned and Johnny harvested the meat and hide. Julie shuddered as she flashed back to the night the couple came to the trading post and attempted to assault her. Ned was there.

Ned was the constant thread through all her memories of her first year at Smoky Flats.

Ned is always there. He's a constant. He is steady and unwavering, Julie thought.

Julie forced her imagination to slow down as she started to consider her feelings for Ned. She knew their lives would at least be like they had been thus far. "Friendly neighbors," Julie whispered to herself, attempting categorize their relationship.

Julie was not completely settled on that category. *What is my problem?* Julie scolded herself.

***

On the sixth night, tears trickled down Julie's cheeks after finishing up camp. She dreaded settling down for camp as much as she dreaded walking. So many workarounds had to be done after they stopped walking; there was no rest to look forward to, because the tasks ahead had become numerous. Getting water, tending to Addison's meal, preparing their meals, washing and sterilizing clothes and bottles, hanging bear-bags... the to-do list for the evening was taxing. Making matters worse, Julie had to do all of her tasks barefoot, in an attempt to give her feet time to air out. She hobbled around, exhausted, well past dark. Sleep deprivation was setting in.

If we were backpacking for fun, this would be fun. We might even give ourselves a break; but we have a strict schedule we have to keep making this work, Julie reminded herself as she wiped her face with her the dirty tail of her t-shirt.

***

Ned was exhausted as well. They spoke very little as they hiked. With Addison keeping the attention of the person holding her, and watching each step, talking was a luxury. He hid his thoughts from Julie. It was easy, since they didn't talk much and they saw very little of each other's faces.

Her feet don't have much left in them, he worried as he tended to her injuries that night. He saw the tears in Julie's eyes from the pain, and wished he had a miracle remedy. It was only going to get worse.

"You okay?" Ned asked softly as he kneeled in front of her, removing that day's gauze layer. From her reaction, he knew it was painful.

"I am not," Julie whispered. "I am choosing to be."

Ned looked at her, unable to hide the concern from his face. He

137

didn't want her to worry, but he knew being in denial about the situation wouldn't help either one of them.

"Ned, are you okay?" Julie asked, studying his face.

"I'm okay if you are, and… clearly you aren't," Ned said through a strained voice. "Your feet are not doing well, Julie. I have no more tricks left in my bag to try. You need to stop walking on them and let them heal. Yet, that is the one thing we cannot do right now." Ned sighed.

"Ned, it's okay. I'll be okay. So what? My feet hurt," Julie said, though the expression on her face said otherwise. "We are both tired, and being hungry certainly doesn't help."

Ned nodded, smiling slightly. Julie was right. They had discussed it at one point a few days ago: they grew hungry, they would become emotional — it was the universal response for everyone who had a plummeting blood sugar level. *Hangry*. Ned recognized that his feelings right now were uncharacteristic… he had to keep it together.

"I understand. But the truth of the matter — even being upset and tired — is that your feet are not good. They are injured," Ned replied, still fighting to separate his emotions from the facts.

"I have no option but to continue, Ned," Julie whispered. "I can't stop. We have two days until the cache with the radios. I can handle the pain."

"Julie, it's not the pain that concerns me. You are at high risk of an infection at this point. I think you're going to get one, and this is *your feet*."

"What do you suggest? Do you want me to stop? If I stop, I'm farther away from help. I need to walk to get to help," Julie said.

"Can you make it one more day?"

"I'm planning to make it two more days," Julie said, sounding determined.

"What would you think of this… Let's go hard tomorrow — pick up the pace a little bit, skip one water break, and go as far as we can. We'll set up camp and stay the night. Then I — and only I — will set out that last day, with the bare minimum on me, and get to the cache. You stay at that camp until I return after calling for help. You'll get the chance to stay off your feet while I get help. You can rest."

Julie was silent, considering Ned's idea. She looked skeptical. "Where is Addy in this plan?" Julie finally asked.

"She stays with you."

"How long do you think it would be before you get back to us?" Julie asked, now sounding worried.

"Twenty-four hours."

Julie found herself swimming in unchartered waters for the first time in years. Being alone, venturing into the unknown, was nothing new to her life… it had just been a while. Being a single parent. Prepping. Protecting. So many things she had accomplished alone with her own intentions and motivations. Agreeing to Ned's proposal on any other day of her life would be an easy "yes"—whatever expedited immediate help and resources. Being alone in the woods—injured, with a baby, for twenty-four hours—gave her pause for thought.

"How do I say this? I'm scared to be in the woods by myself, injured, with a baby," Julie said, followed by a self-deprecating chuckle.

"Julie, this is difficult. We are in a position right now where we can sustain ourselves. If you get to the point where you cannot walk, which will be soon, we risk a lot. I would need to stop and care for you. At that point, our resources run out quickly for all three of us. This is not a rescue, by any means, but it is getting dangerously close to it. There is no one to rescue us but ourselves. I think this is a viable way to do it without putting ourselves at extreme risk."

"This brings its own risks, though," Julie said.

"Yes. Something could happen to me, you, or Addison," Ned answered. "By separating for a twenty-four-hour period, we keep the window for risk short."

"Separating," Julie echoed. "That's the number one rule of backpacking. Don't separate the group. Safety in numbers, and all that."

"There is wisdom in that. But it doesn't account for every scenario. Look, you don't have to decide this moment. You know my thoughts. I just think we should decide before we sleep," Ned replied.

Julie nodded. A tear escaped down her cheek.

***

Julie hobbled around camp finishing the night's sterilizing, and watching for Ned's return from hanging the day's bear bag.

As Ned approached, before she could change her mind, Julie declared softly, "I agree with the new plan."

Ned looked at Julie's wide, red eyes. "This is upsetting to you, I can tell. Do you want to talk about it?" Ned asked as he sat next to Julie at the entrance of the tent. He took Addison from Julie and nestled the sleepy girl in his large arms, giving her a bedtime bottle.

Julie took a deep breath and exhaled slowly. "I know this is the right thing to do. But—I feel like I am quitting a marathon at mile twenty-five. And, if we're being open and honest here, I am also struggling with how I feel about you. I watch how sweet and engaged you are with Addison, and I imagine what it will be like when we get home. I wonder what our lives will be like. I have enjoyed thinking about settling into a new, different life... with you. Ned, you are always in my thoughts. I don't see us just saying 'good-bye, see you in a month' when we return," Julie burst out. "You have done everything opposite of what I assumed you would do when I first met you. You have built me and my family up. You have been generous with your time and skills. Tomorrow, when you leave, you will risk your life for me."

Ned nodded. Julie wished he'd say something, but she didn't give him time to respond before she continued.

"Ned, you did it. You explained this plan to me earlier, and what worries me the most is Addison's safety—first and foremost." Julie felt her lip quiver and her words were just as shaky. "The second thought that scares me the most is never seeing you again."

"Julie, you said that I 'did it.' What exactly did I do?"

"You didn't squander or take from me. In fact, quite the opposite. You have given generously and sacrificially. You let me be independent. By you being you, I have arrived at a point I never thought I would reach in my life... ever. You let me be me, yet at the same time, I want to partner with you and depend on you. I never want this great team we've become on this crazy trip to stop. You got me... You got me," Julie whispered, her voice trailing off. She straightened her back and cleared her voice. "And now you're going to leave me for a day, and that could be the last time I see you. I tell you what, you son of a bitch—don't screw up."

Ned slowly rearranged his seat so he could sit in a cross-legged position. He gently laid a sleeping Addison on his lap. He stretched his arm behind Julie and whispered, "Come here."

Julie leaned her shoulder into Ned's chest as he embraced her. "We got this, Julie. This won't be the last time you see me," Ned assured her.

Julie put her arm around him, and they sat next to each other for several minutes. Eventually, their arms grew tired and dropped, but they didn't move from their position. Julie could hear Ned's heartbeat.

"What does this mean?" Ned asked.

Julie laughed. "If you only knew how much I've been asking myself the same question. It was a struggle to come to the point where I see us together. I wish I knew."

"I think you do know. I think you just said it, but you're just trying not to. I've waited for you to feel the same way about me, and I was not sure it would ever happen," Ned answered. "I think the next step, to answer the question of what this means, is doing exactly what you've been doing in your mind—planning our future together."

"Yes," Julie said.

A weight lifted from her shoulders.

Chapter 79
First Words

Through the night, Julie felt Ned's restlessness as he moved around in the tent, never seeming to fall into a deep sleep. He got up well before first light, when they would usually arise. She watched as he crawled out of the tent. Julie snuggled up to Addison as she heard zippers being pulled in the dark. Julie wanted to sleep, but Ned was up. She felt guilty staying in the tent.

Her mind was fixated on their conversation, which had lasted well into the early morning hours. For the first time, they had lain side-by-side instead of head-to-foot, with a flashlight pointed up as a makeshift lamp.

Ned and Julie had agreed that life would continue its trajectory when they arrived home. They would tell Floyd their plans for their future right away.

"He won't be surprised," Julie said confidently.

"What makes you say that?"

"He hasn't said anything, but he watches me. He watches us. When I come back from our walks around the lake, he gives me a look. No one really knows about our walks except him and Joel. I don't know about Johnny, but Joel doesn't assume anything is… brewing. But I am sure my dad does," Julie explained.

"I think it's great how close you and your father are. It's special," Ned said. "I want that with my kids when they are older — with Addison."

"That reminds me… I'm assuming someday you'll want to adopt Addison, right?" Julie asked, realizing how crazy this all was. "This is so strange and unconventional."

"Of course, I do. After you and I are married. I want to tell Johnny and Joel first and settle in a bit. I might sleep for the rest of the summer after this trip," Ned joked. "Rachel already knows about you."

"Married. That is a word I never thought I'd hear in my life again," Julie said. "Wait, Rachel knows what?"

"When I told her about this trek, she asked about you. Of course, she figured out I had my eyes on you," Ned said.

"What did you tell her about me?" Julie asked with a smile.

"I told her how you have my attention, and about our walks around the lake — but that your feelings weren't the same. She said something that reminded me of you and Floyd. She said something like, 'she sounds beautiful and amazing. I can't wait to meet her,'" Ned said. "I remember thinking that if Floyd found his match, that would be something you would say to him."

"You're right, I would." Julie warmed thinking about Ned's observation.

"I worry about her. The last time I talked to her was about a month ago. I am sure I told you about how she was leaving the Dakotas because her government job was being eliminated. It was dangerous. That is my priority when I get back—to find her." Ned's tone was solemn and determined.

"I agree," Julie nodded.

As they continued to talk nonstop with no set topic, Julie was struck by a thought.

"Ned, this conversation—it's like our walks around the lake. I have missed those. We talked about so much back then, and haven't been able to on this trip. It is nice to catch up with you."

"We won't stop doing them. I enjoy our walks, too."

Julie didn't remember exactly when she had fallen asleep. *Ned must have turned off the flashlight, or the battery died,* she thought as she laid in the dark of the pre-dawn morning, listening to Ned's rustling.

Ned would leave soon. She would be alone for at least twenty-four hours, possibly longer.

"I'll be fine," Julie assured herself.

Factually, she knew she would be. The odds were very good that Ned would make it to the cache, radio Smoky Flats, and summon help. That was the plan laid out to Floyd, Johnny, and Joel.

I'm sure everyone is worried. We are overdue for our window of when we planned to return, Julie thought.

She slowly eased Addison out of her arms, slid from the sleeping bag, and crawled out of the tent. Julie saw Ned, wearing a headlamp and reassembling his pack. They had agreed he would take food for two days, a tarp, sleeping bag, water filter and flask. They were traveling on a trail they had already traversed, and he had traveled many times before. He insisted she keep the map in case she needed to head out.

"Ned, if you aren't back in four days, I'm heading out," Julie said.

"I agree," Ned answered. "I wanted to talk to you about that. We are about ten miles away from the cache. That is a long day with Addison alone, but you can make it. If you get to the point where you have about two meals for each of you, which is about four days, head out. Keep your firearm close by. Don't think twice about killing a predator. The creek is down that gully about fifty yards. I've filtered and filled all your flasks and bottles."

"Got it. I plan to stay off my feet."

Ned stood up, and Julie knew the next thing would be for him to sling his pack on.

"Come here."

Julie stepped toward Ned, but he didn't reach for his pack right away. Instead, he gently took her hands in his and studied them for a moment, before interlacing his fingers in hers. He brought their joined hands to his lips, and kissed her dirty fingers tenderly.

"I love you, Julie Atwood. I love that baby girl in there," he said, nodding his head toward the tent. "We got this. I will see you tomorrow, late in the day."

"I love you, Ned," Julie whispered.

Ned let Julie's hands go and took a step back. He reached down to load his pack, and Julie instinctively stood behind him to help swing it up and set it on his shoulders. It was light.

"I love you, Julie. Bye," he said.

Julie watched as his form disappeared until the light from his headlamp was swallowed by the forest. He was moving at a quick pace, almost a slow jog, and the light extinguished in the darkness.

***

Patrick's already-dark thoughts took a darker turn. He was filling out another job application in the employee lounge of the KOIN tower. He couldn't get Qaatel off his mind, and was having a hard time focusing on the job application.

"Are you willing to relocate for this position?" one of the final questions under "Personal Preferences" enquired. *Hell, yes!* Patrick thought.

Patrick needed to find a computer or a fax machine to submit the application. That was not easy. The worst of the riots and building fires in downtown were over. Danger was at bay, but most street front businesses were either permanently closed, or trying to rebuild. With supply lines of building materials like timber, glass, fixtures, and shop signs compromised, rebuilding was very slow. This would be no easy mission.

There is the place on the eastside where I think I can send a fax, Patrick thought, deciding to walk across the Burnside Bridge and catch a bus the few blocks to the store, hoping to save a little on gas.

He walked over the bridge, looking over the Willamette River, and thought of Qaatel again. Qaatel spoke perfect English, but there were things he said — or maybe it was how he said them — that hinted he knew other languages. *Where is he from?* Patrick wondered. *He isn't white. The name doesn't suggest Mexican or Central American. Somewhere Middle Eastern, but that could be a dozen different places.*

Patrick continued his trudge over the Burnside Bridge. It was morning still, and the heat of the day hadn't set in. He knew as they day continued, the smell from the Willamette River below would become unbearable. Keeping the river unpolluted had been difficult for the city and state, between the homeless dumping their garbage and human waste into it, and the lack of funding to police and clean it. The mayor announced an ad campaign to make it a "top priority" as Portland cleaned up its image. In the meantime, being over the river on a bridge on a hot afternoon was unsavory.

Patrick had a bird's-eye-view of the riverbank below. It was full of dingy tents, which lined the river as far as he could see in both directions. Looking to the north, he watched a woman wash her hair in the river. Turning to the south, he saw a man standing outside his tent, urinating in the river. *It looks like pictures I've seen of India*, Patrick thought. The marina, on the downtown side of the river, normally housed the high-end yachts of the executives, many of whom worked downtown and commuted to their posh community south of downtown. The marina looked abandoned, with disheveled ropes scattered on the wood dock. The wood looked like it needed replacing and hadn't been resurfaced in a long time.

The smell in the air was putrid: a city dump, combined with human waste and dead fish. As Patrick neared the east side of the bridge, he saw a city bus approaching his stop. He ran to catch it, feeling the putrid air burn his senses.

Rushing up to the bus, he smelled an even more grotesque atrocity. *From the skillet to the fire*. Patrick gasped as his olfactory senses suffered a second assault.

Patrick remained standing, doing his best to avoid coming into contact with any questionable surface. He grabbed a bar with his left hand and hung on, hoping the bus driver would get to his destination sooner rather than later.

Patrick arrived at the copier store and logged into a computer to submit his resume. Having about thirty minutes left on his login, he thought about what he could do.

I'm going to find Qaatel.

He logged into a couple of his social media accounts he hadn't looked at recently. It was like walking back in time. *Things were so different just a year ago.* All but a few of his friends were long gone from Portland. Some were dead. Others lost homes to fires. Two friends were hospitalized with serious injurious after getting caught up in riots while trying to navigate Portland during the mayhem.

Patrick looked over the recovery of a friend who had been beaten during a riot after walking his dog downtown. *Wow! Wrong place at the wrong time!* Patrick thought, as a computer pop-up indicated he needed to add more money to his account to continue his session. Patrick quickly made his way to the clerk to pay cash for a time extension.

While he was paying to extend his time, Patrick remembered why he was there, and it wasn't to check his social media. He didn't know Qaatel's last name so he tried a simple first name search in a few social media search engines. No luck. He did an internet search of Qaatel's name and "Oregon." No luck. Next, he tried a search of Qaatel's name and "Portland" and found a few matches, but nothing, really. Knowing he was paying for time on the internet, Patrick thought quickly about any details he might know to help. *Kids! He was with a woman and kids that day. Schools!*

Patrick found a private Muslim school in a suburb just west of Portland, a short distance from the grocery store where he had seen Qaatel with his family. Patrick tried a search of Qaatel's name and the city of "Beaverton," and finally hit success. One news media outlet mentioned a person by that name, no picture, supporting a school fundraiser as a donor.

Patrick took the full name and did an internet image search, quickly finding a picture of Qaatel — the Qaatel he knew. Now that he knew the full identity, he repeated his media and internet searches, and found very little except that the name Qaatel has its origins in Arabic. With that information, Patrick's eyes were opened to the Arabic world, specifically Saudi Arabia. Reading through online encyclopedias and educational sites, his heart raced. Saudi Arabia was a theocracy. There was no codified law, like in the United States. Laws are based upon local clerics' interpretation of their religious beliefs. Saudi Arabia was governed by Sharia Law. His stomach lurched when he learned that while the nation-state of Saudi Arabia does not criminalize homosexuality, Sharia Law does. Under Sharia Law, homosexuality is punishable by death.

Patrick's heart beat hard as he read about cases where people were taken from their homes, had a short and one-sided "trial" before a local cleric, and were pushed off buildings or hanged for the crime of being gay.

"Pushed off buildings...." Patrick's eyes were glued to the letters on the news outlet reporting the tragic deaths.

Patrick's eyes blurred with tears. *I have led a blood-thirsty wolf to sheep. To him, I am also a sheep.*

Patrick analyzed everything he knew about Qaatel. Hanging out at

Kandi's, blackmailing Patrick to gain access to the gay community. Giving Qaatel legitimacy as Patrick's friend at Kandi's, and eventually giving Qaatel access to Kandi herself. *Am I being paranoid? Seriously? This is crazy thinking! A Muslim family man in Portland targeting the gay community to kill them? This is crazy!*

Patrick continued to think as the computer pop-up indicated that his time had expired.

I am being racist for thinking this! Patrick scolded himself. *I'm being judgmental, and everything I dislike, if I keep thinking this way.*

Patrick stood up to leave. Tears streamed down his face.

Chapter 80
Mobilizing

Floyd sat at his base lookout point. After Ned and Julie left, he, Johnny, and Joel had established the lookout points and radio relay communications around Western Lakes Association. It had taken a few days to put together the right locations for maximum clear communications. Between trees, hills, and valleys, getting a good line of communication between posts had taken time hiking between various high points around Western Lakes.

The base of operations was the upper story of Western Lakes' clubhouse. The building was in a clearing at a high point, centrally located on the property. From there, he could talk to the three outposts and relay information to them. They couldn't talk to each other, necessarily.

Since Ned and Julie left, Floyd made a point to man the base as long as he could, before heading home to catch some sleep and come back. He would sleep at the clubhouse if he could, but wanted to be home with Joel in the evenings.

For Floyd, today was worse than yesterday, and worse than the day before that. Julie, Ned, and the baby were overdue to return. Floyd was wound up tight, and running on coffee and adrenaline. He couldn't stop thinking about why they were so overdue with no communications, and wondering what could have happened to them.

The day before, a meeting was held at the clubhouse to plan what to do next. Victor, Floyd, Johnny, and Joel attended. Victor indicated he would call in others if he needed to. Floyd pointed to places on the map. "Here is where the first cache is. That is the key cache with radios and emergency equipment. These two here are food supplies only. Here is Kenney Reservoir. The fact that we haven't heard from them tells me they either haven't made it to this cache, or the radios aren't working for some reason. They were supposed to be at this cache three days ago, radio their arrival there, then be here the next day. In total, they are overdue by four days."

"Were the radios tested?" Victor asked.

"Yes, we did a radio check when they arrived at that cache," said Floyd.

"I have an idea for a plan but what are you thinking, Floyd?" Victor asked.

"I want to put together a team to retrace their itinerary and look for them," Floyd answered. "I know that will stretch our manpower here. I know it could take two weeks to get to Kenney Reservoir and back. I'm concerned for what that could mean here."

"Floyd, this is why we established the comms team and security team we did. For emergencies. Maybe not precisely like this, but nonetheless, we are a team that plans for emergencies. People around here know they could need community help at any time, and they will step up. Don't you worry about filling in security gaps here," Victor assured Floyd. "We just need to plan a team that can get there and back safely, and hopefully find them."

"I would be grateful—so grateful," Floyd said.

"What else are you thinking?" Victor asked.

"That's all I got," Floyd answered with a crack in his voice.

"Okay, this is what I propose. Three of us set out first thing tomorrow morning for the first cache. The next day, two set out for the second and third. We establish the first cache as a post for communications to relay back to here. Do we have gear for this?" Victor looked at Johnny and Floyd.

"We do. I'll get it prepped and ready tonight," Johnny replied. "I have another idea."

"We need ideas," Victor said. "Go ahead."

"Joel and I can use two of the pack horses for the trek. We have access to them from the folks at Lucky Ranch. When we find Dad and Julie, we'll be able to pack them out much easier than if they had to walk out—especially if there are injuries. Plus, the horses would be able to carry more gear—maybe some med kits or something."

Floyd kicked himself for not considering this option. Ever since Ned and Julie left, Johnny had kept his promise of forging a relationship with neighboring Lucky Ranch. In exchange for manpower to conduct their security, they agreed to allow their horses to be used to patrol both Lucky Ranch and Western Lakes. For two weeks, the patrols had been going smoothly. Joel had learned basic horseback-riding skills.

"Splendid idea. Can you secure that today?" Victor asked.

"The McAllister's offered yesterday when I told them that Dad and Julie were overdue," Johnny said.

"Great folks, the McAllister's. Can you arrange for us to have the horses by tomorrow morning?" Victor asked.

"Will do," Johnny said, nodding.

"Radios. Do we have radios for this?" Victor asked.

"We do. I'll get them programmed and operational by oh-six-hundred," Floyd answered. "Radio check at oh-six-hundred."

"Got it," Victor said.

The morning had continued with plans for food and gear. Toward the end of the meeting, Victor's demeanor turned dark. "I need to discuss the elephant in the room."

"Elephant in the room?" Johnny asked.

"Yes. I think we're dancing around it, but I want to bring it up. We have no idea what has happened. We could find them alive with sprained ankles. However, worst case scenario, we find three deceased people," Victor said bluntly. "I've lived in these mountains long enough and have enough memories of rescues turned to body recoveries to know that is a possibility."

"What happens then?" Johnny asked.

"That is what we need to discuss," Victor said.

"I have to interrupt. I know you need to discuss this, Victor — especially you three who are going. I am not going to accept, this early in the game, that I might have lost my daughter and granddaughter. I can't. I am wound up too tight as it is. I need to step out and get some air. If someone could give me a short brief later..." Floyd's voice trailed off as he stood to leave.

"Understood, Floyd," Victor said quietly as the door latched.

Victor turned to Johnny and Joel and solemnly asked, "You boys prepared to see your parents in a tragic way?"

Johnny looked at Victor and met his eyes. "I would want to be the only person to see him that way. It's up to Joel, but I am happy to do the same for Julie and the baby. Everyone around here has great respect and memories of my dad and Julie. We should keep it that way."

"Understood. For both of you, let's remember this — they have enough supplies with them to last them for several days. If they are out there, and conscious, they are probably alive. If they are out there for a length of time, their chances drop, but they are alive. They have food and water, and it's summer. This would be a different conversation if it were November. Unless something catastrophic has happened, I plan for this to be the last time we discuss the worst-case-scenario. We need to be prepared for it, for sure. You two are young men who might have to grow up real quick if it happens, but we're going to do our damndest to make sure it doesn't."

"Got it," Johnny answered.

"Yes, sir," Joel whispered.

"Regardless, everyone is coming home, and I mean *everyone*. One way or another. That is the mission," Victor said resolutely.

Floyd had stood outside the door and listened to Victor's chat with the boys. He was proud of Johnny and Joel and their maturity. It was heartwarming to hear Johnny's respect for his father.

Now, as he sat at the comms base in the second story of the clubhouse, tears flowed down Floyd's cheeks as he remembered the tense planning session only twenty-four hours before. He had decided he would set up a cot at the base so he could be there 'round-the-clock.

"Joel will be with you, anyway. No need for me to be in an empty house for a few days," he'd said to Johnny before the trio left.

Floyd turned his thoughts to that morning, when the remainder of his family had left. *Good grief, Floyd, suck it up. You're being dramatic*, he scolded himself as his emotions welled up in his chest.

The team, and several neighbors, had met at the clubhouse at five that morning as the sky was turning brilliant blue. The McAllisters, Tom and Linda, brought three horses.

"Weren't sure if you wanted three or two, so we brought three," Tom offered.

It was decided to take three.

"When we find Ned and Julie, having the extra horse to carry a rider or gear will be helpful," Victor said. "Thank you."

"All of these horses are experienced in the back country. They have personality. Johnny and Joel have ridden all three. They know their quirks. None of them will give you trouble. Make sure you all have heeled boots when you ride. Hiking boots don't fit in these stirrups," Tom said. He showed Victor, Johnny, and Joel the packs and saddlebags he'd equipped the horses with. Everyone had packed riding boots, and they were all wearing their hiking boots. *Lot of extra weight to bring boots*, Floyd thought.

He leaned over to Joel. "Hey, why are the heels on boots important?"

Joel whispered, "When you ride, you press your heels down and your toes up. Makes it so your legs are flexed and hugging the horse. If you don't have heels on your boots, your foot can slide through the stirrup, and you can end up falling off if you're cantering."

"Good." Floyd nodded as if Joel had passed a quiz, when—in reality—it was Floyd who hadn't known why McAllister had made that point. *Those heels do more than look good at line dancing*, Floyd mused as he watched Victor hoist his frame to mount the buckskin.

Johnny had spent the better part of the time between the planning meeting and that morning's shakedown gathering two tents, sleeping bags, gear, and food. With three horses instead of two, he needed to rearrange gear. When he finished loading the horses, it was time for comms check.

Floyd had a new set of inexpensive radios he had set aside in the cabin the year before. He called them "throw-aways." While useful, if one of them fell into a river, it wasn't a huge loss of money.

"I'll do an hourly status check during daylight hours, or until you get to the first cache. Based on what you've told me, the range after that will be sketchy or nonexistent. I will do status checks with the person at that first location hourly after the secondary team heads out from there," Floyd advised. "This location, Smoky Flats, is Smoky Base on the radio. The first cache is 'Base One' on the radio. Let's use the methods we use on our security rounds for communication. Victor will be Alpha. Johnny will be Bravo. Joel will be Charlie on the radio."

"I'm rusty," Victor chimed in, chuckling and looking at the radio.

"Let's do a sound check and shake off some rust. That might help," Floyd said, smiling and motioning for everyone to step back.

"Smoky Base to Alpha, status," Floyd said into his radio. It crackled across the three other radios.

After a short pause, and obvious deliberation, Victor keyed up his radio, "Alpha to Smoky Base, status," Victor said clearly into the mic.

"Copy, Alpha. Smoky Base to Bravo, status," Floyd said nodding to Victor.

"Bravo to Smoky Base, status," Johnny replied clearly.

"Copy, Bravo. Smoke Base to Charlie, status," Floyd said.

"Charlie to Smoky Base, status," Joel said clearly to his mic.

"Copy, Charlie," Floyd replied, pleased, taking the radio away from his mouth. "Perfect. We'll do that once per hour until nightfall tonight, or when you arrive. I'll be here twenty-four hours a day, but let's not get conversational. We want to conserve battery life as much as possible. However, I would sleep better if you give me any news, even if it's no news," Floyd said.

Victor nodded. "Patsy is on standby at the store. She is 'Papa' on the radio. If things go sideways, she has a radio to call the other associations to make a secondary plan. Those security groups know what we are doing and where we are going," Victor added.

By now, the sun was fully up in the July morning sky.

"Let's saddle up. Time to go," Victor said, and clapped his hands lightly. "Anything else? Think fast."

Floyd tapped Joel's shoulder. Joel turned to him and hugged his grandfather. "You be safe and come home soon," Floyd whispered in Joel's ear. "I love you, kid."

Floyd reached out to Johnny and gave him a hug. "You take care of that kid for me. Feed him a few times. Bring everyone back," Floyd directed Johnny.

"Yes, sir," Johnny said and smiled.

Reaching up to Victor perched on his horse, Floyd gave a firm handshake. "Be safe. I'll see you in a few days."

Victor nodded. In just a few short minutes, they were out of sight on the dirt road leading to the trailhead they would traverse. Floyd felt alone. His entire family was out of his reach. It was midday. The Crew — as he called Victor, Johnny, and Joel in his mind — had been gone about six hours, and all status checks were smooth. Looking at his clock, he realized his daydreaming had eaten up some time. The next hourly status check was due to start in five minutes.

Floyd looked at his map, roughly calculating The Crew's place on it. There was no reason to find them on the map at this point, but Floyd needed something to focus on until the status check.

He stood up and stretched. Deciding it wasn't time for a bathroom break, he walked down the stairs and around the building, then ascended the stairs.

He picked up the radio. "Smoky Base to Alpha, status," Floyd said.

"Alpha to Smoky Base, status."

"Copy Alpha. Smoky Base to Bravo, status," Floyd answered.

"Bravo to Smoky Base, status."

"Copy Bravo. Smoky Base to Charlie." Floyd's voice cracked a little. He wanted to hear Joel's voice.

"Charlie to Smoky Base, status," Joel responded, letting his grandpa know he was fine.

"Copy Charlie," Floyd responded.

Now what to do for an hour? Floyd sighed.

Chapter 81
Relay

Patrick needed no more convincing. He was certain that Qaatel had killed Kandi. And, if Qaatel hadn't done the actual killing, he'd surely participated in it. *There is no doubt*, Patrick thought resolutely.

He sat at the same grocery store coffee shop where he had run into Qaatel and his family days earlier. It was becoming a new hangout for him instead of the KOIN tower downtown. He was comfortable in his new apartment, and hopeful he would have a job soon and could get out of that scene as Portland limped along.

Sighing deeply, Patrick's eye caught an editorial headline: "*Portland 2.0 Set to Launch.*" *What the hell?* Patrick thought as he read about the hopefulness the writer had for Portland's tech and green energy opportunities, rebuilding infrastructures, and solutions for the homeless. *These ideas were what the mayor campaigned on. Wish they worked the first time they were tried.* Patrick turned the page to find something else to read.

As the page settled, he looked up and saw Qaatel and his family. It was like déjà vu — except this time, he knew.

Patrick stood up and got a coffee refill, watching the family pull out a shopping cart and head down an aisle. He inconspicuously followed the foursome to the back of the store, near the meat and deli counter. The children stayed remarkably close to the mother as she pushed the cart. Qaatel walked off to the side, disengaged from the shopping.

Patrick was able to pretend to shop for coffee and cereal while the family shopped for meats and cheeses. He was tucked behind an aisle endcap while they were in the open. Qaatel's back was toward Patrick.

What am I looking for? Evidence? Patrick wondered. Realizing he simply wanted to watch them out of curiosity, he calmed down and started looking at coffee to actually purchase, not as a cover in some covert, Hollywood-inspired operation. *Calm down, Patrick. You're in a grocery store, not a spy movie*, he thought as he took a breath, trying to lower his heart rate.

He struggled to steady his thoughts. *He murdered Kandi! Seriously, that man standing twenty feet from me in the meat section murdered her!*

Qaatel casually turned around as he waited for his sister to shop, and saw Patrick. A sinister grimace came across his face, and Patrick saw it.

Qaatel slowly approached Patrick. As the distance between them narrowed, Qaatel's grimace transformed to a casual smile.

"Patrick, interesting seeing you here," he said in lowered voice.

Patrick nodded, letting his silence force Qaatel's hand.

It worked. Qaatel took the bait. "Hmmm... you seem quiet today. Something on your mind?"

"You could say that," Patrick replied.

"I hope you get it sorted out. Have a good morning," Qaatel said and started to return to his family.

"You're on my mind. I know you. I know what you've done," Patrick hissed, unable to keep it in any longer.

"What I have done? *Me?* What have I done, Patrick?" Qaatel laughed, as if Patrick had cracked a joke.

"I saw you the night Kandi died. You were going into her office with her. She was dead a few hours later. *You* did something to her that killed her. That's what *you* did," Patrick whispered.

Qaatel leaned in closer to Patrick, and said, with same joking smile on his face, "Let's remember, Patrick, *you* have done things. That is the basis for our friendship, after all—isn't it?"

Qaatel stepped back and smiled. "Now, I hope you can relax this morning and find other things to occupy your mind. Enjoy your coffee." Qaatel walked toward his family and motioned for them to move along, out of Patrick's sight.

Patrick's mind spun as he walked slowly back down the aisle toward the front of the store. He looked down, realizing he still had a cup of coffee in his hand. He didn't know what to do next. He only knew one thing: he was angry.

How dare he make this about me?! He killed her! And he'd do it again if he could. He will do it again, I am sure, Patrick thought. His heart jumped as he revisited the truth that he had tried to avoid: Qaatel would throw Patrick off a roof, given the chance.

Patrick zigzagged up and down a few aisles to calm himself. He headed toward the coffee shop to get a refill, and caught sight of Qaatel and his family at the checkout line. The anger came back as Qaatel gave a false, friendly smile and nod to Patrick. Qaatel pointed out Patrick to his sister, who looked up and smiled.

So fake! The appearance of a happy family, and he's rubbing it in my face, like rubbing a dog's face in shit! Patrick thought, and started toward the automatic doors to exit.

Qaatel's family followed behind, with their shopping cart and perfect kids.

"Get away from me!" Patrick said loudly as he realized Qaatel was behind him.

"What?" Qaatel shrugged with a smile. "I don't know what you're talking about."

"You're following me!" Patrick turned and yelled.

"I'm walking out of a store," Qaatel said calmly holding his palms upwards in a show of perceived innocence.

People standing near the entrance of the store started to take notice. Checkers looked toward the loud voice coming from the automatic doors.

"Stay away from me!" Patrick yelled as he stepped off the curb, with Qaatel and his family following twenty-five feet or so behind him. Qaatel's sister simply pushed the cart. The children held onto the cart, watching Patrick, their expressions both curious and bored. One woman near the newspaper stand held her cell phone up and directed it at Patrick.

"Sir, I am not doing anything! I am going to my car!" Qaatel called out to Patrick. "Look, it's over there!"

"Fuck you! You are not just going to your car! You're harassing me! Get away from me!" Patrick yelled as he stopped walking and squared off with Qaatel.

It looked like a western showdown, with Qaatel and his family facing Patrick, a few paces' space between them. They were now blocking traffic. Several people had their cell phones out to record the incident.

"How am I harassing you? I am with my family, shopping. You are the one yelling at me," Qaatel's said. His perfect English was now a thick Middle Eastern accent, for everyone to hear. Patrick was stunned.

"Oh my God, you are a fraud! Fake accent! You are a fraud! You hate people, you hurt them, you kill them. Fuck you! Fuck your family! Fuck your hateful religion! Fuck you! Get the fuck away from me!" Patrick yelled.

Patrick heard a person in the parking lot call out, "Hey, someone call the police!"

Another person yelled, "I'll go get security!" accompanied by the sound of running footsteps.

Qaatel's act continued. His face was crestfallen, as he put his hands to his mouth in a fake gasp as Patrick's words spewed.

"You are insane! How dare you say such insults to my family? Here in America?" Qaatel called out, with feigned emotion in his voice. Qaatel's sister looked horrified as she clutched her children close. They put their arms around their mother in fear.

Patrick broke his gaze from Qaatel, his family, and Qaatel's theatrical performance. By Patrick's quick estimate, he guessed about twenty people stood frozen in their places. They were immobilized next to

155

carts, by the doors of their vehicles, or in their cars with the windows rolled down to listen and watch. It was quiet and still as people watched. Several people had their cell phone cameras directed at Patrick. It was eerie as Patrick realized he was the center of attention—unwanted attention.

Patrick threw his coffee cup in the general direction of Qaatel and his acting troupe, and ran. He had walked to the grocery store, and now he needed to get away.

"Did you see that? He threw hot coffee at those kids!" someone from the parking lot yelled.

Patrick ran to the edge of the parking lot, ducking into the disheveled trees, and found a path downwards into an empty lot with a chain link fence. Looking back, he could see no one following him.

Climbing over the fence, Patrick ran the short distance across the lot and found his way into the neighborhood.

***

I can do anything for an hour, Ned told himself. He was within a mile or two of the cache and the valuable radios. The morning and early afternoon had gone well. After leaving Julie and Addison, he had tried a slow run along the trail, knowing it was risky considering the uneven path. *If I fall and twist or break something, this is now a tragedy*, he thought. Eventually, Ned decided against the slow run and opted for walking as fast as he could, allowing himself to consider his steps.

Many of the trails Ned and Julie traveled had evidence of livestock on them. Livestock and horses were grazed in the open meadows of the Rocky Mountains, including some of the publicly owned lands. A person couldn't look at manure from livestock and assume they were close to civilization, however. Livestock grazed for miles in a seasonal pattern.

Ned crossed the last open field before the cache, and felt the cool shade of the trees envelope him. As he entered the woods, he noticed fresh manure and heard rustling in the trees ahead of him. Taking a second look at the manure, he realized it wasn't cow manure, but horse manure. Cows tended to leave one big pile as they stood. Cows certainly didn't follow blazed trails. *That is from a horse*, Ned said to himself, as his eyes followed the trail of horse manure ahead of him. *Someone is here.*

Stopping in his tracks, prickles went up Ned's spine. He stopped to consider what he was looking at. *Friend or foe?* he wondered. *They could help me or harm me.* Someone on a horse was nearby.

Quickly stepping off the trail, Ned made his way through the sparse trees to find cover behind low scrub brush about forty feet from the trail. He could see anyone passing on the trail, and unless they looked directly at him, they wouldn't see him.

Shedding his pack and laying it beside him, Ned sat and watched. All he could hear was his rapid breath and wind in the trees. After catching his breath, he checked his holstered firearm, making sure to visually check the path.

Several minutes passed. *Dammit! I need to get to that cache!* Ned thought. *This is a waste of time!*

Remembering the crazy young couple who had been hell bent on destroying the trading post, Ned stayed in his place. *Don't need to meet people like them*, he thought, as he considered his options of getting back on the trail or staying still.

Ned estimated he had been sitting in the scrub brush for about thirty minutes, and his exasperation had reached a fevered pitch. He decided to trailblaze through the woods, parallel to the trail, to get to the cache. *At least I'll be headed in the right direction at that point*, he concluded. Hoisting his light pack on and keeping an eye on the trail — not only as his guide, but also to watch for travelers — he set out again.

This is crap. I am too old for this shit, he thought as he climbed over and around rocks, and felt the sting of a branch across his leg. After ducking under another set of branches on a large evergreen, he thought he heard something, but wasn't sure if it was the branches he waded through, or something else. Ned froze in his tracks and crouched down to get out of sight, but also to train his eyes on the path he could barely see.

Movement from his right — bright red and blue colors slowly made their way down the path, skipping through Ned's sight as the moving colors dodged behind boulders and trees. Ned crouched down as low as he could go, and tried to hold his breath, which was noisy in his ears.

As the colors approached the point in the path closest to Ned, Ned saw a beautiful sight: it was Johnny's baseball cap with his school's emblem on the front.

***

Floyd watched the clock on his base camp communications desk. He had eighteen long minutes before the next status check. He was a little sleepy, but couldn't get himself to fall completely asleep. The prior status check had noted that The Crew had arrived at the cache with no indications that Ned, Julie and Addison had been there. Floyd made notes at each status check. Their arrival was the first meaningful note he had written.

While he looked over the notes, he heard static — which was not that unusual, but he listened anyway, just in case. He tuned his ear to the snaps and crackles.

Static… *"Base One, copy… we have…* (static)… *adult male…."* long pause.

Floyd's ears perked up when he heard "Base One." He felt chills when he heard "adult male."

But it could be any adult male, he thought. He closed his eyes, turned up the volume, and concentrated on words he heard break through the occasional bursts of static.

"Bravo…" Static… silence… "Charlie, confirmed, one." Static… "Charlie, copy… returning to Base One with one adult male… standby…"

Floyd's heart thumped hard. He closed his eyes and listened. Laying his head on the hand next to the radio speaker, he prayed, *Dear Lord, let this be Ned.* After what seemed like a lifetime, he looked at the clock. Twelve minutes until status check. *Twelve minutes! They had better not wait twelve minutes to tell me who is returning to base!* he scolded The Crew in his head.

"Alpha to Smoky Base," Victor's voice came across the radio loud and sharp. It cut through Floyd's thoughts, and the room's silence, like a knife. Floyd jumped at the sound and grabbed the mouthpiece.

"Smoky Base, go ahead," Floyd answered.

"Confirmed, recovered one adult male. Female and juvenile are at a secondary location. Last seen twelve hours ago in stable condition. Will be locating them tomorrow. Also," Victor's said through the speaker.

"Go ahead, Alpha," Floyd said as he quickly wrote notes.

"Secondary location approximately ten miles away, attempt to locate today not possible. Adult male indicates female and juvenile have adequate supplies for the night and are in no danger," Victor said.

Floyd wanted to know why Julie wasn't with Ned, why she wouldn't be retrieved until tomorrow, and whether she was safe. But at least he knew the basics: Ned was safe, Julie and Addison were presumed safe and in a safe place. He didn't know the specifics, but he knew enough.

Floyd was not only relieved, but he was overcome with a flood of gratitude, and struggled to clear his voice.

"Copy, Alpha," Floyd responded. Tears flooded Floyd's eyes. All the worries of the last two weeks — of the last few months — were almost over.

"Alpha to Smoky Base," Victor's voice came back through the radio, interrupting Floyd's thoughts. Floyd cleared his throat again.

"Smoky Base, go ahead," Floyd answered.

"Alpha establishing Delta as recovered male," Victor said. "Prepared for status check."

Ned had a radio and was ready to use it. "Let's make sure these stashed radios work." Floyd smiled as he wrote Ned's radio assignment in his log notes.

He had five minutes until status check.

"Smoky Base to Papa," Floyd said, making an indication in his notes he was notifying Pasty.

"Smoky Base, go ahead," Patsy replied.

"Papa, Base One has located and retrieved one adult male in good condition. Adult female and juvenile to be located tomorrow. All in good condition," Floyd said.

"Smoky Base, copy, that is good news," Patsy said.

Floyd could hear cheers in the background. *Must be some folks at Patsy's store,* Floyd thought with a smile.

Chapter 82
The Accused

Patrick walked the three miles to his favorite local brewery. The walk was good for him. He calmed his head and cooled off with a cold beer. The cute girl behind the counter, Paige, had asked if he wanted to start a tab as usual. After he'd enjoyed a few drinks and received the tallied tab, he gasped. *Twenty-five dollars for a beer?!* He decided this would be his last trip to the brewery for a while. Rubbing his temples, he settled in to watch the news, and whatever else anyone put on the televisions around the room.

I need to get a job. I need to relax. And I need to pull my shit together, Patrick chastised himself. *I can't keep obsessing about Qaatel.*

Patrick rehashed the scene in the parking lot repeatedly. He experienced a spectrum of emotions, ranging from vindication to fear from all the phone cameras at the scene. He was paranoid about how the footage of him throwing the coffee would appear to a viewer who only knew half the story.

As Patrick relaxed, his eye caught the local news. Reporters stood at various locations, reporting on the day's hot weather, places to go to stay cool, and how the homeless were faring in the heat.

Patrick rolled his eyes. "Nothing to see here."

As the half hour news report was ending, Patrick's ears perked.

"Now from 'News from You.' Local citizens sent us this footage today of an agitated man at a local grocery chain store, yelling obscenities at a Muslim man and his family. Take a look."

Patrick watched in disbelief as he saw himself on the screen. Most of the footage was from one person's camera. However, as they replayed the scene a few more times, Patrick could tell the news station had more than one person's footage.

"It was shocking. This man was so angry at this family for no reason except that he is Muslim," said an upset twenty-something woman with purple hair. Another interviewee piped in, "It was frightening and yet sad. So much hate is not needed here. I hope they catch the guy."

Catch the guy? Patrick wondered. *What did I do? Lose my cool?*

"We spoke to the victim, who preferred not to give his name," the reporter interjected as the screen switched to Qaatel's face.

"I was so scared. My sister and her kids don't need to hear such awful words. We have lived in America for fifteen years, and love it here," Qaatel said with theatrical emotion, his face distraught.

Patrick was aghast. Qaatel was continuing his fake accent and lies. Viewers not only believed the lies, but sent footage to the news, and now they want to "catch the guy."

The story came back to the reporter on the scene. "Authorities are asking anyone who knows this person to please contact them. He could be facing felony charges of hate speech and assault."

"What?" Patrick nearly yelled. He looked around and realized that a few people were looking at him for his outburst. He sheepishly looked away as the looks subsided.

Paige came to Patrick's table, tapping her fingers twice on the edge of it. "Everything okay?" she asked.

"Yes, thank you," Patrick replied, avoiding eye contact.

"Then, let me know when you're ready to pay, and we'll get you on your way," she said firmly.

Patrick looked up at Paige, meeting her eyes. Normally, she was casual and just waited for Patrick to pay his tab at the counter when he was ready to leave. Her eyes today told him she knew he was the person on the news. Her eyes told him he needed to follow her directions quickly or she would be "contacting police."

***

The following evening, at the brewery, Paige was behind the counter again. Several customers were lined up to order their favorite beer listed on the colorful neon sign above her. It was a busy evening and it was hot outside. The outdoor patio filled up as the evening cooled down. As the busy rush concluded, Paige and her coworker, Aaron, refilled the supply of glasses fresh out of the dishwasher. She was trying to keep up with the customer surge.

"That guy on the news was in here last night, did you see him?" Paige asked.

"I did. Did you see they caught him?" Aaron replied.

"No way? When?"

"I saw it on the early news. Sometime earlier today. You can watch," Aaron said nonchalantly as he grabbed a remote and switched a television to the six o'clock local news.

While they waited for the story, Paige oozed, "He's been here before and I've served him. He seemed so chill. It was weird watching him lose his shit like that. I guess you never know people, right?"

"Never can be too careful," Aaron replied, almost robotically.

Paige refilled a glass for a customer as the news of Patrick's arrest started.

"And now for a follow up report on a story we brought you yesterday. Police have apprehended Patrick Nicks and charged him with hate speech and assault," the reporter said from behind a desk. The Portland skyline was behind her. "Let's take it to Ron, who's been following the story today. Ron?"

"Thank you, Tracy. You are correct. Viewers might remember the story we brought you yesterday on 'News from You,'" Ron said as the video replayed Patrick's verbal tirade.

"We spoke to Mayor Fred Whitlock today, and here's what he had to say," Ron broke in, redirecting the story.

"I am appalled that in Portland, a city proud of its inclusiveness and diversity, there are still people who believe they can conduct themselves this way. I was horrified when I saw the video footage, just like I am sure any witnesses were. I won't tolerate it. We have a zero-tolerance policy for hate. It is a sad day for Portland to have this happen in our midst," Fred Whitlock said, his voice serious and solemn.

"Tracy, we just heard from Portland police that Mr. Nicks has connections with Kandi's. You might remember that Marvin Walter, the beloved owner of Kandi's, was recently found deceased under mysterious circumstances. Police investigators told me just a few minutes ago that they are questioning Mr. Nicks regarding his involvement in Mr. Walter's death. Security footage from within Kandi's establishment show Mr. Nicks was a regular at Kandi's, and was seen at Kandi's the night of her unexpected death. This is an ongoing story, and we'll keep you posted."

"That is crazy!" Paige exclaimed as the story concluded. "That guy? Murder? That is just crazy! I thought he *was* gay. Maybe he was faking it so he could kill Kandi. That'd be trippy, huh?"

"It's crazy," Aaron agreed, halfheartedly listening, but mostly ignoring Paige.

***

Patrick was stressed and sleep deprived as he was led to a meeting room wearing a bright orange jail jumpsuit. He was set to meet with his public defender. *He needs to get me out of here*, he thought. *This is ridiculous. I might be guilty of a lot of things, but hate speech and assault isn't one of them. What they don't know, they don't need to know.*

The jail guard opened the door, motioning for Patrick to sit at a metal table. The room had a rank smell to it. *Better than the puke smell in the jail cell*, Patrick thought, feeling a quick chill up his spine as he recalled the jail conditions where he had spent the night.

"Hello, take a seat," said a man at the table, as he stood and motioned to a bent chair. "I'm Jason Williamson. I'll be your attorney. You are going to be arraigned tomorrow. I'll be there in court with you. You will need to plead guilty or innocent."

"I'll plead innocent, of course," Patrick said indignantly, a little taken aback by this information.

"Alright, so unless you have any questions, I'll see you tomorrow. Stay safe." Jason stood to leave.

"Wait, yes, I have questions. Can I get out on bail or bond or something?" Patrick asked.

"Yes, the bail will be set at the arraignment," Jason replied, sitting back down.

Patrick detected exasperation in Jason for being delayed.

"How much do you think it will be?" Patrick asked, ignoring Jason's obvious need to get to another appointment.

"This case has a lot of publicity, and the judge will be shamed in the news if he goes easy on you. Things like this happen all the time, but you were lucky enough to have it recorded and put on the news," Jason said. "So bail will be high, and it will be public."

"Shit," Patrick muttered.

"You need to prepare for another possibility," Jason added, giving up any hope that he would make a quick exit. "And we'll deal with this when it comes, if it happens."

"What?" Patrick asked.

"You're being investigated for the murder of Marvin Walters; most people know Marvin as Kandi. You are also being investigated for the double murder of Telhas Teeze and his associate—I forget his name," Jason said.

"What?!" Patrick blurted. "I am 'being investigated?' What the hell does that mean?"

"You are being considered as a suspect. If a detective wants to question you, decline. Call me. Do not, and I repeat, *do not* say a word. Exercise your right to be silent. Don't worry at this point, you are simply being investigated," Jason said, assuring Patrick.

"Would you worry if someone told you what you just told me?" Patrick asked Jason.

"I would worry, yes. Let's get through the arraignment and talk next week. I'll be back here at the jail on Thursday."

"I want to be out on bail by Thursday," Patrick stated.

"Do you have the twenty-five thousand dollars needed to post bail?" Jason asked.

"What?" Patrick blurted again. "Why so high?"

"Your bail will most likely be set tomorrow at two hundred and fifty thousand dollars. You'll need to post ten percent of that for bail until your trial," Jason explained. "So, I repeat, do you have twenty-five thousand dollars?"

"No," Patrick answered solemnly.

Jason paused before answering, letting Patrick digest reality.

"Two other things you need to know. First, I will probably be your public defender for the arraignment, and maybe the investigation, if they question you. The county is in the budgeting process right now, and are seriously cutting the public defender pool in half. Also, the courts are really backed up. Criminal trials are two to three years out right now, as the courts catch up to all the crap that happened during the riots," Jason explained, giving Patrick a few more minutes to process.

"I'll see you here next week, Thursday, to discuss what will happen at trial, as well as anything I find out about the investigation," he said. "Take care of yourself and be safe. Here is my card. Call me if you need anything."

Jason stood slowly, heading toward the door. The jail guard let Jason out and motioned for Patrick to stand up. Patrick felt the cold handcuffs being placed on his wrists. *I'm being charged with dumbass charges and investigated for crimes I didn't commit*, Patrick thought. *I am a gay man being investigated for a homophobic-motivated murder and hate speech.*

***

Mayor Fred Whitlock, in response to the inflamed incident of a Muslim man and his family being harassed, held a press conference.

"I am saddened by the events we all witnessed happening right here in Portland. I am saddened by our president's continued policies regarding immigration. Portland, and Oregon as a state, has a long history of being a sanctuary state. Our laws are clear. Our resolve is solid. We welcome all, regardless of race, religion, or gender. We treat everyone as we want to be treated. That is why I want to announce a new city ordinance I will be proposing soon. I will be meeting with community leaders and local clergy to formulate an ordinance to bring before our city's council to recognize Sharia law and incorporate it into our city code. If we are to be the inclusive and welcoming city we claim to be, we need to make room for Sharia law, its customs, and traditions. I look forward to this endeavor. I welcome all input, and my staff is available to receive feedback to put together groundbreaking and progressive policies that will be a shining light for other cities to consider and embrace. I have also tasked my

staff to reach out to cities that have adopted similar laws and policies to find the best practices and the best fit for Portland. We have an amazing city. We are on the precipice of rebuilding from the devastation our President's policies have brought to our city. Embracing Sharia is one more step toward that rebuilding, and exactly the fresh start we need. While I am saddened and angered by the video footage that brought out such ugliness, I am thankful for the conversation it started, the doors it opened, and the opportunities it has presented for our city to be better. On that topic, police investigators have confirmed they are investigating Mr. Patrick Nicks, the subject seen in the video harassing a Muslim family, for other hate crimes, including murder. I am receiving regular updates from investigators on this matter, but right now, we won't be commenting on the ongoing investigation. I am happy this man is in custody until this investigation is complete."

Chapter 83
Stinky Feet

Julie woke up exhausted. *What is my problem? I did nothing to be tired*, she thought as she steadied Addison on her lap, giving her a bottle. The bottle felt like a weight in her arms. Julie had kept a pile of hot embers through the night, and started up a morning fire to get water boiling. It was interesting trying to tend the fire and water, keep an eye on Addison, and not stand on her feet.

Julie's feet... Ever since she'd developed blisters, Julie made a point to have her feet exposed to open air so they could dry out. On chilly nights, with no socks, her feet became cold and sleep was difficult. That night with Addison, they were so cold they ached. As she inspected them this morning, she noticed they seemed a bit more swollen.

"Oh wow, and they really stink!" she said out loud to Addison, as though Addison might understand. Addison giggled. "Do I have stinky feet?" Julie joked and poked Addison's tummy, causing her to giggle again.

After a game of "stinky feet," and applying what little was left of the bottle of sunscreen, Julie slipped on socks, gingerly picked up Addison and a sleeping bag, and carefully picked her sock-footed-way to a grassy spot in the sun about fifty feet from camp. Laying out the bag and removing the socks, she stretched her feet in the sun. *Oh my word, that feels good*, Julie thought as the radiant heat hit her chilled, swollen feet. *Now I need a nap!*

It was roughly mid-morning. *Hopefully, Ned will be back by late afternoon. Hopefully*, Julie thought, planning out her day. *Small lunch and a bottle this afternoon should keep me going. I'll get diapers done early.*

Julie had been looking at Addison and talking to her for days as they'd backpacked. This was really the first day where Addison wasn't confined by a baby carrier. As Julie stretched her legs out, Addison grabbed onto any part of Julie she could and pulled herself up to barely a standing position. Her legs stiffened and her hips swayed as she tried to balance.

"You look like you're ready to twirl a hoola hoop!" Julie said as she let Addison try out her legs, keeping a hand nearby to catch any falls.

Julie enjoyed the relaxing morning with Addison. She played freely, staying close to the laid out sleeping bag. *Reminds me of taking Joel to the park when he was a baby*, Julie reminisced. As Addison climbed busily all over Julie, Julie studied her. *She looks a little like Joel did as a baby. I definitely see Steve in her*, Julie thought. *I only saw Mandy a few times, so I am not sure if I see her in this face.* Addison grabbed onto Julie's t-shirt and scrambled her way to a barely standing position. As she began to straighten her legs, Addison laughed, promptly losing her balance and falling onto her rump. Julie laughed, making Addison laugh harder.

Late morning turned into early afternoon.

"I am so tired. I can't shake it. We should get out of this sun and get some lunch. Come on, little lady," Julie said to Addison, as she started to slip on her socks to return to the tent.

When Julie stood and put weight on her feet, shooting pain went up her legs from her blistered soles.

"Oh!" Julie exclaimed. "Wow!" The unexpected pain caused her to buckle her knees and sit down again. Slipping off a sock, she looked closely at the balls of her feet, where the pain seemed to come from. The largest blisters were there. They looked like they hadn't healed at all. They looked bigger, in fact.

"Whew! Stinky feet!" Julie exclaimed, as she contorted her leg to see as much of the bottoms of her feet as she could. Addison giggled, grabbing Julie's shoulder and pulling herself up to a standing position. "Something is wrong with these feet, Addy. This isn't good," Julie said, worriedly. "Let's get back to the tent. Momma will need to stay put."

Julie slowly slid the sock back on her foot and carefully stood. The pain shot up her legs again, but she expected it this time. Picking up Addison and the sleeping bag, she crept to the tent.

Addison started rubbing her eyes, and her cheeriness had subsided. "Time for you to have some lunch," Julie said. Crawling on her hands and knees, she opened a prepackaged meal and added water to the freeze-dried mashed potatoes portion. "It won't be hot, but you'll like it."

Addison watched Julie intently, knowing food was coming soon. Julie spooned mashed potatoes to Addison, watching as she rubbed her eyes in between bites.

"I think it might be nap time soon," Julie said, touching her cheek.

After taking a few bites of the leftover potatoes, Julie stowed away all the gear for meals and cooking.

"Let's be ready to go when Ned gets here, okay?" Julie said as if Addison understood every word. Addison just rubbed her eyes. Julie grabbed a baby bottle filled with water and a serving of formula, scooped up Addison and sat up straight on her knees. She scooted toward the tent on her knees to avoid the pain.

Scooting her way into the tent, Julie plopped down the bottle and gently set Addison down. She focused on the med kit. *Need to open that after she is asleep*, Julie noted.

After shaking the formula in the baby bottle, and Addison crying for its contents, Julie spread out the sleeping bag that had been warmed in the midday sun, and laid on top of it with Addison curled up in the crook of her arm.

Addison's red, puffy eyes focused on Julie's eyes, only a few inches away. Julie smiled. Addison smiled as much as she could as she slurped the bottle's contents. Julie was taken in by the girl's beautiful blue eyes, rich red lips, and soft white skin.

"You are a pretty little girl, Addison," Julie whispered.

Addison blinked a long blink. As her eyes opened, they were somewhere else in a dream. Her eyelids fell closed again in another drawn out blink. Her face relaxed and the bottle slipped out of her mouth, as Addison let go of being awake and succumbed to sleep. Julie couldn't help but be drawn into Addison's peacefulness. *I'll get the med kit later*, she thought, and let herself fall asleep.

***

"Julie! Oh my God, Julie! Can you hear me?"

Julie could hear Ned faintly as she pulled herself out of a dead sleep. She struggled to answer Ned.

"Yes, Ned. I hear you," Julie mumbled as she opened her eyes. "Ned! You're here."

"Julie, are you okay?" Ned asked, sounding worried.

"I think so. You made it. Ned, I'm so glad you're here. You made it!" she said excitedly, yet softly.

Her excitement was muted by her exhaustion. Julie propped herself up on her elbows. Ned was next to her on his knees. She could barely muster any energy.

"You scared me for a moment. You sure you're okay?" Ned pressed.

"I am. Wait! Where's Addison? She was here," Julie exclaimed, looking around frantically.

"She's outside with Joel and Johnny," Ned said.

"Joel and Johnny are here?" Julie yelled, and started to scramble to get out of the tent. As soon as she put a foot under her so she could stand, she stopped.

"Ned, wait. I take that back. I am not okay," Julie said, looking behind her.

Ned was poised to follow her out of the tent. Before she could explain, she put her leg behind her and crawled out of the tent, straightening up on her knees once she got out.

"Joel! Come here!"

Joel was near the fire circle, holding Addison. She looked so small in his arms, and he looked so big.

"Mom!" He quickly walked to Julie, who had sat back onto her heels. He gave her a funny look when she didn't stand up to hug him. "Mom, you okay?" Joel went down on one knee with Addison in his left arm, hugging Julie tightly with his right arm.

Julie squeezed Joel hard. "I think something is wrong with my feet," Julie said softly in his ear as she hugged him. "Don't worry, we'll figure it out. I have missed you so much." Julie held onto Joel and hugged him for a long time, putting her arm around Addison, too.

"Bravo to Alpha." Johnny was near the tent with a radio to his mouth.

"Alpha, go ahead."

"Alpha, we have located one adult female and one juvenile. Adult female with possible foot infection. Beginning evaluation for transport," Johnny said.

"Copy, Bravo. Any information on the juvenile?"

Julie released Joel and watched Johnny.

Ned had brought the med kit out of the tent and whispered to Julie, "Let me see your feet."

Julie sat on her rear end, swinging her feet in front of her, still watching Johnny.

"Alpha, juvenile requires no aid," Johnny answered. "Plan to load subjects in thirty, ETA to Base One approximately four hours."

"Copy, Bravo. Information to be relayed to Smoky Base. They will be glad to hear the news."

"Copy, Alpha," Johnny said with a smile and clipped the radio to his belt. Johnny looked up and started toward Ned and Julie. "How are you doing?" Johnny asked.

"I am not sure. I have felt exhausted today. I sat with Addison out in the sun to dry my feet off and warm them up."

"They're infected," Ned said looking at them. "I want to get them really clean. I think we have a little bit of rubbing alcohol, which will sting. Then let's apply antibiotic ointment and wrap them in light gauze. You are not putting any weight on them. Plus, I don't want them in the dirt. The key is to keep them extra clean and sterile."

Julie nodded. "How bad is this?" she asked, worried.

"I don't see the telltale signs that it's spread. I think we can nip it. I

169

have stashed antibiotics at home. If it gets worse, we'll have you take a course of them," Ned explained.

"Thank you."

Ned sprinkled the little bottle of rubbing alcohol over Julie's feet, and she immediately gasped in pain. "That is worse than when I stood up on them earlier!" She gritted her teeth, clenching her eyes as the wave of burning hit a peak, then dulled to a slow, steady sear.

Ned blew on her feet to try to take away the sting. Julie just gritted her teeth as the alcohol settled into the angry, oozing sores and evaporated.

As Ned tended Julie's feet, she heard bits and pieces of Johnny's radio.

"Alpha to Smoky Base."

The response was mostly static, but Julie thought she heard a few words.

"Johnny, what is going on?" Julie asked, as Johnny helped Ned by handing him gauze out of the med kit, so Ned's hands could stay sterile.

"Alpha is Victor. He's at the cache where you stashed the radios. He is signaling your dad at Smoky Flats that you and Addison are okay. You'll only be able to hear Victor. Your dad is too far away," Johnny said. He pulled the radio off his belt and held it up for Julie to listen. Ned listened in as he wrapped gauze around Julie's feet.

"Smoky Base relay from Bravo, adult female and juvenile have been located. Rendering aid to possible foot injury. All expected at Base One in approximately four hours."

Julie recognized Victor's voice as Alpha. Static followed Victor's message.

"Copy, Smoky Base, will advise when all subjects are back at camp. Confirm, injuries are believed to be minor and not life threatening," said Victor. Garbled static followed. "Copy, Smoky Base." Victor concluded his message.

"Your dad has been strung up tight worried about you," Johnny said, "especially when you didn't return on time."

"Johnny told me that when they left to come find us, he parked himself at the radio tower in Western Lakes, and practically hasn't moved since. He's been there 'round-the-clock for about the last two days. They said he even brought in a cot to sleep on," Ned said.

"Can I talk to him on the radio when we get there later?" Julie asked.

"Of course. He would appreciate that, I'm sure," Ned said with a warm smile.

Joel held Addison next to Julie, while Johnny and Ned quickly packed up the small camp and extinguished the embers in the fire.

"I'll get water. Can you get the horses ready?" Ned asked Johnny, who nodded and disappeared behind the tree line.

"We have horses?" Julie was surprised.

"We do, Mom," Joel answered, explaining the offer of the use of the McAllister's horses for the trek, and the newly improved security patrols with the use of the horses.

"How cool that you've learned how to ride!" Julie said.

"I've learned enough to ride," Joel said. "I'm no expert."

Julie looked intently at Joel for a moment. In a few short weeks, he had gone from being a gangly kid, to a young man. He seemed mature and focused.

"No, but you will be," Julie said with confidence.

"Mom, I was really scared when you didn't come back on time. I mean *really* scared," Joel said softly, fear in his eyes.

"Honey, I know. We knew. I couldn't just call or text you. I wished I could reach out to you and tell you and Grandpa I was okay," Julie said, reaching out to Joel and giving him a hug.

Johnny approached them, leading one horse. "Joel, can you hold him a moment?" Johnny asked, holding up the reins.

"Sure." Joel handed Addison to Julie, who watched as Joel confidently stood to the left side of the horse, holding the reins. Johnny retreated to where he'd come from, and brought two more horses into the mix. Ned returned with four full flasks of water. Within a few moments, Johnny and Ned had the extra gear strapped down to the horses or stowed away in saddle bags.

"This will be fun," Ned said, "getting you onto a horse."

It was agreed that Ned would carry Julie up next to the horse. He didn't do it until she saw Johnny and Joel demonstrate how to mount a horse.

"Mom, you stand on the left side of a horse and look to its rear," Joel explained. "I know it seems weird, but it'll make sense." He showed how he twisted the stirrup a half turn, inserting the tip of his boot into the stirrup. "Put your weight on the ball of your foot on the stirrup, not the arch of your foot. Then you hop on your right foot and take a big step up." Joel did it as he spoke, and showed how he bounced up, put the weight on his left foot, then swung his right foot easily over the back of the horse. He settled easily into the saddle.

"Putting that kind of weight on the balls of my feet—" Julie said. "This is going to hurt."

"Wait," said Ned, "let's do this differently. Julie, you'll be barefooted except for the gauze. I'm not sure that is a great way to get you on."

It was decided that Johnny and Ned would lift Julie up from her knee and have her swing her right leg over the horse. "Don't put your feet in the stirrups," Johnny said, "Just let them hang. But you'll need to hang on tight to the saddle horn. You won't be able to grip the horse with your legs as well, and you'll get tired from bouncing all over the saddle."

Ned rode the third horse, and Johnny walked next to Julie's horse and led her mount by the reins.

"Take the lead, Johnny," Ned said. "Joel, you follow your mom. I'll carry Addison with me in the rear."

As soon as Johnny got a wave from Ned, he nodded and started to lead Julie's horse in a brisk walk—toward home.

Chapter 84
Unexpected Regrets

Ned sat with Victor and Johnny around the campfire. They had been at Base One for a few hours. Julie, Joel, and Addison were in a tent.

"I'm glad I have the two of you together," Victor said, gazing at the mesmerizing waves of orange across the coals. The sky was turning deep blue with streaks of orange as the sun set. "I have something to tell you, and I don't want to," Victor said.

"What's wrong?" Ned asked, alarmed by Victor's serious demeanor.

"Chalmers arrived in Smoky Flats about a week ago to check on his property," Victor explained. "You are both aware that Barbara had been living at his property since last fall." Ned and Johnny nodded.

"She came to town during the winter to visit the trading post," Ned said. "Julie encountered her."

"I remember," Johnny said. "Julie let her stay in one of the cabins at the trading post so she wouldn't have to walk back to Chalmers's, only to turn around the next day and come back."

Victor nodded. "Sounds about right. Chalmers had arranged for Barbara to occupy his property to discourage vagrants and squatters, especially after the pair we had problems with early last winter. When he went to check on things last week, well... I don't know how to say this. He found her deceased," Victor said solemnly. "I wanted to be the one to tell you both, privately, before you got back to Smoky Flats and heard the gossip."

"What?" Ned exclaimed, with sadness in his voice. "How?"

"I did an initial investigation. Looks like she starved to death," Victor explained. "Chalmers thought he had supplied enough basic food in his pantry for her, but apparently not. From the scene, it looks like she fell asleep and didn't wake up, and she probably expired sometime in May. I am sorry."

Johnny leaned his head down and rubbed his temple with his fingers. He began to quiver.

"Johnny," Ned said, "come here." Ned stood, and motioned for Johnny to stand up, too. Without a word, father and son embraced. Ned felt Johnny's shoulders shake as he cried.

"Son, I am so sorry," Ned said as he held Johnny as close as he could.

Ned felt as if someone had poured ice water over him. All of his nerves went cold at once. He felt light headed and his fingers and toes tingled. Johnny sobbed against his father. Ned's eyes blurred; he felt his throat burn as his emotions took ahold of him. Odd thoughts came to his mind as he held Johnny. *I need to get ahold of Rachel. I need to be strong for Johnny. Johnny just lost his mother. I don't want this to impact Julie. Julie...* Ned thought.

"Hey, Victor, can you do me a favor?" Ned looked at Victor, still holding Johnny, his eyes welling with tears.

"Anything, name it," Victor said, putting his hand on Ned's shoulder.

"Can you tell Julie? Tell her as little as possible, and that I'll be with Johnny if she needs me tonight. I don't think she will," Ned whispered.

"You bet." Victor nodded, patting Ned's shoulder as he turned away to leave a father with his grieving son.

"Dad, I was irritated and frustrated with her, yes. But I never hated her. I never wanted *this* for her," Johnny sobbed as they headed toward their tent

"I know," Ned replied, resting his hand on his son's shoulder.

Johnny and Ned settled into their tent.

"I should have visited her. I should have talked to her more," Johnny cried as he spilled his heart — his regrets.

"Johnny, shh... I don't need to hear your regrets right now. I want to hear the good memories, the respect and admiration," Ned said, trying to redirect Johnny's emotions.

Johnny lifted his head and took a deep breath. "I appreciate how much she supported me in sports and school. She was at every game, drove me all over for practices and meetings. She gave rides to my friends. When I wanted to quit because of someone's drama or whatever, she told me to stick to it," Johnny said, wiping his face with the back of his arm. "She did the same for school. Mom never let me get away with slacking off. I hated it when she got a phone call or email from school that I had missed some assignment or something." Johnny smiled and shook his head. "She'd be on my ass for it. She'd say I could do better."

Ned and Johnny stayed in their tent that night. Ned wasn't that hungry. Johnny's emotions subsided. Father and son stayed close to each other.

***

Julie could hear upset voices as she talked to Joel about Addison. *Should I check on everyone?* she wondered.

174

"Mom, she's smiling at me," Joel said excitedly. Addison was sitting on Joel's left knee. She was trying to grab at anything to do with Joel—his t-shirt, his ballcap, his earlobes. Joel tried to distract her with the sleeping bag zipper pull. Addison wasn't sure if she wanted to play with the zipper, or Joel's face. Regardless, she liked playing with Joel. Julie enjoyed relaxing. Ned had explained that her fatigue was her body fighting the infection.

"We'll have you on antibiotics soon. Just keep off your feet, and we'll keep them clean," Ned had assured.

"Joel, you okay for a minute? I'm going to check what's going on," Julie asked.

"Sure, Mom," Joel answered. "We're fine."

Julie crawled out of the tent and perched herself on her knees. Victor was walking toward her.

"Hey, Julie," Victor said as he approached.

"Hey, Victor," Julie replied. "What is going on?"

"So hey, Johnny and Ned are talking in their tent," Victor answered. "I need to fill you in on a couple of things, but I know voices carry and walls are nonexistent. Can we maybe talk at the campfire?"

"Yes," Julie replied. "Don't tell Ned, but I am going to walk on my feet, okay?" Julie reached back in the tent to grab a pair of socks and slip them on.

"Deal," Victor said, reaching out to help Julie to her feet.

***

After breaking the news to Julie and letting her know how Ned and Johnny were faring, Victor slapped his knees. "Before I forget, let's get you on the radio to your dad," Victor declared. Julie's mind was heavy with worry about Ned and Johnny.

"Can I?" Julie asked, welcoming the momentary diversion. "I don't have a license or anything."

"Don't worry," Victor assured, unclipping his radio from his back pocket.

"So how do I do this?" Julie asked nervously.

"Couple of things to remember," Victor explained. "Don't give actual names over the radio. Keep sentences super short and informative. This isn't a phone conversation so much as relaying information. Difficult, I know, since you want to talk to him. Keep in mind, others who have radios near us can hear you if they are tuned into our frequency."

"Okay."

"Also, you heard us talking earlier. On this trip, we have established our names based on the NATO phonetic alphabet." Victor explained the names and locations. Julie nodded, trying to remember every detail. "Interestingly, your NATO name is Juliet," Victor said with a smile. "Should be easy to remember."

"Got it," Julie said.

Victor nodded, lifting the radio to his mouth. "Base One to Smoky Base," said Victor.

"Smoky Base, go ahead Base One," Floyd responded.

"Smoky Base, Base One establishing retrieved adult female as Juliet," Victor instructed.

"Copy, Alpha Base."

Julie took the radio that Victor handed her and keyed up. "Juliet to Smoky Base," Julie said clearly into the handset.

"Smoky Base, go ahead Juliet," Floyd said, cracking a bit under the emotion as he heard his daughter's voice.

"Smoky Base, all is well. Minor injuries delayed travel. All are stable and accounted for," Julie said.

"Copy, Juliet," said Floyd. Julie heard the gasp of emotion her father made before he was able to finish his words.

"Smoky Base, be advised, ETA is in approximately eighteen hours. Rally point to be at Smoky Base comm center," Julie said.

"Copy, Juliet. Be safe," Floyd responded.

Julie handed the radio to Victor, put her face in her hands, and cried. Victor put his arm around Julie.

***

Julie sat on the deck of the cabin with Addison in her arms. She had been home for two weeks. It had been two weeks of experiencing a wide range of emotions. Many times, Julie found herself astounded that she could feel sheer happiness and despairing sadness at the very same time. *I know why people say, 'I don't know whether to laugh or cry,'* she thought as she cuddled up with Addison.

It was later in the day, probably around nine, and the sun was spreading out another one of its breathtaking orange-and-blue sunsets.

"It's August, we won't be able to sit out here much longer to watch this," Julie told Addison. Already, Julie was taking note of the early signs of fall. Aspens were getting a slight tinge of the telltale yellow on some of their leaves. By October, they would be painting the landscape a golden yellow.

Julie's feet were healing, and she was able to walk around the property easily. Ned had given her a course of antibiotics when they'd arrived home, and she'd started them right away. Julie remembered Ned's face as he stood at her back door with the bottle of pills. His face was strained and fraught with emotion.

"Julie, I know Victor told you. I know we have a lot to talk about, but I need to focus on Johnny right now. He's torn up," Ned said quietly. "Promise me you'll take these just like I wrote on here. These are true antibiotics, and aren't effective unless you take all of them."

"I understand, Ned," Julie said, touching his shoulder. "If you or Johnny need anything — and I mean *anything* — please let us know."

Ned nodded. "I am sorry, Julie," Ned said. He slowly shook his head, and Julie could sense that he was trying to keep his composure.

"Ned, please," Julie whispered. "You have nothing to be sorry for."

"I wanted our homecoming to be memorable," Ned said as he wiped his sleeve on his cheek. "We kicked ass out there. To use your metaphor, I wanted to cross the finish line with fanfare and cheers. I am sorry that we didn't have that. You didn't have that."

"It's okay," Julie said, smiling. "That would have been fun. Yes, we kicked ass out there. Our fanfare will be our own. We know what we accomplished. Johnny needs you right now. I am here, taking care of my feet and a new baby. I'm right here if you need me. I mean it."

Ned nodded, and they sat for a moment in silence, each in their own world.

"Ned, I will always be here for you. I meant what I said about planning our future. Our future is now. We haven't formalized anything or told anyone, but my commitment is solid. You tell me what you need, and I am there," Julie said. She reached out to Ned's shoulder and pulled him to her. He threw his arms around her waist and squeezed. And cried.

Julie teared up as she remembered that night two weeks ago, saying goodbye to Ned as he tended to the tragedy that had greeted them then. It was the first of many sad moments, as Smoky Flats dealt with Barbara's death. Many people knew her from the years she'd attended city council meetings, school sports and events, and parenting activities. Her death stunned everyone.

Julie hadn't known Barbara, and felt bad for not feeling as sad. Julie's heart was broken thinking that more wasn't done to make sure she had what she needed to live at Chalmers's property. *It pisses me off that Chalmers didn't check on her more often, or make sure that if someone was going to care for his place, he had provided at least adequate supplies,* Julie fumed.

Many times, Julie felt guilty. She had known that Barbara was not doing well. *I saw her last year. She looked gaunt then. I could easily have asked Johnny or Ned to get to Chalmers's and check on her. Hell, I could have gone to check on her,* Julie scolded herself. Many residents of Smoky Flats had had similar soul-searching conversations with themselves. Many of them had come to the same conclusion: anyone could have reached out to Barbara, but didn't. It was sobering.

At the same time Smoky Flats was grieving, Julie was nesting with Floyd, Joel, and Addison. Addison was extremely easy going, and adapted to change surprisingly well.

"I think she had to, considering all the places she's been to in her short little life," Julie mused with Floyd as they talked over dinner one evening.

A surprise delivery had been made while Ned and Julie traveled to Pierce Point. Patsy came to the cabin the day after Julie, Ned, and Addison arrived home.

"Patsy! This is a surprise! You here to see Addison?"

"Of course! But I have something to give you, too," Patsy said, giving Julie a hug.

"You don't have to give me anything," Julie said as they sat down on the sofa.

Patsy laughed. "Well, it's not me. I'm dying to tell you about a delivery that came for you while you were gone."

Patsy explained that a small Conex container was delivered to the post office in town. "I agreed to sign for it, and had them park it behind the trading post, since it was for you," Patsy explained.

"A Conex? What is a Conex?" Julie asked.

"It's like a small shipping container," Patsy replied.

"A shipping container? For me?" Julie was dumbfounded.

"It came with this." Patsy handed a large envelope to Julie.

"This is so mysterious. What is going on?" Julie asked looking at Patsy questioningly.

"I honestly don't know. You know as much as I do at this point," Patsy said, shrugging. "Not gonna lie, honey, I'm here to see the baby, but I'm also here to find out what is in the mysterious thing."

Julie opened the envelope. Inside was a portrait of her former in-laws. "Oh my word," Julie gasped. "Is this from them?"

Unfolding a letter, Julie read:

Dearest Julie,
When you read this, the mission will be complete. You will have traveled to Pierce Point, adopted Addison, and returned safely home. We (Bentley Atwood,

my wife Rose, and Steven's mother Kathleen) celebrate your homecoming. You have put yourself in grave danger in uncertain and unstable times. We are forever grateful to you for taking such a risk for our granddaughter.

While we know you have adopted Addison and she is your daughter now, and that changes the dynamic of family relationships, in our hearts she is still our granddaughter. She is the granddaughter that you took the risk to save from a dangerous existence and a future marked by danger. Part of this endeavor was to provide for Addison's physical needs. You will find basic supplies that a small baby and growing child will need in the container this letter accompanies. In these uncertain times, we couldn't guarantee that we would be able to send supplies to you in the future, and did our best to provide as much as we could for now. A shipping container, as extreme as it may seem, was the best option for a growing child's needs.

If you ever need anything for Addison, please email me at the email address below. We've included a picture of us, hoping you would share it with Addison. Please be sure she grows up knowing that we love her dearly. Your homecoming and her future is the legacy we leave in this world that we are most proud of.

Bless you,
Bentley Atwood

"Oh my word," Julie whispered again. "That's how he did all of this—his parents." Looking up at Patsy, Julie handed the letter to her. "It's from my former in-laws, Addison's grandparents. It's all from them," Julie said, as Patsy scanned the letter.

"Special folks." Patsy nodded, with a warm smile.

Julie spent an afternoon going through the Conex. It contained a massive supply of baby formula and food.

"That's a huge relief," Julie said to herself as she looked at the cases of formula. There were organized boxes of clothing, with a small supply for each stage of a young girl's life. There were various books, and some toys. There was a collection of encyclopedias. About half of the Conex contained items specifically for Addison. The other half was food supplies.

"I told Steve I wanted food supplies, and here they are." Julie was amazed by the canned, powdered, and freeze-dried foods. She made a point to put a solid lock on the Conex door. Later that night at the cabin, she and Floyd made plans to relocate and organize those supplies into the cabin over time.

Julie's eyes burned as she remembered the day she explored the Conex. *That is out of the movies, it is so crazy,* Julie thought, smiling. The sun was almost behind the tree line, and the air was getting chilly.

"Let's get inside, little lady, and go to bed," Julie said, gingerly standing up with Addison.

Chapter 85
Titles

In the weeks since Addison had been home, the beds had been rearranged in the cabin. Floyd and Joel slept upstairs in the loft on the single beds. Julie slept with Addison in the first-floor bedroom. Addison easily settled into her new portable crib, which had also been sent in the Conex.

As Julie watched Addison drift off, a slight knock came to the door. "Come in," Julie called.

Floyd's head poked into the room. "Hey, Julie, Ned is here and wanted to have a word with you. You go ahead, I'll watch her," Floyd said with a wink.

Floyd had done nothing but dote on Addison since he met her. His care for her had allowed Julie to stay off her feet, sleep off the infection, and gather items from the Conex.

"Oh, wow—yes, thank you." Julie was surprised by the visit. She stood quickly, handing Floyd Addison's bedtime bottle as she exited the room and headed toward the back door of the cabin.

Ned stood with his back to the door, hands in his pockets; it appeared he was looking at the barn.

"Ned," Julie said as she stepped out onto the small porch. "How are you?"

"I'm well," Ned said and smiled. It was the warm smile of the Ned Julie knew.

"Good," Julie said returning the smile.

"Can we take a walk around the lake? Or maybe as far as we can go before it gets too dark?" Ned asked, holding out his elbow.

"I would like that a lot," Julie said. "Let me grab a jacket."

Julie came back out of the cabin in a jean jacket and instinctively slipped her hand in the crook of Ned's arm.

"That feels good," Ned said.

As they approached the road, Ned asked about the previous two weeks. Julie filled him in with details on her recovery, the Conex, and settling into baby life.

"But that's enough about me," Julie said, "tell me about you. I've been worried about you and Johnny."

"Yes," Ned said. He explained how he and Johnny had been faring. "Johnny has taken it hard. I have taken it hard," Ned said. "There's guilt there. A lot of folks in Smoky Flats feel guilt." Julie nodded in agreement.

Ned went on to explain that Barbara's brother was planning for her remains to be transported to a family plot somewhere back east. "It's a difficult process right now with travel being unstable, but he thinks he can do it. It will take some time," Ned said.

"That's a much better option for her than what Smoky Flats had last fall," Julie said.

"No kidding," Ned said. "I would have stepped in and done something at that point. Her brother is a nice person, and we've had some good talks. It's helped me settle this in my mind. We've been a good support to each other in this."

"Glad to hear," Julie said.

"I also heard from Rachel, thankfully," Ned said, visibly relieved as he gave Julie the update. "She's with Barb's cousin in Cheyenne. I broke the news to her, and she's pretty torn up, too. We're working on getting her here soon."

Julie nodded and smiled sympathetically as she absorbed the updates Ned was giving her. "I can't wait to meet her," Julie said softly.

"Funny. When I told her about you awhile back, she said the same about you," Ned said, and chuckled.

Ned took a deep breath and exhaled loudly. "Julie, that is not all that I wanted to talk to you about," Ned said. "I want to pick up the conversation from where we left off a few weeks ago, when I left you in the tent."

"If I recall, the last thing we said to each other was that we love each other," Julie said.

Ned turned to Julie. "Julie, I want to marry you. I feel foolish asking you to marry me. I know you will. More than anything, I wanted to tell you that I am ready to marry you. I've talked to Johnny about it, and he thumped me on the shoulder and told me it was about time. He and I also both agreed it would be a fresh start we could both use after the last few weeks. He's looking forward to being a part of our future," Ned said, looking intently at Julie. "I think I've demonstrated this, but I will say it aloud—I promise to not squander or disregard you, and the gifts you bring to those of us who enjoy your presence. I promise to be a man who partners with you and looks to make you shine. To be traditional, Julie Atwood, would you marry me?"

"Ned Collins, yes," Julie said. She reached up to Ned, placing her palm on his cheek, and kissed him.

Opening her eyes, looking tenderly at Ned, Julie said, "I have an early wedding present for you—for us. Want to see it?"

"Of course," Ned said, surprised. Julie pulled an envelope out of her pocket, unfolded a document and held it out to Ned.

"The deed to the trading post property? You're kidding? It's yours!"

"It's from the insurance settlement of my property in Oregon. I got lousy pennies on the dollar, but I got a sum that the bank that owned the trading post was willing to take. Victor put the deal together for me while we were traveling. You told me once to let him deal with the bank, and he did it. He gets all the credit."

"Wow, Julie, I don't know what to say…"

"This is my home, here in Smoky Flats, with you," Julie said. "There is a lot of uncertainty around us. We got a hard lesson in that from Colonel Matson. His words continue to echo in my mind. I have no control over the collapse happening around us. None. I have control of where and how I live—and I choose here, with you."

www.ingramcontent.com/pod-product-compliance
Lightning Source LLC
Chambersburg PA
CBHW050846180626
46814CB00007B/2648